THE THOUSAND YEAR QUEEN

APRIL SAVAGE

SPLASH TIDE
—PUBLISHING—

Contents

The Primordial Moon

Every thousand years, a hunter's moon bleeds the night sky with crimson and breathes a Primordial. The one chosen as a fated mate is given to a wolf king to take it. That kingdom enjoys vast prestige, solidifying it as a dominion of power. This time, fate does something unexpected and the one chosen does not bend nor relent. This time, the one chosen comes to make that kingdom repent.

The Endowing Curse

It used to twist their spines and break their bones. They hurled in pain with aching moans. The moon demanded a horrific fate, so the seers rebelled and bled hate. They breathed an endowing curse on the wolves and laid waste on the humans. Instead of twisting spines and breaking bones, the wolves reveled in renewed hope.

The wolves changed like a breath of wind and back again. The strongest of them, the Primordials, were given seer power to bend the wind and earth at their will. As these powers passed down the ages to their offspring, they became formidable rulers. With these endowments, the wolves rose and took the lands.

In time, the kingdoms became subjected to their endless breaths of rage and rule. As oppression took the humans, the seers of old died off. All that remained were kingdoms dominated by wolves, and the humans who could not fight back bowed to them.

So begins the tale of The Thousand-Year Queen.

Chapter 1
The Thousand Years Begin

Brovina stood on the tower overlooking the river and endless forest. The evergreens stretched for miles and kissed the mountains rising in the distance. Her gray eyes peered into the wild, her wrinkled face clenched into the sunrise coming to kiss the city. She gripped her staff and sighed as her auburn and white hair glowed in the dawn. Her long black robes kissed her short-rounded frame. Her shadows stretched from the tower down the corridor to King Meltivi. He emerged beside her, his silver crown sparkling like diamonds in the light.

Brovina did not look at him. She closed her eyes and met the wind in her face. "Last night was the hunter's moon. The thousand years have begun. It is time to prepare the human faction for war."

Meltivi took a deep breath. His royal blue and white robes blew against his tall, slender frame as his long gray hair and beard blew behind him. He gazed into the rising sun with gray eyes and listened to his older sister. "So be it."

He turned to go, leaving Brovina clutching her staff. Her heart beat like something burst from the deep and ate her from the inside out. "Oh, child. I am so sorry." She closed her eyes, her desperation riddled upon her grieving face.

King Meltivi marched down the corridor from the tower and straight into the throne room. His general Louve met him there and bowed, his black beard swinging to his chest as his silver breastplate kissed it. Serkily's kingdom crest on his armor was all-seeing eyes from a mane of hair like the sun rising, and the walls were hung in these flags.

He pressed a fist atop his long sword hanging in his sheath at his side, his gauntlet squeaking in delight. The king met him there and nodded. "It is time to prepare Serimi and Galin."

Louve nodded. "We leave straightaway, my king."

The king turned to gaze upon the warriors who stood with his courageous general and smiled at them. The men were in full body armor, their pauldrons spiked and tall on their shoulders. Their graves and sabatons adorned their muscle-ridden bodies from head to toe. Their backs sported short spears, bows, and arrows in sheaths, and a broad sword. As Louve turned to go, the king called at him again.

"Steer clear of the mountain passes and Alaric's wolves. Stay on the river, away from Conri's hoard also. Stay safe my friends."

Louve pursed his lips and huffed, splaying his arms out his sides, smiling. "Bring the wolves onnnnnn!" His men laughed with him.

Meltivi watched them go, but he was not smiling. The rising dawn had brought a new thousand-year age, and now the white wolf was in danger. The humans would continue falling to the wolf kings, serving and enslaved by them. This time, Meltivi prepared. This time, he would not allow his city to fall to the wolves or his people taken as it was with his ancestors.

Brovina slithered into the throne room. The ivory pillars crossed over them like fingers into the heavens. Their shadows reflected clear on the stone floor and looked as if there were two of them. Meltivi turned to his sister and swallowed.

"Send the falcons to intercept her. We must protect her at all costs. If we are to defeat the wolf kings, it is now, and now alone."

Brovina sighed, nodding. "I have already sent them this morning and for Randon to watch her."

Meltivi shook his head. "We do not need two primordials together. That is a catastrophe, my dear sister."

Brovina turned to go. "We do not need Alaric becoming more powerful either. I had no choice. We already know Randon is pure."

"But is she?!" Meltivi wondered.

"Tala raised her. She is pure."

Meltivi sighed. "Whether we live or die, the wolf kings must fall."

Brovina turned to face him. "We have no choice now."

Louve catapulted from the city streets out of the gate. The flowing river waters roared beneath them under the drawbridge as wide as the street. Fifty warriors on horseback lunged behind him. Their helmets adorned with silver spikes made them look like demons. When they crossed the wide river, Louve led them in a full gallop through the forest heading west.

Serkily's human war leader Serimi stayed west with a vast army. They would race through the wilderness along the river to get to him. They had two days. On the way, they hoped to run into the outskirts of the traitors' villages. The traitors were not human. They were wolves not loyal to the wolf king Alaric. Louve hoped he could bribe them. These wolves were suspicious of humans, but they hated Alaric more.

Louve had two days to do the impossible before the wolf king began the hunt for his fated mate. Alaric would fill the lands with pain and suffering to get the white wolf. Louve faced an impossible task, but he had to save his kind. If he failed at saving his kind, the lands would continue falling to ruthless cruelty. The lands would continue falling, and the humans would die out to the wolves.

The human war leader Serimi's army stretched through the west on the warring plains. White tents dotted the rolling land in the thousands, and fires burned of wild game and stew cooking. Serimi leaned his muscular frame atop a long table strewn with maps. His red hair spiked over blue piercing eyes as he pressed his freckled hands atop the maps. He stared at them and clenched his jaws.

His war council surrounded him. Their shiny black metal body armor pressed shadows across the white tent walls. The walls blew in the winds coming off the mountains. Serimi pointed to a cavernous territory in Alaric's realm and sighed. "The wolves of Worgen will come from there, his kingdom."

He stopped talking as a tall man peeked in with sparkling brown eyes, his long blonde hair braided over his shoulder. He wore the black armor of the human warlords and smiled as he entered. "The falcon arrived pending Louve's arrival tomorrow. What is your command."

Serimi sighed and glared at the maps. "We do not know who she is, but Randon will know."

Galin huffed. "Ah, come on."

"I know you two have differences, but remember, he is a primordial wolf. He can track her before the wolf king takes her."

Galin laughed. "He is loyal only to his kind."

Serimi yelled at him. "He is loyal to the human faction and not the wolf king! That makes him our ally. You will summon him to come. He needs to track her, guard over her, and keep Alaric from taking her."

Galin blinked his eyes and turned to go. "Fine then. But he still owes me money, and I am not thrilled with him right now."

From across the table, another warrior chimed in. "He owes me money too."

Serimi huffed, ignoring them, his face stern at Galin. "It is time to call Randon."

Galin disappeared, leaving Serimi huffing at his back. He turned to gaze at the maps again and his war council, biting his lip. "The wolf king of Cayden will want her. His commander Conri will hunt her. It will be a hunt to see which one takes her first. This worst-case scenario for humans is also a war between the wolf kings."

One of the men spoke up. "Wolves not loyal to Alaric need to be summoned. We must go to the traitors' villages beyond the mountains."

Serimi scoffed. "And risk losing our men to Alaric's wolves?" But then he paused, thinking. "Yes, you are right. Alaric will be hunting her, and his wolves will be consumed with that and warring against Cayden. This could work."

He pointed to a section of the map winding around the mountains. "Here. Take one hundred men. You must travel by day only, for they hunt at night. Spread out once you have cleared the mountain passes. Find the farthest traitor wolves you can find. Do not stop until you have secured them to fight with us."

Serimi paused. "They will be rewarded as Serkily's kingdom coffers do not run dry."

Five of his war leaders bowed and then disappeared. They would ready their warriors to travel deep into the mountains and go over it. They would travel to the farthest northern villages in the unexplored territories, where wolves and men cohabitated. Serimi stood upright and crossed his bulky arms over his chest, his keen eyes gazing over the maps.

"Where is the white wolf." He whispered. "Where is she."

Galin marched out and up the street to his horse. He lunged up the street in the rolling plain for three miles until he reached the end of their tent village. The warriors posted at a stone tower nodded to him as he gazed up.

"Call him." He commanded.

The warriors protecting the tower pulled their horns to their lips and blew. The shriek echoed through the plain as if something had awakened. Galin sat atop his horse and waited as the bellowing shriek filled their ears. It echoed over the plain and into the valleys. It roared over the rivers and tributaries.

It trickled into a valley kingdom brimming with stone houses where a wide river boasted rocky shores.

The bellowing howl raised the hair on Galin's arms as he leaned back on his saddle. His brown eyes followed the call over the plains, his fists clasped over his lap. He clenched his strong jawline and narrowed his brows. They blew two more times, the three horn bellows carrying for miles. It called to Randon, the primordial wolf needed to help the humans find the white wolf queen.

Randon stood at the water's edge one hundred miles away. He pulled River Rock out with his wolf-size broad sword. The blade was as thick as his arm and tall as himself. Even in human form, he was over six feet. Naked from the waist up and barefoot, he used his blade to pry the stones out. He was using them to build more houses and stables for his village. He tossed a flat stone in a pile behind him on the rocky shore as sweat drenched his bulky chest.

His black hair was drenched with sweat as he wiped it from his brow. His choppy hair stuck up like his head was obsidian spikes. He needed to shave, his tanned face dark and shadowy.

He peered through the forest in the valley and sighed until his ears perked at an echo. The sound echoed into the valley and made his back rigid. He stared through the trees along the river toward the village in silence. His blue eyes glowed with the recognition of the bellowing horn calling to him.

He walked up the incline and burst through the trees. He stared over the village that sprawled below him. Everyone stopped working, stopped fishing, or mending nets. The women with the children froze as their eyes met the horizon. Randon froze. Other wolves covered with sweat and half-naked from hard work gazed at him from the street. Their eyes shimmered in amber as they met his.

Randon sneered. "Damnit."

He stood there clenched to his broad sword, his back heaving. His deep breathing made his muscles shimmer on his physique. The hair on his arms stood up, and a shiver chased his spine. Something had awakened deep inside him and clawed its way out. He clenched his jaws, his eyes shimmering. His face was hard as he stared straight over the plains and valleys to the call.

Chapter 2
Tala's Rebellion

Tala stood in the sunrise gazing at the river village. It sparkled like diamonds below her on the rolling knoll. They were miles away from it, and no one was up yet. The bustling waters flowed like sparkling fingers sprawling through the woodlands. Her amber eyes sparkled as her ears perked up to a fleet of horses coming for them.

She pressed her braided brown locks off her neck and peered back to her god-daughter, Ashina. She heard the shrieking bellows from the wolf king's army. Alaric had come for her, and they were fleeing. Tala pulled her satchel packs upon her back and kicked the stones at her feet, turning back to slide down the knoll.

Ashina stood taller than her at five feet nine, tall for a woman. But this was no woman. Ashina was the white wolf queen, destined to take the wolf king Alaric as her mate. Ashina gripped her satchels that hung off her back. Her long white hair braided down her back in a thick knot, her hazel eyes shimmering in the sun. She pulled at her black leather breastplate and sighed. Her long wool skirt split over her tight trousers and danced to her boots.

Tala sighed. "Ready?"

Ashina sighed back. "Ready."

Tala warned her. "You must continue to train. It is pivotal to your power. We have one chance. I would rather die than waste this chance."

Ashina sighed, turning one last time to look at the village, her eyes tearing up. "I will miss them. The humans are my family."

Tala swallowed. "They know this and will miss you too. They sacrifice themselves so I can get you out. The hunter's moon came with no warning last night. I hate this thousand-year curse." Her voice was deep and harrowing.

They turned and lunged east into the unexplored forest. They rushed away from Alaric's Mountain kingdom of Worgen. Their backs were heavy with provisions and weapons. Their sheaths sported daggers and swords and a battle axe on their backs.

They crept through the forest under cover of the dark canopy, away from Hildenia. It had been a beautiful place to raise Ashina and yielded plentiful fish and crops. It was an all-human faction. Tala felt it had helped keep Ashina safe all these years she had to raise her by the court of Alaric's parents.

But she did not raise her how the court expected her to. And year by year, Ashina had grown stronger and learned to defend herself with weapons.

Ashina closed her eyes and clenched her thin jawline. She gazed at her human family, her eyes lighting up in anger. She could not go back because they would take her. They would take her to a fated mate she knew deep inside was not his to take. But now they would take her human sisters as mates instead. She bit her lip and seethed inside, letting the agony of choices eat her from the inside out.

For miles behind them, Tala and Ashina heard shouts of rage and hate. Alaric's army plunged into the streets from the wood line across the gentle river. The wolf king Alaric's wolves were formidable and strong warriors. They lunged into the village by the hundreds. Alaric was going to ensure he got his queen.

His wolves were not in their wolf form, but they were intimidating to look upon regardless. The women stood outside their houses, holding their breaths as the wolves gazed upon them. Their eyes lit up as their scruffy faces sneered smiles as they pillaged the houses and boats.

The women of the village stared at one another. Their eyes stayed determined to accept their fate to these wolves who would take them. There were fourteen human women under thirty years old in the village and they were not married yet.

Alaric's commander Rieka eyed his wolves as they pillaged the village and searched for Ashina. He clenched his tattooed fists, his amber eyes burning inside him. The wolves pulled every human out until they stood in the street alongside their houses. The village was small, and around fifty humans lived there.

Rieka leaned on his stallion and peered around, his bald head kissed in dark blue tattoos as if fire seethed within him. The wolves wore stone coats of armor in bronze-colored metal and were armed. It was needless for the wolves to be armed as they were brute wolves, but they kept weapons in case they ran into human warriors. Rieka watched as one of his wolves yanked an old man from his house and tossed him to the ground before him.

The old man hit his knees and raised his arms, "Please! We are peaceful here and no threat to the wolves of Alaric."

Rieka sighed. "The guardian Tala swore to honor the mating agreement and surrender the white wolf after the hunter's moon. The child came here twenty-five years ago for her to protect."

Silence pestered them as Reika glared. "She would be thirty years old now."

Reika leaned over the mane and peered down at the human. "Where is she?" His voice echoed as the silence pestered the humans.

The women stood by one another and eyed each other in silence. Their long tunics hung to their ankles and flowed like their hair spilling down their backs. Their tanned skin and bright eyes exhibited the only youth in the village.

Rieka's wolves' eyes were dark and insidious. Their long beards and tattooed arms and faces were sinister. They eyed the women, flexing their naked forearms on their horses. The women found themselves gazing upon these wolves. Their bodies were rugged and looked carved from the mountain, fine-tuned warriors.

The old man swallowed. "I have not seen them today; I have only woken up. Please have mercy on us."

Reika took a deep breath, his amber eyes glimmering down upon him. He gazed around at his wolf army as they surrounded the humans. They had not found Ashina or Tala.

Reika took a deep breath. "Tala is treasonous, I see." He nodded to the wolves behind the women.

They lunged around them, pivoting their horses to lift them up. The wolves pulled the women up in their laps by their waists. They twisted them around like they were weightless humans and pressed their backsides into their chests, forcing them to sit against them. The women did not scream as the wolves gripped them tight against them. Alaric always let his wolves take the women.

"No! Please no! Not our daughters!" The old man grieved.

Reika laughed. "We always take the women, old man." He eyed the women sitting calmly in their laps, his brows furrowed. He watched their expressions and noted they were not afraid.

"They are not afraid of us. They are not upset about us taking them." He glared around and fixed his stare upon the man again.

"When was the last time you saw them." He demanded.

The old man shook his head, but Rieka turned his horse to face the women in the wolves' laps. The women grew stiff and wide-eyed. as he approached them. Rieka stopped his horse at one young woman with long blonde hair. As he pulled it out and sniffed it, she held her breath.

He glared in her face, his amber eyes glowing. "Hello, beautiful. When did you last see the white wolf? Ashina, that is her name."

The woman did not respond. Rieka glared at her face, waiting.

"What is your name?" Rieka demanded.

The wolf sitting behind her pressed her into his chest harder and lunged her head back by her hair. As he revealed her neck, Rieka pulled her tunic off her shoulder, ripping it down her arm. The wolf holding her bent into her skin and breathed on her neck. His fangs burst up and she held her breath. Instead of biting her, he kissed her neck gently.

He laughed against her skin and whispered. "You are mine, beautiful."

Rieka leaned into her face. "Do not be stubborn. The wolf sitting behind you has claimed you as his mate, and he will bite you here in front of everyone." Rieka whispered in her face. "Do you know what happens once we bite our chosen mates?"

She grimaced, her chest heaving.

Rieka smiled. "We get this insatiable desire to breeeeeddd." His voice was deep and bellowing.

Anna squirmed and clenched her face at him. She sneered, her eyes rolling over to his. "Anna." She belted out, defiant still.

Rieka leaned back, his face hard. He nodded his head to the wolf gripping her hair and released it.

Rieka sighed as it dawned on him. "You human women are defiant. I think the white wolf and Tala encouraged you to behave this way." Rieka turned and glared at his wolves and then shook his head at the human men. They were dirty and older.

"Hmph." He bent into Anna's face again and whispered against her cheek, his fangs erupting. "When did you last see the white wolf, Anna."

Anna swallowed. "Last night, after the hunters' moon came."

Rieka bent back up and growled. "Damnit!"

"Take them!" The women squirmed, but there was nothing they could do. They could not fight the wolves. They were strong and the women were only human. They would go to

Alaric's Mountain Kingdom and get bitten by the wolves taking them and mated to them.

"Please, no!" The old man begged.

"We always take the women." Reika turned his horse away shaking his head. "Burn it all down. Tala has rebelled against our king."

A wolf sneered across from him. "And the men?"

Rieka sneered. "Kill them all."

The wolves who did not have women in their laps lunged off their horses and began tearing into the men's throats. The women closed their eyes and grimaced, and a few cried. The wolves pulled them tight against them and raced back over the river with their prizes.

The old man scoffed at Rieka as his wolves killed the villagers. He stood up to face him. "You may take our women to breed, but you will never take our queen!"

Rieka turned to go and then froze. He craned his neck to glare at him, his black brows sneering across his slender face. He clenched his jaws, the blue veins on his bulky tattooed arms bulging.

"That sounds like the white wolf is refusing her mate."

The old man scoffed. "She will not serve Alaric. You are all doomed. You will die."

Rieka slid from his horse as fangs burst up.

He yelled one last time. "The white wolf has come! She is powerful and your kingdom will burn!"

Rieka lunged at the old man and ripped out his throat. As blood pooled in the street, he growled. His eyes glowed like a black fire breathed within him.

"Alaric will have his queen, or every human dies." Reika turned away from the body, his face flowing in blood as his resolve lit up to find Ashina for his king.

He jumped on his horse again, sneering at the houses burning into the sun. He watched the human men bleeding out on the road while their homes burned. They did not put up a fight or even try. Even the women did not try running, as they always ran when the wolves came. Chills rushed up Rieka's arms as it dawned on him.

"She flees the king on purpose. She stalled us. Alaric will have to hunt her." He rolled his eyes. "Stubborn white wolf."

He turned to his wolves. "Spread out and track them. They could not have gotten far."

He clenched his teeth and turned off the road. His army followed him while the wolves with women in their laps headed back to the mountain. Behind them now, bodies were strewn over the fields and street as the village burned.

At rising dawn two days in, Tala had led Ashina away from the mountain. They tracked into the unexplored woodlands to the east. They stayed away from the river atop the plateaus, their keen eyes watchful for movement. They had climbed rock faces and hills and put many miles between them and Hildenia. There was no movement, only the forest animals foraging for food.

Tala and Ashina stood on the edge of a plateau overlooking the world at dawn and bent into the rising sun. They breathed in the warmth and power of its presence. They bent as one in tune with each other and nature. As their bodies flexed, their strong limbs danced into a silent heaven. Tala had taught Ashina her whole life to do this, as it kept her limber and helped hone her power.

Tala led Ashina as they swayed in their pivotal formation. They sliced their fists into the air and stretched their legs as if they were in battle. Ashina closed her eyes into the rising sun and breathed in deep. The forest lingered in her soul, the sounds of movement or the wind caressing her intuition.

"Nature will guide you. Nature breathes within you. You will sense it calling to you Ashina, warning you. You will feel it in your soul." Tala stretched her arms out and breathed in deep as Ashina followed. "You are not like any wolf ever born. You are the only white wolf female primordial born in our world, as the others have all been black wolves. That makes you more dangerous to your fated mate Alaric. It makes you dangerous to the kingdom of Cayden."

"The wolf kings only crave your power. They will take you and bend your strengths to their will..."

"When you came to me, I vowed you would not be a breeding queen. I vowed you would be strong and free." Tala told her, and Ashina took a deep breath. "You were taught to stand up for yourself and others. The wolf kings will take and destroy. You will build and lift others."

Ashina breathed in Tala's words.

"You are of the Hunter moon but born of the light. Even though your wolf bloodline is empowered with ancient seer magic, you must be cautious how you use these powers." Tala stopped moving, opened her eyes, and stepped back to watch Ashina bend into the sun.

"You will always fight to do what is right." Tala whispered.

Ashina was still moving as if dancing in the sun, her eyes closed, her breathing strong and calm. The rays kissed her white hair, her olive-toned tanned skin, her pouty lips firm and res-olute. Tala watched Ashina swish her arm from her back and jut it straight out. She flexed with power, and the wind moved around her. Something awakened from the deep of the earth, and it followed her.

The oak leaves kissed at her feet, and the trees swayed toward her. The forest bent toward her will with her movements. Tala watched it as if fingers had pried something loose. She peered up into the forest lingering around them. The sun continued to rise upon her god-daughter, and chills rushed up her spine.

The leaves swished in the air following Ashina's movement and followed her hands. The dirt beneath her feet shook as if the ground had awakened. The trees bowed to her and rolled back up again. The sun surrounded her body with crimson fire like the hottest inferno burned within her.

Ashina swished her fist out again, flexing her arm. She stretched it out and froze. The leaves at her feet blasted away from her and lunged down the plateau over the ravine. It split

the forest below them for miles as the rushing wind bellowed

through it. The trees blasted away from it and shook, sliding

back to form the canopy. The forest moved in its wake as every

bird in the trees darted up, and the sky became black with them.

When Ashina opened her eyes, they lit up in a fiery golden from

within her.

Tala widened her shimmering amber eyes. A sense of dread

filled her heart. The wolf kings must never touch this queen,

but now they would find her.

Tala swallowed, realizing what this meant. "Come, we must

track further into the wild. Alaric's court stretches wide, and

the kingdom of Cayden will now be on the hunt."

Chapter 3
Where the Hunt Begins

Alaric stood with his hands clasped behind him. His sun-kissed blonde hair flowed down his back in waves as he turned to face a dozen of his wolves. They bowed upon one knee, their faces to the stone. Alaric's green eyes sparkled like the emerald woodlands filling his mountain kingdom. His blonde beard and mustache accentuated his strong jawline as he clenched his face. Aside from him, the mountain throne opened to an expansive wall he built inside a cavern. The cavern wall opened to the forest as the mountain rose around them.

His leather breastplate kissed his bulging chest. His naked arms bulged and riddled with tattoos dancing to his shoulders. He was tall and slender, but his presence was more demanding than any wolf in his kingdom. The tattoos snaked across his chest under his armor. The intricate designs danced up his neck like flaming embers and branches.

"She did what." Alaric held his breath.

As they met their king, they were in wolf form, black as the night and ribbed from head to toe with bulging muscles. Their claws pressed into the stone at his feet. Their bodies sang in breastplates of shining silver and leather. Their broad swords kissed the scabbards on their backs.

"Sire, she fled into the wilderness with her guardian, Tala. The villagers knew and stalled us." A wolf said, his snout sighing at Alaric. "They did not put up a fight, and the women did not run. It is as if they had planned this all along." His bellowing voice echoed deep and scathing.

Alaric turned away from them and stared out the open cavern wall. He watched the trees move, and they sang to him. He closed his eyes, letting nature call to him. "Cayden will be after her. The humans will want her. She will be hunted by all wolves and man by the end of the week."

He walked to the edge and took a deep breath. "Ready the Dakitae humans. I will need them to help find her. Let Serk know I will demand his army, as the human warlords will be assembling by now. I will need them to cut off Serkily."

He craned his neck to stare at them, clenching his jaw. "I will track her myself." Then he turned back around to face them.

"Have Rieka split the army and hunt her in the wild. We will meet Cayden's wolves with swift vengeance."

The wolves bowed and lunged to do his bidding, and Alaric warned them again. "Do not bite those women you have taken yet. Put them in the stone house and guard them until we find my mate."

The wolves scoffed but then nodded, agreeing with him.

Alaric stood there, his green eyes glowing, his face stern, thinking about his mate. "Why do you run from me." He wondered.

He turned to ready himself to head into the wild, his arms flexed as if power bled through his veins. His wolves stood up, towering over his human form, bowed, and Alaric watched them go.

The ground quaked below him in the forest as his army plunged from the mountain on horseback. One hundred thousand would ensure the wolf king Cayden would not get her. His commander Conri and wolves were formidable. Though they were farther out, Alaric would ensure his wolves surrounded the territories they tracked.

"I am coming for you, white wolf," Alaric told himself, marching to his horse.

In the tent, Serimi stood with a slew of his war leaders as Randon popped his head in. Randon recognized Louve from Serkily and ducked to enter as the leaders gawked at his body mass and tallness. Randon wore full earthen hue body armor, etched and inscribed with flowing trees and wolves. He wore an axe over his back along his broad sword. His wide waist belt sheath housed daggers and a long sword. He had a black cloak attached around his neck, so when he loomed in on them, they thought a werewolf king had joined them.

Randon's eyes shimmered in blue back at them, and he loomed over them with his tallness. Serimi sighed. "About time."

Randon met his sigh with one of his own. "Who are we attacking now." He asked.

Louve glanced at Serimi and Randon froze.

Galin lunged into the tent to join them and Randon rolled his eyes at him. "I do not owe you money. Stop telling people that."

Galin huffed. "Denial. Typical wolf behavior."

Randon turned his stare back to Serimi and Louve, his face amused. "You will not accompany us to battle when that time comes," Louve told him.

"What."

"We need you to track the white wolf queen. A primordial, like yourself." Serimi chimed in.

The room fell silent as Randon's face drained of color. He held his breath, narrowing his brows. Then he let out a burst of laughter, his voice thunderous. "You are mad, mad humans." Randon stopped laughing as the silence filled him with dread.

"No." He shook his head, his eyes narrowed.

Serimi cleared his throat. "We need to get to her before Alaric does. We need you, Randon. You are the only primordial who can track her fast and sense her presence."

Randon huffed. "You ask me to hunt the white queen, the one chosen for the most powerful wolf king. The wolf king has maintained power and prestige for thousands of years in our lands. Alaric has a vast army of wolves and men, you know. He and Conri will use all their resources and power to hunt her. Plus, he would already have a head start on me."

Louve walked up to him and patted him on his leather vambrace. "You are fast. We need you, Randon. We need you to intercept her and bring her to Serkily. We can protect her better there until we defeat the wolf kings."

"You will draw the wolves and the Dakitae humans who serve the wolf king Alaric. They will come from the farthest reaches upon you. The city will not survive." Randon warned them.

Louve cleared his throat. "Well, our seer says otherwise. So, we need the white wolf at Serkily."

Randon scoffed at them. "His wolves outnumber all our men and wolves combined, you know. He will more than likely get to her before I can. This is death in the making what you are asking me to do."

Serimi sighed, his fervent jaws clenched, his cheeks red as his hair. "Serkily's tower seer has given us the order, and Meltivi is initiating. Louve's men are tracking wayward wolves to join us."

Randon scoffed at them, folding his bulky arms over his chest, and thinking, "And then what."

"What do you mean?" Serimi questioned.

"Are you hoping to wipe the wolf kings out? To take their kingdoms? What is the end game here."

Serimi gazed at the maps. "For too long, they have ruled our lands and taken humans, leaving decimation in their wake. They have killed and fed upon our people. They have taken our women to bite and then breed!" Then he turned to Randon. "You and your rebellious wolves are nothing like them. You fight back. That is why you must do this, now more than ever."

Silence, and then Serimi shouted. "We will fight until the death to free our kind from the wolves!"

Randon felt chills dart up his spine. "The white wolf queen. So, the thousand years has come again." He sighed and closed his eyes, flexing his forearms.

Serimi nodded. "We can have peace among our kind, but we must rid it of the wolf kings' power first, and the white wolf queen can help us."

"How do you know she does not want Alaric." Randon wondered, his face clenched. "The fate bond is powerful. He will pull her to him, no matter how hard she fights it."

Galin laughed. "We received word from a scout at Hildenia who fled as Rieka came. The white wolf has fled into the wilderness with her guardian. Alaric now hunts her."

Randon rolled his eyes and laughed again. "She flees her fated mate? Great. So, you want me to track the white wolf while keeping her from Alaric? You know Alaric has the gift where nature bends to him, right?"

Serimi nodded. "I know. You are also a primordial. You are the only one we can depend upon whose strength and power can protect her, even from the wolf kings."

"What say you." Galin cheered.

Randon glared at him even as chills darted up his spine and stared at the maps. They had placed the marker where Hildenia was and suggestive markers where she may have fled. He leaned over and bit his lip. "Her guardian would have taken her north from the mountain and east to the unexplored. That is the safest territory to keep her, for now."

Randon smiled. "This guardian lets the world know the white wolf will not bow and calls for humans to come to their aid. She is letting you humans know the white wolf is on your side. Impressive. She is wise doing this, leading her deeper into the wild."

"So, you will help us?" Serimi pleaded.

Randon gripped the hilt at his side, his leathers squeaking. A fire lingered and lit up inside him and spread into his bones. Something clawed into his backbone and sprouted like fingers were growing there. "I will get her." His eyes sparkled blue, his jaws clenched. "I will bring her to Serkily." His voice echoed as a strength poured out of him.

Louve took a deep breath. "Good."

"What does the seer want with her?" Randon demanded.

"Why?" Louve asked.

Randon clenched his face. "She is my equal. I need to know what your city plans on doing with her before I bring her."

"Ah. Protective of her already, eh?" Galin smiled.

Randon took a big breath, his face flat, staring at them.

Louve cleared his throat. "She will break the fated mate bond and set her free. If the bond breaks, she will not be drawn to her mate to serve his lust for power."

"What." Randon laughed again. His laugh stopped as quick as it started, and something itched his insides. He closed his eyes and shook his head.

"She can try. Never been done before."

"If this works, it will give us a white wolf queen and court of her choosing to work with humans to build a new world," Serimi added.

Randon froze when he said it and turned to go. He nodded at Galin. "Before I forget, I brought fifty wolves to help you." He patted Galin on his shoulder and smiled. "I sent word to gather them from the farthest northwestern lands also. They are weeks out, be forewarned."

"I do not need your filthy wolves to help me in the army."

Randon laughed. "Yes, you do, human. They stand outside and await your command."

"We humans have done fine!" Galin complained. "We have crafted the best armor to withstand your strikes and created weapons to take the wolves down!"

Randon laughed at him, turning his head to glare into the tent. "Very impressive, yes." He paused, craning back to stare at him. "We are brothers in spirit, you know. No matter how stubborn humans are."

Serimi, Louve, and the war leaders laughed, but Galin stood wide-eyed with his face clenched. "Damnit."

Randon exited the tent, turned to his wolves who wore the same body armor as him, and nodded to them. "Protect them with all you are. We have one chance to get this right."

They nodded at him, their eyes lighting up at his face. Randon jumped on his horse and turned east to cut the white wolf off in the wilderness. He would push the horse until it could go no further, then track her on foot. He would go into a part of their world they did not explore. It was the perfect place to hide, it was the perfect place for war.

Louve and Serimi stood outside and watched him go. "Will he get her?" Serimi mumbled.

Louve nodded. "He will get her; Brovina chose him for a reason."

Serimi nodded. "The wolf kings will bleed. Finally."

Galin popped out and watched Randon disappear over the plain, his black cloak whipping behind him. Then he turned to see the fifty men who were his wolves staring at him, and he cleared his throat. "We have work to do."

Just as Galin began to lead Randon's wolves, a scout pummeled up the road at them. "Serimi!" He He hollered, gasping for breath atop his horse.

Serimi, Galin, and Louve met him on the road. The scout pointed his arm west of the plain. "The kingdom of Cayden is coming! They ride fast over the western plains east, led by their commander, Conri. They will be north of us by nightfall. They number in the tens of thousands."

Serimi held his breath. "Damnit. We need to hold our position so if they ride upon Serkily, we can flank them in."

Galin sighed. "Randon has only just left!"

Louve began saddling his horse again. "I must ride back to Serkily and ready the kingdom! The Dakitae are never too far behind that wolf king! They will come and try to overrun our city."

Galin nodded, turning to the wolves Randon left behind. "Help me gather the army. We set up a perimeter to protect the plain and prepare to ride to Serkily if the worst should happen."

Serimi agreed. "The warring over the white wolf begins."

Galin lunged his arms out either side of him and hollered. "We are at warrrrr!" He filtered down the street with the wolves to the plain to ready the men.

On a rolling plain wide open to the world, the wolves of Cayden bent their heads into their horses' manes. They were formidable to look upon. The wolf kingdoms relished in the burly muscular forms of their human sides, with long beards and body-scathing tattoos to match their sinister natures. There were one hundred thousand of them.

They sported crimson cloaks that snaked in the air on their backs. Leading them was Conri, his black spiky hair twisted on his head over dark eyes. For miles, a crimson tide spilled from his warriors decked in obsidian armor. Their crimson cloaks filled the horizon like a blood wound had bled out.

Only this blood wound was alive and coming. They split the plains wide open, their swords and axes shimmering on their backs. They would ride over the human warlord faction, barely missing the plain. They rode due east and would pass under Alaric's Mountain kingdom and north of Serkily. That put them in direct line for war from the humans. Conri did not care.

His wolves would fill the plains and territories with a vengeance of pain. Conri's blue eyes sparkled in the daylight left as his fists clenched tight to the reigns. His heart was on the prize of the white wolf. He clenched his jaws and furrowed his black brows. His bulging muscular body glided atop his stallion as if floating in midair.

Alaric would know the kingdom of Cayden was coming now. The Dakitae humans serving Alaric would also be ready. The thousand years had begun. This time, Cayden would take the white wolf, and Alaric would fall.

Chapter 4
The Wild Reprieve of Fate

They were days in, and Ashina followed Tala upon another ridge. It overlooked endless rolling valleys and plateaus, and the forests drenched them in emerald kisses. They were nearing the heart of the unexplored eastern lands. They were far east of Alaric's Mountain kingdom and northeast of Serkily. They were getting closer to the heart, where Tala needed to take Ashina.

Ashina pushed her braid off her shoulder and paused, her hand atop the hilt of her sword. "Why is this not inhabited."

Tala stood beside her and smiled. "It was, once. My wolves had a settlement here by the falls in the heart."

"What happened to them."

They continued following the ridge.

"Alaric's father lured the leaders of my people to the Mountain with promises of peace and freedom. Then he killed them all and came for me. They put me in Hildenia and brought me you." She stopped walking and turned to face Ashina.

"You were only five."

Ashina swallowed, her face clenched. "I remember that day."

"Primordials take more time to come into their season because your kind are the most powerful. Alaric's throne has taken all the primordials for thousands of years."

Ashina bit her lip and narrowed her white brows.

Tala sighed. "You were crying and very upset when they took you from your pack and chose you as the next mate for Worgen. It was then I knew I had to rear you differently than the others. Worgen lied to my family and destroyed my home."

Tala scowled. "No heir of Worgen will ever take a primordial again."

Ashina turned her head to stare into the sunrise again, the warmth beating her face. "You have trained me well."

Tala took a deep breath. "They do not like women to be warriors or strong. They want them to be submissive breeding queens. They will find you, Ashina." She turned to stare at her again. "You have skill, but the wolf armies have expert trackers. Alaric is one of the best. He is strong and handsome. Do not let him fool you with his cunning."

"Let him come." Ashina glared at her, her face hard.

Tala turned to walk again. "Alaric and Conri will war against one another now, with the human warlords in the middle. They will kill one another and decimate each other's wolf armies. That will give the human warlord faction a reprieve for once. I hope."

Ashina huffed.

"This was the only way for me to let Serkily know you need help to be free. The seer there is very wise. Alaric will know you will not bend to the bond with us running. We have started a war." Tala huffed, gripping the leather straps at her chest. "They need to know you are on the human side and their ally."

"I am. Our lands have been at war between the wolves and man since I can remember." Ashina scowled. "Humans are suffering at the claws of the wolves."

Tala sighed. "Alaric will hunt you, Ashina. He will not stop. He is the strongest wolf; you must be wise and use cunning with him."

Ashina swallowed. "I will not let him take me."

Tala held her breath. "You may not have a choice, but you know what to do if he does."

Ashina sighed. "Unfortunately."

"You have never experienced the power of a male wolf when he wants his mate. He will lure you to accept him because of the fate bond. I have done my best to train you otherwise." She swallowed. "They are powerful and persuasive."

Ashina held her breath.

"If we flee deep enough into the wilderness, it will draw the wolf armies away from the human villages and cities. I hope. They have suffered enough loss with Alaric's menacing wolves. No more."

Ashina agreed. Her eyes rolled back over the vast wilderness they loomed over in silence. "By doing this, you have doomed yourself to death if Alaric finds you."

Tala breathed through her nose and closed her eyes. "It is too late to stop now. I will die a happy wolf if I know you can be free from bondage or oppression. That is what matters for our kind and the humans." She turned to her. "Never forget that."

Ashina followed as Tala turned to lead her on, but a part of her heart panged deep inside. She walked on the ridgeline, craning her face into the sun. Her soul lighted alive with something sprouting wings deep inside her. She paused on the ledge as a whisper of a powerful voice called to her, and her back went stiff.

Ashina met the call with wide eyes as her whole body froze on the plateau. She stared into the abyss of the forest and rolling plains, her heart beating fast. A whisper called her again.

"Ashina."

The movement atop the plateau opposite of them, ten miles over the rolling plains, caught her eyes, and she froze. Her amber eyes lit up. The trees bent as if something lurked beneath them, and they were breathing and alive. The forest swayed like fingers were prying it apart, looking for something. The birds lunged from the forest, spreading like black fingers in the sky.

Tala took a deep breath, her heart falling to her knees. "Alaric has found you already!"

Ashina raced behind Tala across the ledge deeper into the forest. They followed the ridgeline toward the winding river and the massive cavern waterfalls. She felt a tug deep inside, and her eyes kept craning back to glare at the forest, moving like something followed her.

Alaric froze on the ledge under a canopy of trees, his eyes following the lingering movement across the valley. The movement lunged on a plateau ten miles out. He had tracked her for days from the mountain. Alaric was swift and had lunged in his wolf form to track her. In his human form, he hunched on his legs.

His face clenched as he watched Ashina. "I see you." He whispered, his heart lighting up at her presence.

He turned his gaze to his wolves and craned his neck to the human Dakitae warriors. They waited in a wooded clearing on foot below him, and their black body armor and dark tattoos danced up their faces and arms. They shaved the sides of their heads and had tattoos on them, too. They gripped their long swords and axes and nodded to Alaric.

Alaric was fortunate he had kept a sect of them in this wilderness. The kingdoms were all fools to think he did not have eyes and ears everywhere, even in desolate places. He should have known the guardian, Tala, would take his mate here. She was wise in drawing the armies away from Serkily to protect the humans.

"Do not touch my mate," Alaric commanded. "I will take her."

Serk bent down aside Alaric, scowling. "What of the guardian."

Alaric sneered, his eyes lighting up. "Treacherous wolf. Hunt her."

Serk turned to go as Alaric called after him. "Serk. Prepare your army for Conri and the warlord Serimi. I know they will come to flank us and try to take her."

Serk nodded, his black eyes sparkling. "They can try, but we are ready, my king."

Alaric took a deep breath as his eyes followed Ashina. She disappeared over the ledge deeper into the forest. "No one takes my wolf."

He stood up, his face hard, as his eyes shimmered golden. He followed the ledge on the rolling plateau under the canopy of darkness, his eyes ever watchful for Ashina. He lunged through the forest to cut her off at the falls.

Tala and Ashina lunged over the plateau and around boulders through the winding forest. Their hearts beat wildly as Tala's backbone burned. They both turned as a bellowing horn sounded behind them. Tala froze and glared through the forest.

Ashina huffed. "The Dakitae! Alaric must have a sect of them here already."

Tala turned to run again. "Hurry to the falls straight ahead! There are caverns where you can hide until Serkily comes for you!"

Ashina watched Tala veer away from her. "What are you doing?!"

Tala lunged into her and hugged her in a fierce embrace. She kissed her head and pressed her palms against Ashina's cheeks, staring into her eyes. "This is where I leave you, white wolf. I will draw them off, but you must hide under the falls, follow the cavern passes through the tunnels. The scent of you will not reach Alaric there."

"Alaric comes also. This is to get you to divert from me." Ashina warned her, clenching her jaws. "Alaric will find me."

"The Dakitae will think you are still with me. I must draw them off now, or Alaric will force you to the mountain today. My people have used that place as protection for centuries. Trust me!"

Ashina watched Tala lunge away from her toward the bellowing horn. She turned and raced with all her strength straight ahead until the roaring of water filled her veins. Her head throbbed as she reached the end of the bellowing woods miles down. It opened to a lagoon with raging falls that loomed over her for what seemed like miles into the heavens.

She raced around the lagoon and climbed the rocks. Her back burned with an itch she could not describe, and her ached. She pulled herself higher until the falls roared by her face and she was soaked. She saw an opening doused in light and stepped onto a stone ledge. She followed it and stood alone in a vast cavern as the falls fell before her face.

There were no cavern passes. "What are you planning, Tala?" Ashina questioned, backing herself against the wall.

A mile out, Tala stood atop a boulder and whistled. She watched as the forest came to life with the Dakitae. She jumped away from the boulder to a ledge leading back to the plateau as they chased her there. They emptied the forest floor for miles. She would lead them south away from Ashina and the wolf king who hunted her.

A shina held her breath at the splendor of the power of these falls. She gazed around the high stone ceiling cascading over her and turned her neck to see carvings on the wall.

She meandered at it, saw painted drawings and wondered if Tala made some when she was a child. Being ripped from her guardian so suddenly made her weary. As a shadow loomed in on her, she stood silently contemplating her life.

She widened her eyes as Alaric approached her from the path, and chills darted up her spine. His eyes were as powerful as his strong face. His blonde hair was in long twisty braids down his back, his beard trimmed to frame his handsome face. He pressed a fist atop the hilt of his sword by his side and walked toward her cautiously, studying her eyes.

His long leather robes split at his legs over trousers laced with buckles and daggers. His black wardrobe danced at his boots and adorned his full body armor of inscribed leather. His naked arms bulged under his breastplate, riddled with elegant tattoos that spilled up his arms over his chest.

He paused as he neared her, his eyes lingering upon her face. His eyes rolled up and down her body to acknowledge this was his mate. He lit up at her presence, his face firm. Ashina knew someone had followed her since dawn. It had pricked her backbone all morning. She let him linger closer, her eyes on his face, studying him.

As he neared her chest, she jerked her long sword out and met his throat. Alaric froze, his eyes meeting hers. She met his eyes as he loomed over her, her strong fist clasped against her hilt. He pressed forward anyway. She pulled her dagger and pressed toward his groin.

Alaric sighed at her face. His sigh was weary, full of contempt. "Your guardian trained you to be a warrior. That is unfortunate." His voice sounded deep and echoed, rich and powerful.

Ashina sneered at him. "Unfortunate for you." She threatened him, her face hard.

Alaric's face was flat in disappointment yet amused with her. A slight smile of intrigue lit his eyes up. "Yes." His face clenched.

Ashina met his intrigue with wide eyes, noting his brazenness toward her. "You will not take me." Her voice sounded like a rushing wave that echoed.

Alaric curved his lips to smile and then froze, his eyes determined and his jaws clenched in her face. "I am your mate." He whispered in her face.

He leaned away from her. "And you know it." He eyed her with suspicion.

"I did not choose you." She belted out. "The fated bond lies."

Ashina continued to push her blades out at him even as he lingered toward the falls away from her, studying her. "The bond never lies. It draws us to one another. Did you think the forest would not have allowed me to sense your presence? I have tracked you for days."

Ashina froze as he continued. "You are not the only white wolf with powers. There is a reason you were chosen for another white wolf."

Ashina lowered her sword for a split second, her eyes wide. "It betrays me then. If you are also a white wolf."

Alaric huffed at her, his body flexing, his face studying hers. "You dare to defy the fated bond? In thousands of years, it was never defied."

Ashina swallowed. "I defy it. I will break it."

Alaric eyes lingered into hers as he stepped closer again. His eyes were adamant at her face. "You are very brave to defy me."

His glare at her sent Ashina's knees trembling because he was enjoying her defying him. "But you cannot defy fate. Your guardian was chosen unwisely."

"She has saved me," Ashina warned him.

Alaric approached closer, and Ashina saw his power as he loomed over her, his aura filling her with weakness in her knees.

"We belong to one another, white wolf." He whispered into her, his breath on her face.

His eyes sparkled emerald at her face. He studied her as if reading her thoughts and feeding off her emotions. Ashina found herself drowned in the strength he exuded over her. Then she remembered what Tala warned her about the luring power of the fated bond.

She plunged her blade against his throat again as he pressed closer into her, and they faced one another off again. He did not pull his sword. She cut a sliver on his throat. He held his breath and sneered at her as blood trickled down to his armor. Ashina held him there by her blade even as fangs burst up from his gums, and he roared over her into his white wolf form. She fell back against the wall as he transformed like a wind had pressed her back and dropped her weapons.

She stared into his golden eyes, his ears flat on his head. She stared at his wide snout full of dagger-like fangs as his broad, bulky, muscular form loomed over her. He raised to the ceiling, towering over her several feet. Every inch of him was perfection, power, and beauty.

She swallowed at first as terror filled her heart at his presence, her eyes meeting his. "I see you." She whispered up at his face, a rage of glory basking in her from him.

His ears perked, and she saw his eyes waver at her. She stood to face him, gazing upon his magnificent form that lured her closer. She lingered on him and gazed at his snout as his eyes met hers. His breathing was calm and firm as he lowered his snout to gaze upon her.

He bellowed out, "I see you, white wolf." They stood there and stared at one another while the roaring falls sang behind them.

He held his paw out as she took it in her hand. Alaric watched her graze her steady fingers across his leathery pads and took a deep breath as she pressed into the fur. She compared her hand to his mighty paw, the breadth of it engulfing her.

She caught him staring at her and felt his breath upon her soul. Before she could say anything, Alaric turned back to human as if he had been born of a mighty wind. His armor was still snug to his body as he met her eyes.

He gripped her hand in his strong clasp and took a deep breath in her face. "I would never harm you." He pleaded with her, his voice echoing. "You are my mate. We will mate for life."

She tried to pull away but he held onto her hand and pulled her against his chest. She fell into his arms, her body stiff at his strength. Ashina felt the power in his arms as he pulled her into him, and she held her breath at his face. His eyes lingered in her eyes and fell to her lips. "I need you to trust me, Ashina. My strong warrior white wolf."

Ashina swallowed. "The world hunts me."

Alaric huffed. "I will hunt the world to keep you safe. I will burn it down to protect you. You belong with me and no other."

Alaric pressed into her lips, and for a moment, she wanted to meet him there. His breath was hot and very powerful. As his fangs burst up, she knew he would bite her to begin the bonding. She bent away from his lips even as he leaned in deeper to taste her, his mouth open.

She pried her hand from his grasp as he let her go, but he could have forced her to relent. She knew this. Alaric was being cautious with her. She pressed her back against the wall and slid down to her butt. As she propped her knees up, something lit up inside her. She stared at him as he met her face with anticipation, his body flexed.

He studied her, his eyes lingering all over her. He watched her mannerisms, his jaws clenched. He held his breath at her strength and bravery. "You are beautiful." He whispered at her face as his muscular body loomed over her.

Ashina raised her eyes and stared into him, her heart ravaging her chest at his presence. She did not like it. Tala never told her it would feel like this. Ashina bit it down deep inside her and breathed deeply.

He would not let her leave the cavern, and she was not ready to transform. Alaric knew what he was doing. He hunted her, tracked her there, and subdued her. Ashina let her heart sing to her at this moment, but her soul lit a fire within her edged with caution.

He stood by the falls, his shadow stretching over her like a blackness had fallen upon her. It was a deep darkness that filled her with a weakness she hated. His words seemed promising, but his intentions lied, and she knew it. His sweet words soured in her mouth.

"By dawn, you will accompany me back to my kingdom. We will consummate this union as fated mates, and the thousand-year reign shall begin again."

Ashina did not respond to him. She studied his mannerisms, the way he walked and held himself, his facial expressions and his deceiving eyes. He was a mighty hunter and tracker. His werewolf form was magnificent, but something lurked deep inside. Ashina breathed him in like a plague. It filled her lungs alive with death and pinged her guts like a relentless dripping of water.

Tala trained her well, or she would have fallen into his arms. She would have let him take her as his mate. No wonder so many had fallen to the realm of Worgen. But she could not. Her mind went back to Tala and whatever else was coming to hunt her. She would accompany him in the morning and travel to his kingdom. She would play along with him for a bit.

Then after, she would be his fall and not relent.

Chapter 5
The Ambush

Serimi and Galin lay flat on their stomachs and peered over the mound toward the plain. The ground shook beneath them with the wolves of Cayden coming. Serimi peered through the darkness with Randon's fifty wolves. The wooded hills behind them filled with the warring humans. Wolves not loyal to either wolf king were there, but they only had about two hundred wolves. They needed thousands upon thousands more.

They waited until the plain filled with Conri's army. The breadth of the horizon lit up the darkness as their wolf obsidian body armor glistened in the night. He watched his commander Galin crane his neck and blow his war horn. Behind them, the horizon lit up from their flaming arrows tipped in wolfsbane. His archers pillaged the night sky, and it became as bright as dawn. The arrows flanked the wolf army and hit them on horseback. The bodies began flailing onto the plain, the riderless horses slowing down.

"Again!" Serimi commanded.

As Galin sounded the horn again, the flaming wolfsbane arrows filled the breadth of the plain over their heads.

Conri did not slow down. His army fled from the flaming arrows. They veered north away from their sights, with the line getting hit behind him. The wolves hit by arrows flailed off their horses and pulled them out. They transformed into mighty black wolves to rush Galin's army.

"They are strong!" Galin complained and pressed into the horn again

From the woods behind them, slinging silver blades thrust into the night. The ballista's flung blades to cut down the wolves in battle. The blades swished and twisted in midair, and cut their heads off, severed their limbs.

The black wolves fell as their legs collapsed under them. Galin raised to peer out again, his eyes wide. The blades sunk into the ground after they hit the wolves, and the silver shimmered into the moonlight. As the bodies filled the plain with blood, Serimi, Galin, and the wolves followed them down the incline. They slid down the hill onto their horses, and the army with the wolves lunged back up it on horseback.

When they met the wolves on the plain, Serimi and Galin lunged their long arms out and gripped their magnetic swords. The silver blades flung up out of the ground away from them. The diamagnetic properties of the silver made their weapons formidable against the wolves. The silver blades repelled against their swords.

The human warriors with the wolves roared onto the plain as silver cut down Conri's wolves. The shimmering blades filled the breadth of the plain like shards of broken glass. The blades looked as if they had erupted from the earth as the wolves lunged in midair at them.

They met the wolves at the plain and throttled into them. The wolves on Galin's side transformed and met Conri's wolves in midair. The plain was horrendous as roars echoed into the dawn, and Galin met the wolves on the plain. His ten thousand warriors and two hundred wolves lunged into them. But it did not matter because Conri continued his hunt for the white wolf.

As dawn arose, Serimi and Galin sat aside one another on horseback covered in blood. They had injuries that needed stitches, but they had killed twenty thousand of Conri's wolves. Even with the help of their wolves, it was not enough. Conri still headed into the wild to hunt the white wolf with his thousands upon thousands. That meant he and Alaric would be warring in the wilderness soon.

It would be a miracle if Randon could get the white wolf out.

Chapter 6
The Denial of the Bond

Randon let the horse go once he reached the unexplored forests. He took a deep breath and tracked north toward the heart. Hours later, a bellowing horn blew through the darkness, tingling his spine. He hid under a thicket as the Dakitae lingered under the canopy in the darkness. They had beat him to her, and by now, Alaric had her.

They came as dark as the night. He counted fifty of them, held his breath, and slithered out in the open behind them. His transformation was like a wind catapulted through the woods.

They turned slowly as the twelve-foot wolf Randon met them there. His muscle-riddled body filled the path, his black fur as pitch as the night. He loomed upon them as his blue eyes shimmered under the canopy, and his black ears perked atop his head.

He flayed into them with his claws, his broad sword cutting them down on the path. Their screams echoed into the night.

He flung their bodies over the rolling slopes, surrounded them in the woods, and pressed away from them as they all died. He would stay in wolf form at night to track the white wolf. The path behind him filled with blood and severed bodies as he ripped into them. He paused under the canopy as he emerged on the plateau.

"I know you are there." He moaned, sighing. "You have watched me for some time, old wolf."

He turned to see Tala come from the darkness, but she was not in wolf form. "I knew Serkily would send a wolf to hunt her. And a primordial at that."

"You are the guardian? Where is she."

Tala led him on. "Alaric has her by now. He is much faster and would have found her at the falls."

"What."

"I had to get the Dakitae off her trail. Alaric had been tracking her all day before they came. I could not tell her. If I had not done that, he would have drug her out to his mountain then."

Randon huffed at her, shaking his snout. "Yet you let me kill them all. You led them to me. Fifty of them."

Tala shrugged her shoulders. "He also has his wolves with him and has sent them on the hunt away from him. That gives us a chance. There are many more where we are going, trust me. I discovered Alaric has settlements in these lands filled with them. I will have my turn. I need you to help me get Alaric away from her now."

Randon turned to follow her, shaking his snout. "You guardians are something else, did anyone tell you that?"

Tala sighed. "Yes. Come, great wolf. We need to get her to Serkily. Alaric will be leaving with her at dawn. We have little time."

"You want to break the bond. I was told." He followed her, his paw clasped around his broad sword. "You want to make her queen and build a new world..."

"Yes, and you will need to help her break it." Tala stopped walking and stared up at him, but Randon widened his eyes and snarled his snout at her.

"No."

"Yes. You are the only primordial in the world with Ashina. It takes two of that powerful blood to break it with the help of a seer." Tala informed him. "It is now or never."

"You picked me to track her for this reason. You want me to bond with her. That sounds like treason."

Tala nodded. "No, the seer Brovina did." She turned to walk again. "This is the only way the humans will ever be free of the wolf king's brutality. And yes, she needs to trust you. It is not treason to do what is right."

Randon took a deep breath as his knees grew weak and his spine tingled. "You force me to face Alaric."

Tala took in a deep breath. "You have no choice. You will do what is right because that is what a virtuous wolf does. We do what is right for our wolves and humans."

Randon stared at her, his wolf form looming over her by several feet. He stared into the cloudy night sky and shook his head, his ears perking in the silence. He said nothing else, but Tala sensed a strength pouring from his backbone she could not explain. She gazed back at him one last time as they continued, his eyes sparkling of resolve and determination.

They had not slept. Alaric stayed alert all night, watching and listening in the woods. Ashina stayed awake with her back against the wall, watching him. Tala had trained Ashina in the ways of the alpha wolves. If she had fallen asleep, given the chance, she had no doubt Alaric would have bitten her to begin the fate bond. After a mate got bitten, the attraction would increase. If consummated, she would bond as his mate. She was not ready for that to happen right now.

The roaring waters filled their heads with resounding echoes. A wind moved in as a pressing storm lingered over the plains. Ashina watched the sunrise as if it bled through the falls, the crimson glory warming her face. Alaric stared at her as the sun touched her face and recognized her strength. He clenched his fist atop his knee and watched her.

The light kissed her skin as he gazed upon her face. Her eyes lit up in hazel diamonds, shimmering with hues of yellow. She bent her head to peer at its glory and raised her chin as the sun kissed her face. The sun gave her strength and glory. She took a deep breath as it calmed her heart, a fire surging within her.

Alaric bent his head at her, stood up, loomed over her, and blocked the sun in her face. "Time to go, my beloved."

She stood up and did not take his hand when he offered it. He watched her, leery, as she denied it. As she walked by him, she froze and glared in his eyes. He held his breath and met her stare as their bodies pressed against one another. He clenched his jaws at her face, his eyes bright and powerful. Ashina sensed his weariness for her. He had not expected to chase his mate days into the wilderness.

"I will not harm you, Ashina." He bent around her to lead her down, his whole backside tense.

She followed him down the rock wall to the lagoon as the roaring falls calmed her heart, but her ears itched. Vibrations rang up her legs to movement, and she turned her ear towards it. Something was coming. She craned her neck and let the sun kiss her face again. She blinked her eyes into its brilliance. Her face was clenched and strong, her eyes firm, her lips pouty.

When she turned back to follow Alaric, she met his chest like a wall hit her as he pressed his blade against her throat. She froze at his face, his eyes firm at her.

The Dakitae emerged from the darkness of the forest and surrounded her. She pulled back, but it was too late. She grabbed the hilt of her sword, but Alaric pressed his blade harder against her throat. "Your weapons." He glared as they surrounded her.

She held her breath and swallowed, his blade against her throat swift and brutal.

"I know you will hunt them," Alaric added. "I cannot allow you to do that."

Ashina craned her eyes to gaze at the human barbarians and sneered. "You side with these cruel humans."

"They serve me, yes." Alaric watched her unbuckle her belt and remove her weapons with his blade still on her. She unbuckled the leather straps around her chest and let her scabbards fall at her feet. She caught Alaric undressing her with his eyes as she did that.

Ashina handed her axe and sword to Serk. She sighed, watching them walk off with her weapons, and rolled her eyes. "You know they commit brutal acts upon innocent people." She tested him. "And your wolves take their women."

Alaric froze when she said that and did not remove his blade from her throat. He bent his face into hers, his fangs showing. "They do not harm wolves as we rule the kingdoms. My wolves are loyal to the mates they choose with the human women..."

Ashina held her breath when he said that, her face hard. "Yet the Dakitaie are human."

"Yes, but they serve me. That makes them brave." He removed his blade and turned to walk past the lagoon with her. She huffed at his back, counting the number of the Dakitae filling the falls around her by the dozens.

"And the human women you take? Are they brave?" She questioned.

Alaric stopped walking, his back tense. His naked arms writhed in muscles and flexed when she said that. She got a good glimpse of his powerful backside and broadness. She had hit a nerve with him deep inside. She watched him take a deep breath as she said that.

"Or are they brave because you give them no choice?" She demanded, her voice echoing over the falls.

Alaric's heart pricked him when she said that. He eyed her from the side, his face clenched. "You do not approve."

Ashina met his stare with narrowed brows. "A virtuous kingdom would not do that."

Alaric stopped again and turned to face her, his eyes hard and cold. "You know nothing of the mountain, white wolf."

"Where are the women your commander took from my village." She demanded.

Alaric did not answer her. She bit her tongue and said nothing more. He turned to lead her on again. She turned her head to face the sun and breathed it in. Anger filled up the hole that had lingered deep inside her. She closed her eyes and filled her lungs with fire. Something burst out of her that had laid dormant her whole life.

She growled from a pit in her soul as her white wolf form emerged and loomed above Alaric. It blew over her as if a mighty wind blasted around him. As she did that, it blew away the slew of Dakitae following her. They slammed into the rocks hard, their chest plates crunching, injuring them.

Alaric's long blonde braids flew around his neck like a whip as he lunged around to see her in her wolf form, his eyes wide. His eyes went from her paws to her snout, enthralled by her beauty. She lunged at him with her paw and blasted him away, where he flew midair into the lagoon. She turned and roared at the Dakitae lingering around her like an endless plague. She cut into them with her fangs and claws atop the rocks, killing them.

Alaric lunged up out of the water in his white wolf form. He catapulted over the rocky shoreline, snarling. He wrapped his long arms around her and pulled her off the bodies. She ripped them up, but Alaric's size and muscle mass engulfed hers. As he picked her up, he pressed over her shoulder.

His breath was hot on her neck, and Ashina roared. He was going to bite her here.

"You will not bite me!" She bellowed, her back to him.

Alaric growled, pushing against her power, which surprised him. "I will!" He roared, his eyes on her neck.

Ashina blocked his fangs with her claws and pressed his snout off her. She lunged into his chest, and he gasped for air. He twisted her around in his arms to face his snout, and he growled at her face.

He pressed her long arms out hard to bite her, his body flexed. Ashina head-butted him. She catapulted off him sideways and went air-born past the shoreline into the trees. He was stronger, more muscular. Alaric watched her, his fangs itching for her neck.

Her back hit a tree and it cracked, sending shards of oak splinters like darting arrows around her. Alaric had not anticipated her strong wolf form or her power. He took a deep breath to compose himself to take her, snarling.

"Where are the women of my village, Alaric!" She roared at him.

Alaric bent down, his back forming a ridgeline of hair standing straight up, and roared at her face. Ashina had landed on her paws, digging into the soil beneath her to steady herself. She lunged her snout to the ground and growled. She roared at

Alaric's face, her fur standing up all along her backbone to form spikes.

"You dare defy me!" He roared at her, stretching his paws as his claws slithered out.

"I dare defy you and your kingdom." She roared back, her beautiful white snout snarling to her pristine blue eyes.

She lunged into the dirt and ripped the earth up with her claws. She spread her paws, protruded her dagger claws, her eyes a fiery hate upon Alaric.

"I will kill you all." She loathed him. "For what you have done to humans."

He stood back, taking a deep breath and growling deep inside him, waiting for her. He stood taller and stretched his neck, sneering his snout at her. His eyes filled like a fierce gold flame had lit within him. "You would kill your mate?! Your chosen fated mate!" He roared at her. "We wolves rule! We have power in these lands."

"You are evil!" She roared at him.

He bellowed at her. "You do not know meeee!" His roaring voice was deep and dark. "You are giving me no chance."

"Using the Dakitae is evil! It is not hard to do what is right!" She commanded, her wolf voice riveting up Alaric's spine. "Trying to bite me when I am unwilling is not right!" She warned him.

Alaric stood taller, his whole wolf form tense, his eyes lit on fire. "You are my mate," He moaned, exasperated at her. "You do not get to question me bonding to you, our kingdom, our power, or the choices made to keep it thriving."

"I was not given an option. I reject you as my mate."

Alaric growled, his laugh an assault on her. "You are not released of our bond. You are stubborn, denying me."

As she reared up to attack him in midair, a black wolf plunged over the rocks through the forest into Alaric. It lunged into his shoulder and knocked him back into the water. Alaric went flying again and landed under the falls against the rocks.

This black wolf was broader than Alaric. Ashina paused as she gawked at him. A fire broke inside her as this wolf appeared, and chills darted up her spine. She let the chills push deep inside her as she watched this wolf attack the wolf king.

He turned to her and growled. "Run! Run, Ashina!"

Ashina blasted through the Dakitae and flayed her claws into them as she lunged away from Alaric. Randon stood tall and stretched his neck as Alaric pressed through the falls. Alaric stood in the water, his eyes glimmering a fiery gold. His snarl wrinkled on his snout to his peering eyes as he rose from the lagoon and growled. He seethed at Randon as he walked out of the water, his claws engorged.

Randon growled at him even as the remnants of the Dakitae rolled in around him. "Traitor wolf," Alaric growled. "You dare come between me and my mate."

Randon growled, towering over Alaric by a foot. Alaric huffed at him. "A Primordial. You come to hunt my mate?" He demanded.

Randon laughed, his deep roar echoing. "She rejected you."

Alaric snarled, his eyes narrowing over a wrinkled snout full of vengeance. "She is mine and mine alone."

Randon continued to circle him at the lagoon, snarling, his whole body flexed. "She will kill you."

Alaric was magnificent to look upon but Randon was broader. His primordial blood line was evident as Alaric faced him. Alaric bent down to lunge at him and belted back suddenly. An arrow shot through his shoulder from the tree line. He flew back away from Randon as the shaft plunged through him.

"Run, Randon!" Tala shouted from the canopy.

Alaric roared at the pain and fell back into the water again. Randon split the Dakitae behind him and lunged through the trees to get away and follow Ashina. Tala pressed another arrow into her bow and fired and began taking out the group of Dakitae. She paused as Alaric catapulted out of the water again. He seethed and roared toward her. Tala lunged away from him and transformed into her gray wolf form to get away.

Randon picked up Ashina's scent and bent his wolf head to track her. He pushed himself hard over the plateau she had taken opposite the falls. The incline rose and the roaring falls cascaded in rainbows around him in the forest. These falls spilled into a wide river basin flowing into Serkily. Randon huffed, his eyes dead set on her trail.

Tala led the Dakitae with Alaric on her paws over the other plateau opposite the one Ashina had taken. She had Ashina's scent on her to draw Alaric to her, hoping he would think he was chasing Tala and Ashina. She craned her neck to stare back and noticed Alaric was not following her anymore. She slid down the incline to the river below the plateau. The hordes of Dakitae emerged from the woods and could not follow her down the sloping incline.

She dug her claws into the earth, sliding down in a desperate race, and belted out a resounding roar. Across the plateau, Ashina perked her ears up and recognized Tala's warning.

Ashina galloped hard and slowed down as she neared the end of the plateau. The waterfalls met there with a cliff beneath her. She pressed into the rocks and stopped on the ledge, taking a deep breath.

Her wolf eyes followed movement as Randon lunged from the woods, airborne at her snout. He plunged into her waist, his eyes hard and focused. She growled at him, swiping his muscular back. But it was too late. Randon pulled her over the falls with him into the river. He gripped her hard and would not let her go even as they fell.

Ashina burst up from the frigid rapids in her human form and gasped for air. Strong arms wrapped around her waist still. This black-headed man pressed up at her face and took a breath. He pressed into her waist and put his face in hers. She met his eyes as the water pulled them under again. They bobbed together, his strong arms clasped around her waist like a clamp.

His blue eyes beamed into hers as he nodded in her face, his jaws clenched and hard. "We go down the river toward Serkily. This is the fastest way!" He pulled her through the rapids, his body mass and bulk overpowering her.

"Tala!" Ashina screamed.

Randon pulled at her again to stay against him. "She will come!"

Ashina let the rapids pull her downriver with Randon. For twenty miles, they raced as the current pulled them up and down. They took deep breaths and rolled into one another. The deep vat of desperation trying to get away filled them with dread. Randon would not let her go. The power of his grip filled her mind with a desperate furor, and she noticed it in his eyes as he fought to get her to safety. Every time he bobbed up again to breathe, his eyes were on her and their surroundings.

Hours later, they had reached the outskirts of Serkily along the rolling plains. There were no Dakitae, but they would hike and take two more days. Randon pulled Ashina with him through the water. They collapsed along a sandy shoreline, spent of energy. The silence of the woods with the evergreen trees rolled over them to form a sacred canopy. They lay there for endless moments, their breaths loud with exhaustion.

Ashina heaved in and out and turned her head to look at this wolf who had saved her. He laid on his back, his chest heaving up and down. Randon turned his head to stare at her, his eyes roaming over her face and long white hair. She met his eyes, and he froze as he stared at her.

He closed his eyes, turned his head, and sighed. "Damnit."

Ashina glared at him, her face drawn and tired.

"I am Randon. I will take you to Serkily." He moaned, sitting up slowly.

He reached over his shoulder, pressing a wet hand on his back, and pulled it away with blood on it. Ashina eyed the slash she gave him. "I am sorry." She belted out.

Randon sighed at her face. "We have two days of hiking left." She watched him stand up and stretch his back, his body armor squeaking in saturation. "The Dakitae will head to Serkily to cut us off. Conri will be coming for you. We must hurry."

He popped out a fist, and she stared at it. She swallowed, her eyes meeting his, and took it. Randon pulled her up and paused as she lingered her eyes upon him. She saw the man, but his wolf form seared in her mind. He bent his head to acknowledge her and waited, watching her expression on him.

"You are a primordial." She whispered, and she met his eyes.

He leaned into her face and whispered, "I see you too, white wolf." He half-smiled at her, and his eyes lit up.

She met his smile with a slight one of her own and followed him through the wilderness along the river. He turned his head to stare at her as she followed. Ashina gazed upon the power of his magnificent backside and looming tallness. She quaked inside, her eyes wide. Before Randon could turn again to look at her, she rolled her eyes behind them. She wondered where Tala was or if she was even alive.

Alaric stood on the plateau gazing at the rapids, pulling at his shoulder. He had veered away from Tala once he sensed Ashina was not with her. He let the Dakitae chase her, but they lost her down the ravine into the river. He stood in his human form again, clenching his jaws and fists. Serk approached him from behind, bowing.

Alaric did not look at him. "Take the army to Serkily. Prepare for my arrival there to take the city."

Serk widened his eyes. "Yes, my king."

Alaric sneered. "Serk." He called back to him.

"Hunt the guardian Tala. She has disobeyed me for the last time."

"What shall we do with her?" Serk wondered.

Alaric sneered. "Kill her."

Serk agreed. "We will begin today, my king."

"Do not fail me again. My commander Rieka will see to it you succeed."

Serk bowed to him and turned to go, leaving Alaric seething over the falls, his eyes filled with rage.

"Go ahead and run. I am coming for you regardless." He belted out, his face clenched. "And you will be mine."

Chapter 7

A Relentless Assault

Louve arrived the night before with fifty warriors. They faced the daunting task of ridding the kingdoms of Alaric. It was harrowing as the impending blackness headed their way beyond the horizon. Louve stood on the tower, glaring aside at Meltivi and shaking his head.

The Dakitae were coming and were a week out. The blackness ebbed and flowed like a river flooding in on them, and it would come with harsh pains for the city. Louve pulled his gloved fingers through his long black beard. His brown eyes glowed yellow in the sunrise, his fervent hope adamant. He turned to his warriors guarding the wall behind him and sighed.

"Get the women and children into the cavern pass before war comes. Prepare the warriors to guard the walls and gates. We are now at war."

Meltivi watched the horizon, envisioning the army pressing in closer. The unexplored forest was vast, and the plateaus fell to roaming plains, allowing quick travel through the forest.

Louve huffed. "Conri comes across the plain from the wilderness. If Randon found the white wolf, he will have a hell of a time getting her here now."

Meltivi agreed. "We have a short time to help the white wolf who can free us of the wolf kings' reigns. Are you ready, dear friend?"

Louve smiled. "Serimi and Galin plan to flank them with the wolves. They outnumber us, but we humans are brave warriors. We will succeed."

"Alaric will also come with his army of wolves." Meltivi shook his head. "He will be warring with Conri for his mate."

Louve laughed, his booming voice echoing. "Bring them on-nnnn!" He shouted and marched away from the king to ready his army. "Been dying to try our new weapons on the wretched wolves serving these kings!"

Meltivi stood and stared into the horizon, watching Louve be diligent and courageous. He sighed. "Hurry, Randon. Our fate depends on you getting the white wolf here safely."

Serkily was impenetrable from the rolling plain. A rising plateau behind it had endless caverns leading into a mountain range under the river. The river snaked around the kingdom and then back up again toward Alaric's Mountain kingdom. The plain of Serkily was engulfed with towering stone walls from the mountain. They succeeded because of their defensive position and the prowess of their human warriors. Their weapons helped them thrive with the wolves in power for thousands of years.

Brovina's foresight ensured their protection. She ensured their human war leader Serimi and his commander Galin split away from the city. They took over the unexplored plain in the west. They did that in case war came, then the human faction could flank them from behind. The time was now at hand. Humans learned to be meticulous when fighting the wolves throughout the centuries.

Serkily stood walled with stone pillars rising over a raging river, with a broad city-drawn bridge over the waters. The river was deep, roaring, and very fast. It would be hard to breach it. The towers rose into the heavens and the warriors manning the walls had keen eyes. Catapults and archers were ready by the thousands.

The lands suffered, and the wolves bound humans. Their city streets filled with families fleeing into the mountainous caverns. King Meltivi took a deep breath, and Brovina joined him. They watched the horizon fill with blackness coming for them.

"What do you see, sister?" Meltivi asked.

Brovina gripped her staff, her hip aching. "I see the wolf kings bleeding as the white wolf comes."

Meltivi grew chills. "Good. Let them bleed. Humans have bled long enough for these wicked wolves."

Beyond the horizon on the open plains across the river, the Dakitae filled the lands. A black veil thrust upon it as the human warriors serving Alaric seethed with Serk led them. Black Flanchards draped their horses and their Chanfron's sported obsidian spikes. The Dakitae black metal strip armor fitted their fine-tuned bodies. Their form-fitting helmets had horns built on the sides of them. They looked like demons on horseback.

Their spiral tattoos danced up their hands and arms to the edges of their faces in pitch black. The men wore full beards braided to their chests and shaved heads. Black paint glazed under their eyes, and their bodies looked carved from their armor. They plunged over the plain like a river had bled out from the depths.

The attack would be a short burst of power, and Serkily would fall. If the white wolf was there, Alaric would take her for his mate. He was a formidable war leader and wolf king and it was evident with his human faction. His wolves were even worse.

Behind the Dakitae army, four horses pulled catapults. They had two on each side, and stretched over two miles wide. Behind the catapults were the ten thousand archers on horseback. Alaric spared no expense on his human faction army, and it increased yearly. It had helped cement him as supreme wolf king, and the lands suffered because of him.

Ashina did not know what she was up against. She dared to defy the most powerful wolf king in the world. Although Alaric had her in his grasp, he failed at biting her. If he failed at biting and keeping her, what other hardships would he face to get her or even keep her?

Chapter 8
The Brutality of Conri

Randon pulled Ashina through the wilderness along the river. They melted upon a rolling plain where the forests bled out under the moon. It was a week's journey into Serkily from the unexplored lands, and they were nearing closer. They hunched on their knees on a hill and peered through the trees in the darkness. Their wolf sight shimmered in the darkness as Randon felt the earth vibrate beneath them.

"An army goes to Serkily already. My guess is the Dakitae. They try to head us off."

He froze and glared down at her. "Alaric's power is vast and wide, and he will take Conri's armies too."

Ashina huffed. "I hate them all."

Randon stared at her in the darkness as she leaned into his forearm and pressed against him. "I feel your hatred." Then he paused and stared at her face. She met his stare as he continued.

"Into my shoulder. With your bony shoulder blade." He smiled and then turned to stare out again.

Ashina pursed her lips and pressed harder into his arm with her shoulder. She dug into his armor, her weight into him. Randon grunted and took it in stride, shaking his head and noting her sense of humor.

Ashina cleared her throat. "Be thankful my leg isn't in your back, big wolf."

Randon glared down at her, his face wide and amused. "Why would it be all the way up there?" His eyes glowed at her.

She did not answer but narrowed her brows, realizing what she said. A smile lingered on Randon's face. "I know what you meant."

An awkward silence followed them until Randon bent down. "There is a cave in the woods to the west across the river from Serkily's gate. It lies under a boulder shaped like a gravestone. It goes under the river into the city. That is where I am taking you to get you around the army."

Ashina nodded, as he continued. "It is well guarded and they are expecting you."

"Us," Ashina added, meeting his face.

Randon peered at her, even as she leaned harder into his arm. "Us, Randon. I do not leave wolves behind. Except Tala, but she is stubborn and has a plan."

"What if I am dead." He pestered her.

Ashina swallowed. "That would be a great loss."

"You would mourn me." He whispered.

Ashina nodded. "Yes. I also need you to break the fated bond since you are a primordial. I am certain that is why Tala sent for you and you alone."

Randon sighed in her face, shaking his head. "You just want me for my blood."

Ashina glared at him. "It is better than what I am wanted for."

He bit his lip. "True. You win."

Silence overwhelmed them before Ashina swallowed. "Thank you."

Randon stared into her as she met his eyes again, her face soft and powerful. "For saving me from Alaric. Thank you for that."

Randon took in a deep breath at her, his eyes lit up. He reached up with his arm and patted her forearm in his palm, but she gripped his hand with hers.

Ashina held her breath at him. "Who sent you."

Randon sighed. "Serimi, the human warlord. But this order comes from King Meltivi in Serkily. His sister is the seer there..."

Ashina swallowed. "I was raised with humans. Tala became my wolf guardian, but sometimes I question why the throne of Alaric would put me there like that."

Randon huffed. "To make you weaker and in no position to reject Alaric. That is why."

Ashina sneered. "So, I would have gone with his commander the day they came..."

Randon nodded. "Yea. You would have. Tala is very brave; it is a good thing she taught you our ways."

Ashina took a deep breath. "To overcome something powerful, you must make it believe it is weak..."

Randon jerked his head to glare at her when she said that. "Yeah."

Cloud cover moved under the moon as darkness filled the rolling wooded plain. Randon stood up, and Ashina followed. In the distance, the falls roared, and the flowing river would lead them to the gates. They also felt vibrations and echoes. War had come to Serkily because of her.

Ashina clenched her face in the darkness and narrowed her eyes. She clenched her fists until her knuckles were white. Randon got chills up his spine as she filled with anger. She hated oppression, cruelty, pain, and suffering. She was strong and virtuous.

Randon swallowed because a part of his heart ached, worrying about her and what could happen if the wolf kings got her. A fire lit within him and raged through his bones.

"Ready. We run together. We make it across, we will miss the army. The first sense of danger we must get to the water."

Ashina nodded at him. Together, they lunged under cover of darkness through the forest over the rolling plain. They had five miles to go before they reached the thick forests of Serkily. Randon had them running along the edge of a cliff basin where the rolling plain leveled out to the river. Waterfalls lingered to their right, where the river spilled into the lands. The white-tipped rapids roared and echoed through the forest.

Randon did that in case they needed to lunge into the waters again. It would tire them out but may save their lives if needed. Three miles in, Randon slowed down as his ears tickled. Ashina growled, but it was too late. Randon turned into Ashina to drive her to the rapids as slivers of arrows darted into them. The shafts lunged at them through the darkness and two of them hit Randon in his shoulder and forearm.

The arrows catapulted him away from Ashina even as the forest before them lit up for miles with flaming arrows. Ashina widened her eyes and froze, turning to Randon. An arrow hit her in her shoulder, knocking her to her side away from him.

Randon rose as Conri's hoard blasted through the trees at them. He got hit again, fell off into the darkness, and the rapids swallowed him. He plunged up from the waters in pain and ripped the arrows out, his mind racing with the ambush. His eyes changed to a fiery blue in his rage, and he belted a roaring hum from his soul. His whole face clenched in vengeance. He plunged his wolf form through the rapids and met familiar shadows looming upon him at the bank of the river.

Ashina pushed herself to her knees just as another arrow plunged between her neck and collarbone. As she belted out cries of pain and rage, weakness overcame her. Her eyes lingered upon a tall figure with black, spikey hair and a beard trimmed to match. His crimson cloak hung on his black obsidian armor as sinister as his amber-glowing eyes. He bent down on one knee at her face as if snakes had bent him to their will. She screamed as he twisted the arrow in her shoulder.

"Hello, white wolf," Conri commanded. His eyes lingered up and down her body, and he met her face again and smiled.

He clenched his jaws at her as his wolves picked her up by her forearms and pulled her into the woods behind him. Ashina held her breath, her eyes darting around as his wolf warriors split up to form a path. Their eyes were upon her as if they had found a priceless treasure. She breathed through her pain, glaring at the back of Conri. He was taller than Alaric and more muscular, built broader but of the same harshness.

She sensed his cruelty by the stone-cold way he walked. He exuded power and malice and kept turning his eyes back to stare at her. She was just an object of power and not a being. They pulled her into a tent, and Ashina realized this war had not only begun, but that Conri was good at it.

They dropped her to her knees, their power pressed over her. shina lunged up to pull an arrow out, but the wolves grabbed her arms and held them behind her back. She yelled in pain again, her face red with anger as she fought against them. Conri sighed, watching her.

"I see you have a temper. My king will be taming that."

"Release me now!" Ashina warned him, shaking in pain.

"Or what? You will transform? Your wolf guardian dispatched into the rapids will come for you?" Conri walked over and lunged into her face again. He took her chin in his fingers and squeezed hard. "Anyone coming for you now will die, white wolf."

"I have injured you, so you will not change into your wolf form until you have healed." He bit at her.

"Who are you." She demanded, her face clenched.

Conri sighed. "I am in charge until my king comes for you." He raked a finger down her cheek, smiling. "My king was not expecting me to get you first, but I did. He will not be happy you are injured, but war is harsh, and we had to get rid of your guardian."

She held her breath at his stern glare. His black beard and mustache matched his armor and mood. His dark eyes bled fervor at her. He gazed over her face and her long white hair disheveled down her curvy back. He lingered his eyes up and down her body again until she sensed bugs crawling inside her.

"You are beautiful." He stared.

He clenched his mouth in her face, and she saw fangs, his eyes lighting up with power. "I know who comes to hunt you. Alaric's kingdom is coming to an end."

"I do not belong to you nor anyone." She raged at him.

He pressed into her face, his breath hot at her mouth. "You will belong to me before this night is over. I can promise you this."

"Your king comes for me..."

Conri laughed in her face. He pulled her hair and bent her neck back. "He is arriving too late to stop me."

Ashina pursed her lips, snarling in his face. "I will kill you." She whispered in his lips.

He whispered back into her lips. "Not if I subdue you, white wolf." His eyes loomed into hers, his face hard and clenched.

Conri grazed his fingers down her cheek to her neck as Ashina gasped. He dug his fingers under her leather pauldron at her shoulder. She moaned in pain and jerked away from him. He pulled it until it snapped off and took chunks of the arrow. She screamed. He gazed at her tanned skin drenched in blood, and two arrows still plunked through her. He ripped her armor off her shoulder and stared at her naked neck. Her tunic was ripped down her bloody arm and she shook in pain.

"After you get bitten..." He breathed into her lips. "You will be bonded to me. You will submit." He moaned, excited. "The king will lose you to me." He bragged.

"You are not the king! I will not submit to you." She growled, but Conri laughed.

Ashina grunted as his men held her. Her blood boiled, but she could not turn. Her injuries made her weak, and Conri knew what he was doing. He bent into her bloody neck and licked the blood from her, his eyes glowing a fierce yellow tasting her.

"Just a taste of your power..." He moaned. "Alaric's reign is over." He moaned against her skin.

Ashina closed her eyes, his breath hot on her neck at her shoulder. From the pits of her mind, a whisper called to her.

"Ashina."

Ashina bent her head toward the voice. She held her breath and waited for him to bite her, but he lunged up away from her. Shouts of rage echoed outside and filled the camp, his wolves assembling for battle. Ashina felt the ground vibrate beneath her.

One of his wolves barged in and yelled. "Alaric comes!"

Conri belted out in rage and stood up. "Damnit!"

They yanked her up, and Ashina was never so thankful Alaric had come. Conri sighed as she stood before him, and he loomed into her face. He gripped her naked, bleeding arm in his palm, his face clenched into hers. Ashina swallowed at his presence. A darkness grew in his eyes, and a fear shot up her spine. She would die before he took her to the kingdom of Cayden.

"When this battle is over, you will submit white wolf. Then you will come to Cayden, where you belong."

Conri pointed to the back of the tent. "Take her to the reserves and protect her there. Our king comes soon to get her."

Ashina turned and glared at him wide-eyed as they dragged her away. Who was their king?! She fretted. Conri watched her. His face screamed he had won the hunt. His face clenched as he raised it at her, his eyes shimmering, his chin doused in her blood.

Ashina held her breath as something lurked inside her that pricked her backbone. She moaned in pain, the arrows protruding from her as they drug her back. Her mind wandered to Randon, and her eyes teared up. They pulled her out of the tent under the canopy as torch lights filtered in her face. They pulled her to the back of camp by the river toward the flowing plain. Her eyes grew dim and weak, and she was desperate to pull the arrows out, but they would not let her.

Conri would keep the arrows in her all night if he had his way. He would subdue her in his cruelty. Ashina's hair rose on her arms as a sudden blast of wind pelted over her, and an awakening hit her. Her back grew rigid, and she craned her ears to hear. Ashina fell limp in the wolf's arms, slumping to her knees. They paused as they dragged her through the woods to stand her up.

As they were pulling her back up, arrows plunged through the darkness into them. They slithered to her feet with arrows through their skulls. Ashina clenched her jaws and pulled one arrow out but the other broke off. Conri ensured she would not be able to fight that well. She would have to fight as a human. She turned as a familiar whistle beckoned her from the darkness of the woods, and she lunged through it to meet Tala.

"Randon! Where is he!" Ashina cried.

Tala pointed. "There."

Ashina turned to see Randon and a dozen of his wolves lunge into the camp from the rapids. They emerged from the darkness and raged like fire. They ripped into the wolves along the tents, roaring retribution. And then Conri came out.

"I cannot turn! An arrow is in me!" Ashina worried. "I cannot get it out."

Tala swallowed. "Back to the rapids! Now."

Ashina turned to run and follow Tala as Conri emerged on the path. He transformed into a raging black wolf right after her. Randon lunged into the wolves at the wooded path to the reserves. His twelve wolves with him broke through the army and lit the path on fire with their blood.

Alaric plunged into them behind the army coming from the north. Conri's army split between fighting Alaric and dealing with these wild wolves who had come for Ashina. As Conri roared into Ashina, Tala changed to her wolf and met him in midair to block him. Tala plunged her claws toward his chest but Conri was faster and bigger. He flayed her shoulder open down her arm with his claws.

Ashina screamed, "No!" She reached in behind her to try and grab the arrow but it was of no use. She could not reach it. A raging desperation filled her heart with dread.

Tala met Conri again, bleeding out. "To the rapids! I love you!" She screamed.

Ashina turned and ran under the canopy, her heart beating wild. She heard Randon and his wolves flayed into the army, their rage echoing. Alaric's wolves sounded their battle horn, and the wooded plain roared. Ashina's head pounded as she rushed to the rapids, but Conri's wolves followed her. He rendered her weak and useless until her thoughts lingered upon Tala.

She stopped running, her eyes lighting up in a flaming gold. She took a deep breath and turned to face a dozen wolves lingering at her from the darkness. They had changed to their wolf forms and loomed over her like shadows bred from black pits of despair. She closed her eyes, her heart beating her chest to death.

When she opened her eyes again, they lit up like a golden flame had burst inside her. The trees whipped down like they had grown daggers. The branches gored the wolves as if they had become extensions of her fingers.

Conri picked Tala up by one hand and gripped her throat, choking her. Randon lunged atop his shoulder and tore a chunk out, pivoting over his head in mid-air to pry Tala from his grip. Tala sunk her claws into his chest and roared at his snout. He belted out in rage, pushed his fist into her chest, and ripped out her heart. Randon roared as he and his wolves got surrounded, but then a wind blew through the woods.

Alaric lunged into Conri's army on horseback, bending the trees to his will to find her. He sensed her near and bleeding to death. He sensed her weak and in pain. He raised from his horse as a wind blasted over him. He changed into his wolf in desperation to find her, and his wolves rose and changed with him. They lunged into Conri's wolves in midair horseback, and beat Conri's front-line back.

Conri's wolves paused the attack on Randon and his wolves then. As Alaric pressed into them, he decimated their lines. Conri dropped Tala's body and broke away from Randon and his wolves to meet Alaric. Randon heaved and moaned, picked up Tala's body, and fled with it to Ashina.

Ashina watched Randon burst toward her with a dozen wolves. They lunged over the wolf bodies she killed splayed around her. Randon pushed Ashina with him into the raging waters again, even as Ashina began crying at Tala's body.

"Tala!" She raged.

They hit the waters and let the rapids carry them again, the bitter cold biting their desperation. Ashina lunged up from the cold with a wide mouth and screamed. "No!"

Randon pressed into her as Ashina clung to his wolf chest. He and the wolves loomed in the water, swimming away from the battle. Ashina cried against his chest, her hands shaking as she grabbed Tala's paw.

"Noooo!" She moaned, her bellowing ache painful and throbbing in Randon's heart. "No! Tala!" Her face grieved in pain.

Randon turned to see his wolves behind him in the water as they remained watchful. His snout met Ashina's tearful face, twisted in pain as he moaned with her. The rapids carried them into Serkily, even as their beating hearts raged from the loss of Tala. Randon's trusted brothers had come for him, and they saved their lives.

Tala gave hers so Ashina could escape from the cruel Conri, the brutal commander of Cayden. He would have forced himself upon her and taken everything she ever was.

As night fled into dawn, Randon pressed hard into the wilderness with Tala's laid over his shoulder. Ashina clung to his wolf chest as she bled out, her pain resolute. A resolve of anger filled him with a roaring rage, his wolf form tense as he held Ashina against him.

At dawn, bellows of roars and death filled with the silence of the wilderness. Alaric had come at the right time for them, and it saved Ashina's life. Randon laid Tala's body down by him in the leaves and pressed Ashina against a tree. He was still in his wolf form as his brothers kept watch. Ashina stared at the lifeless body, and tears spilled down her face. A pain she could not describe haunted her.

Ashina's shoulder and arm were bloodied and weak, her armor ripped off. She would need new armor. Randon gazed at her naked neck and shoulder and sighed as he did not see any bite marks.

Randon swallowed. "Need to get the arrow out. You have lost a lot of blood."

Ashina nodded but said nothing. Randon pressed his snout at her face and sighed. He gripped her shoulders in his paws and pulled her forward. She held her breath as he lunged her back against the tree.

She belted out a low moan as tears filled her eyes. The arrow pressed out her front, and blood spewed from the wound again. Ashina clenched her face and gripped his strong wolf arms in her palms but did not scream. Randon pulled it out of her and then turned to his wolves.

"One of you carry Tala. I will carry Ashina. She is too weak to walk."

Ashina watched one of the wolves bend down and gently lift Tala's body, her eyes blurry from her tears.

"Tala." Ashina cried, her lips trembling.

Randon pressed over her, his eyes blurry from tears. "I'm sorry." He moaned, his snout quivering.

He paused as Ashina gripped the hair at his wolf chest, her face stern. Randon let her grip his hair as his muscles flexed at her grasp. Her grasp was weak, but her resolve strong.

"I will kill them all." She spit.

The other wolves stared at her, the anger on their snouts snarling of retribution. Ashina grabbed his paw, gripped it in her hand, and pressed it against her heart. Randon froze as his paw pressed against her heart. Her eyes screamed into his, her face in pain laced with anger.

Randon stared into her and nodded as a growl filled the space between them, and his ears stood alert. She let Randon push her matted white hair off her face with a paw. He rubbed the blood off her cheek with one of his wolf fingers and sighed at her face. She closed her eyes, the softness of his fur as if he kissed her by a warm light.

He pulled his paw from her, plunged his strong wolf arms under her legs, and held her lower back. He lifted her in his arms, his eyes staring into her teary ones. The sunrise kissed them in tangerine and warm yellow hues, warming their bones. Ashina breathed it in.

She met his snout and stared into his big blue eyes, leaning her head into his chest. Randon pressed his snout into the sun and gripped her tight. His whole wolf body flexed as he eyed the rest of their journey.

"We will kill them all, white wolf." He whispered into the sun.

He led his party along the river, their strides filled with anger. The Dakitae began their march at dawn, and the window was closing for them to get to the wooded tunnel. They would be in the city soon, and then war would come. The war brewing in the white wolf was coming, too, and her retribution lit like a fire from hell's lair had burst open.

Chapter 9
The Wolf King's War

Alaric did not see Conri in the battle last night. That coward split off from his raging wolves and headed south to Serkily. Alaric had pushed through them to the reserves and cut them down. Conri's wolves were raging beasts, and Alaric's were tactical warriors. It put Alaric almost a day behind him. He would push his wolves hard to meet them at Serkily.

The fog lingered on his bloody boots, hiding the blood and body parts strewn in the forest surrounding him. The rushing sound of the falls echoed in the distance. It was there he tracked the scent of her heavy in the air. She was injured and bleeding out, and his blood boiled.

He bent down and tapped a finger into a pool of blood where she had stood and closed his eyes. He sensed her pain and weakness, and his knees trembled. His heart raced, her blood singing to him a story of the terror she experienced. He stood up, his eyes a flaming golden fire.

His wolves and Dakitae overcame Conri's camp with decisive brutality, but Conri was good at playing games in war. He took his reserves away from the heat of the battle before Alaric could penetrate them. Conri staged his tactics in layers to stall the kingdoms, and it was a bitter assault upon Alaric.

He knew Conri would be chasing her for his king.

Alaric seethed. "Where is your wretched king? He has hidden far too long."

Conri's main goal was to cut a path through them to get to Ashina, which he did. Alaric's commander Rieka would flank Conri soon, his armies numbering hundreds of thousands. They would march upon Serkily's gates and break them down, walls and all, and take Ashina.

Alaric kicked a wolf's head and sighed. If they died as wolves, they stayed as wolves and did not turn back to their human form. He glared toward the raging rapids, his heart heavy. He should have bitten her when he had her. He should have taken her then. But something in her eyes as she looked at him held him back, and a lingering prick grew up his spine.

Ashina would not go by force. Conri tried, and it did not go well. Alaric took a deep breath, his heart craning to Ashina. "Why do you run to Serkily?" He questioned.

His heart pinged him as a roaring ache filled him with dread. "You will try to break the bond with that damn seer. No doubt your guardian told you it could be. That is not how it breaks." He shook his head, sighing. "You will see I am going nowhere, white wolf."

Alaric clenched his jaws as his eyes craned through the forest toward the plain at Serkily. He closed his eyes in the sun streaming down upon him as the trees bent toward him in a slight breeze. The sun warmed his face and filled him with strength. He remembered the look on her face as she gazed into the sun beaming through the falls. He turned back to face his wolf warriors and the remaining surviving Dakitae.

Serk nodded at him. "Rieka approaches from the western mountain, my king, with one hundred thousand. The others wait for your command at Worgen."

Alaric's eyes lit up. "Good. We march upon Serkily in a week. We kill Conri and his army remaining."

Then he huffed, looking at the falls. "He is desperate to take her and almost succeeded if I had not shown up. And now a primordial has her."

He gripped his chest, resting a palm on his breastplate. His heart ached. From the time the hunter's moon had risen, he awoke in the night. It called to him. It ached his bones deep inside. He could feel her presence and sense her thoughts and fears. He had ensured his commander Reika raced into the darkness out of the mountain to get her at first light.

Last night, as he plunged into Conri's camp, he had a terror overcome him for her. He sensed her draining and desperate. It was as if she had no power to protect herself, and then Alaric seethed inside and called to her.

That was how the bond worked. For thousands of years, once the hunter's moon had risen, his ancestors had taken their fated mates. They had officiated the bond by consummating their marriage and bearing offspring. Alaric stood and stared at the falls again, his heart raging like the white tips blasting the rocks.

An ancient Primordial had come for her with Tala's help. That was a problem. The wolf would take her to Serkily, to the seer. The Primordial would be the only powerful thing to break the fated bond and woo her. That wolf was strong. The humans knew what they were doing. They would try to break the bond and make Ashina the white wolf queen to rule the wolf kings. She would rule them all.

Alaric narrowed his brows and growled from a pit of sorrow deep inside, and it echoed like the wind.

"She will not rule me, but I need her alive," Alaric growled. "Ashina..." He called to her. "Keep breathing, Ashina..."

"Do not give up..."

Alaric needed her alive and well. He could not bite and mate her if she was not well, and if he could not mate her, he could not control her power.

Conri was not going to lose. He never lost a battle, no matter the losses. His king would not bend either. The white wolf was ready, and it was time to take her.

When Cayden's wolves had plunged north of the human warlord faction, that was a small taste. Conri lunged through the forest to the open plains south of Serkily. He had thousands upon thousands who survived.

Alaric was formidable in battle with his wolves and human warriors. But the kingdom of Cayden beat them in strength. His strength lay in his brute force.

Cayden's wolves marched north of Alaric's kingdom of Worgen. The mighty wolves of Cayden plunged east over the Black Plains, and there were two hundred thousand of them. They fled the obsidian earth from the mountain kingdom there.

They filled the horizon with a darkness drenched in malice. They marched east intending on turning south through the Eastern Unexplored Forests. They were thirty days out.

They would follow the raging river over the open plain and melt into the forest at Serkily. They would outnumber man and wolf. Conri slowed the army down under the forest canopy, following orders from his king to be meticulous. They could not lose the white wolf.

Conri harassed her last night and knew the penalty for that when his king found out. It was too late now. He wanted her and would have taken her. He would beg for forgiveness from his king and move forward regardless.

Behind him, Alaric would be surveying the battle scene and tracking Ashina's scent. Conri had lost wolves and would mourn them in time. Conri clenched his face. He sighed in the wind, the taste of Ashina's blood still in his mouth. He raged. He would get her and he would take her to his king.

The Black Plains in Cayden rolled out before the kingdom, and light did not linger upon them. Light fled those black plains, and darkness bred there like the blackness of the empirical fur of the wolves. Ashina may be of the light, but the wolf kingdom of Cayden breathed in the night.

Serimi readied his armor and weapons as his eyes craned to Galin. He peered in at him, his long blonde hair slung over his shoulder in a braid like his beard. His brown eyes lit up at his warlord commander, and he nodded.

"We have seventy-thousand. Eighty-five if we need to use the archers and catapult warriors to join in combat with us at the front lines."

Serimi rolled his eyes. "Barely enough to break the wolf hoards. These damn wolf kings have bled us of men for far too long."

Galin agreed. "We have better weapons and seers. They have their stealth and strength and size..."

Serimi froze and narrowed his brows.

Galin rolled his eyes. "Yessss, yessss, I know. We can beat them with the wolves coming in from the plains at Randon's village. We have three hundred so far."

Serimi slid his long sword into his sheath at his side and pulled his gauntlets on. "Empty the plain. We end this war with the wolves when we reach Serkily. It is time for man to overcome the wolf kings."

Galin smiled.

"Any wolf coming to serve does so under my command. If they are not committed to the human faction, they are not welcome to serve the army."

Galin bowed his head and left the tent.

Serimi followed him with his eyes, his face clenched, his red hair as strong as his bulging arms under his armor.

Galin pulled his horse and marched with Randon's wolf warriors in tow. Their eyes lit up afire as they followed him. They would transform into wolves when the battle started. Galin walked to the end of the row of tents and they eyed the rolling plain of humans. They readied their formations atop their horses to march. He turned to the wolf warriors; his face hard.

"The assault will start at the back line from the archers. After that, we need the wolves to break Conri's and Alaric's lines."

The wolves eyed one another and nodded, agreeing with him. Galin counted the catapults and archers numbering in the thousands. They had seventy thousand men and ten thousand archers.

Galin could not let the worst happen. They could not let Serkily fall. They must not let the wolf kings win at all.

By nightfall, the plain was empty. Eighty thousand human warriors and three hundred fifty wolves on horseback headed east. They would reach Serkily in a week. They would flank the Dakitae already marching upon them and face Conri and Alaric's hoards. The odds were against the humans.

Randon had the white wolf, and two Primordials at Serkily could mean disaster for the wolf kings. Galin hoped Randon had found her and made it safely to the city. As night fell upon them, they filled the plain with shadows of wonder through the night. Their vibrations filled the earth, matching the human hearts hoping to catch a reprieve from the oppression of the wolf kings.

Chapter 10
A Haven for Healing

Ashina opened her eyes as a whisper called her name. "Ashina." It went away and came back again.

Her eyes lit in gold as she craned her neck to follow the voice. Her chest heaved with her labored breathing. As it called her again, a breath from Alaric's lips touched her. Her heart raced as Alaric called to her. She listened, and something grew inside her as he continued whispering.

"Keep breathing." He called to her. "Do not give up."

She took a deep breath as her head fell back again and breathed deeper. Randon glared at her as she shook in his arms. He was running out of time. She needed medicine and the seer to help heal her now. Conri hit her twice with arrows and moved one around on purpose. It made the hole bigger and made it bleed worse. She was bleeding out and had no time for her wolf power to heal her.

Randon questioned why Conri would do this unless he hoped to bond her to himself. To force the fated mate bond upon a wolf as powerful as Ashina would bring upon great pain for the wolf taking it, even death. Randon knew this, so Conri had rebelled against his king, or he did not care. The king was not even there, and Randon questioned why. He bent his snout and stared at Ashina.

Ashina remembered the sun burst through a thick canopy overhead as blackness fell upon her in waves. She heard the wolves grunt as they moved a stone. She heard human voices, and their whispers echoed in a damp tunnel. Ashina opened her eyes to see Randon perk his ears up, his snout in her face, his eyes wide with fear.

"Bring her to me." A woman's voice called out.

And then she heard the most pitiful moan of all as Randon bellowed. "She is dying."

Ashina closed her eyes and let darkness fold over her mind. Her body went limp in Randon's arms as her breath left her.

Randon sat with his fists clenched atop his knees in his human form. Night had fallen, and on the plains, the Dakitae army folded in around them. Brovina used medicine to help heal Ashina but she needed to rest for the next day or two.

Randon stared at her lying on her back as her long white hair spilled over the side of the bed and touched the floor. Brovina and her healers stripped Ashina naked and washed her of the blood when Randon brought her in. They stitched her up and wrapped her breasts, shoulder, and arm with a stretchy material. It covered her nakedness and would allow her to heal.

Her tanned skin accentuated her high cheekbones and was as striking as her powerful stance. She had thin lips and a strong nose that accentuated her white brows on her dark skin. She was beautiful, and he sighed, closing his eyes. He bent his head to his knees until Ashina woke, and he met her staring at him. She smiled, her face weak, her eyes lit up like fire.

"Randon."

Randon bent aside the bed, pressed his forehead against hers, and breathed against her skin. "I feared I failed to save you."

Ashina raised her good arm and cupped his thick black hair in her palm. "You saved me."

He raised to look at her. "You scared the shit out of me. You are so damn brave." He kissed her forehead and gripped her head in his palm.

She closed her eyes as he kissed her, gripped his forearm, and sighed. "I would not be here if not for you."

"How are you feeling?" He leaned into the chair again.

"I will live. Conri hurt me, and Alaric came, and then Tala..." Tears filled her eyes.

"I have her body, Ashina. We will give her a proper wolf funeral, I swear it."

Ashina nodded. "Now help me sit up." She jerked the blanket off and then froze. "I am naked."

Randon pursed his lips, pulling the blanket up over her groin as she jerked it off at his face. "They had to. King Meltivi making new clothing and armor for you as we speak. You will have it by morning."

"Good." Ashina sat up anyway and pulled the blanket around her waist. She paused at the thunderous roars and drums beating days out on the horizon. She stared at Randon.

Randon lifted back up into the chair across from her. "The Dakitae are coming. They will be here in six days."

"You brought me here just in time." Ashina sighed. "We have another problem also."

"What."

"I am bonded to Alaric. He called to me. I must break it." Her face was pale from blood loss, but her resolve made Randon widen his eyes.

"The fate bond has never been broken. Alaric can feel your pain and torment. It torments him the same." Randon warned her.

"You do not agree with breaking it?" Ashina whispered to his face.

Randon stared at her, his face clenched. "It hurts. Fate brings the mates together; it is fate that holds the bond. It calls, it encourages. It pains me as an alpha male to see it broken. It could kill him."

"Do you have a mate?" Ashina asked.

Randon leaned against the wall. "No."

Ashina stared deep into his face as her eyes lingered over his facial features and then roved over his broad body. "Why not?" She whispered.

Randon let out a laugh and then froze, swallowing at her face. He sighed at her but did not answer. He crossed his arms over his chest and shook his head at her, refusing to answer.

"You will help me break this bond. Alaric is evil, and his wolves keep taking human women to bite and make them breeders. It stops with me. That is not a bond I will serve. If you are a virtuous alpha wolf, you would not want any woman serving it."

She bit at him again. "His commander Rieka took the women of my village. They were my friends. I will get them back."

Randon opened his mouth as if he wanted to say something and then froze, his eyes wavering at her. His eyes roamed her face as his mouth fell open at her. He lingered his gaze on her lips.

"Do you want women serving this wicked bond, Randon?" She demanded, her face as hard as her eyes.

Randon swallowed. "No." He whispered.

Ashina sat higher in the bed and let the blanket fall to her waist. It showed her muscular, naked stomach and curvy waist. As her hair slipped down her back and over her shoulders, Randon sighed at her. He closed his eyes and let his head lean against the wall.

Ashina sat there staring at him, a half-smile on her face when he did that. "Brave wolf." She whispered to him.

Randon lunged his head up as she said it and met her stare, leaning into his knees again to melt into her eyes. She called to him deep inside, beckoning him to come. Randon held his breath at her face as a truth hit him. She was an alpha. His blue eyes filled with fire as he met her eyes, his heart roared.

"What do you want, white wolf." He whispered into her face, his backbone and guts filled with shivers.

"I choose my fate." She whispered back. "Fate has no right to choose me."

Ashina's eyes lit up at him, and she smiled. Randon smiled back at her but shook his head like he could not go there with her. He would not let himself go there with her because he sensed the power she had linger into him, and his knees grew weak.

"Yes, you do." He answered her.

As they stared at one another, Brovina lingered in on them, her eyes lit up. The round tower room overshadowed them in ivory pillars and oak beams like fingers on the ceiling. "Hello, white wolf queen." She bowed to her, holding a tray of a large chunk of rare steak and green juice in a goblet.

Another healer walked in and handed Randon the same food, and his mouth watered. He took it, his eyes wide.

Brovina smiled. "You must eat, both of you. We have also fed your wolves, Randon. You need to heal first. I cannot break the bond until you both are at full strength."

"What is this green goo?" Randon asked.

Brovina smiled. "That is what you need in you both to begin the breaking. You have two days of this."

Brovina and the healer leaned over Ashina and pulled the cloth from her wounds. Brovina huffed. "Good. You are healing fast, as expected. Rest tonight. Tomorrow, you should be stronger."

Ashina gazed at her and smiled. "Thank you for saving me, seer."

Brovina stared at her. "You are strong and virtuous and will make a powerful queen. Tala raised you right." She turned to go and left them alone again.

Ashina picked up the meat and tore into it with her hands, her body ravished. Randon smiled at her and did the same, the blood dripping from their chins. They held the goblets up and dunked the thick green goo down their throats in big swigs.

Ashina sighed and raised her eyebrows, but Randon sneered as if he had drunken sour lemons.

"This tastes like shit." He gulped it down and then gagged, shaking his head as Ashina laughed at him.

"The taste of freedom." She joked, but inside, a part of her had died.

Randon froze and met her stare. "I am doing this for you." He finished the contents and then shivered all over as it went down.

"I know you are. I owe you now."

Randon set the goblet down and wiped the blood from his stubby chin. "You do. I was working on a stone house, and the rainy season was upon us. I will dig the stones out again because the river will wash them downstream." He smiled.

"Tell me about your wolves. Do you help the humans? Or do you hide in the villages? I know there is a sect of wolves not loyal to the kings, but stay hidden."

Randon cleared his throat. "My wolves and I help the warlords and Serkily. A sect of us rebelled against Alaric over a hundred years ago. We have been gathering our brothers to help us in case war came. It is here now, so Serkily will have my wolves to help fight soon."

Ashina sighed. "Good."

"And you." He asked.

"They took me from my mother when I was five. Tala was appointed my guardian for the kingdom of Worgen to prepare for my mate. She raised me at Hildenia. Tala led me away. She saved me..." Her eyes teared up.

"She did not adhere to their standards and raised me to fight. She taught me to listen to nature and draw strength from the sun. I can do as Alaric does with nature and sense things..."

Randon swallowed, listening to her. "What." He froze, acknowledging what she said, and then blurted out again. "What?"

"Sometimes the ground moves beneath my feet like something is coming up inside me. The world hears me, and things happen."

"What happens." Randon's face clenched.

"Something calls to me..." She froze and then sighed, her eyes closing. "Nature becomes an extension of me and my rage. I do not understand it, but it killed the wolves at the river before you came..."

Randon blinked his eyes, his mouth open. "You need to rest." She listened to him as he leaned over her to cover her up. As she rolled over and closed her eyes, it was then he noticed a tattoo in the middle of her naked back at the base of her neck. It looked like a tree that had caught on fire but breathed from the inside of her. He held his breath and lunged down the corridor away from her.

King Meltivi stared at maps and battle tactics in the throne room, his shadow lingering over the massive wood plank table. Louve lunged up to see Randon looming in on them. "Ah. The primordial. Glad to see you and the white wolf have come."

Randon narrowed his brows. "Where is the seer."

Meltivi and Louve froze. All the humans around the table met his stare as silence filled the expansive room.

Meltivi cleared his throat. "You look as if you have seen a monster."

Randon swallowed, his body tense. "I have! The monster is here. What have you humans done."

Louve huffed. "Ah, yes. That." Then he glared at Meltivi. "Told you he would not like this."

Randon scoffed at them. "You lure me out to bring the thousand-year queen to you. The one with ancient seer powers in her bloodline to bend nature to her will. She will destroy us all. That is why Alaric has ruled so long, and his family powerful for thousands of years."

Louve bit his lip. "Yesssss, but she will not do that because we had Tala raise her to do what is right. Alaric was not raised right." He rubbed his long black beard and stared at the maps again. "I mean, look at him. He is evil." He shivered.

"She is Alaric's mate! She is powerful like him, and he will destroy this city to get her." Randon bellowed at them.

Meltivi walked to Randon and patted him on the arm. "And you saved her from Alaric and Conri. You are now bound to her by fate, brave wolf. And two primordial's too! How lucky we are."

Louve rolled his eyes. "Yessss, two primordial's, what could go wrong!" He hollered at them from across the table.

Randon sneered. "You humans know I am the only thing that can control her if she loses her shit. This was not some random ask you conjured up. You sought me out for her."

Meltivi stared at him. "We had no choice, Randon."

"She will destroy this whole kingdom," Randon warned them. "You humans and your deceiving ways."

Brovina emerged from behind him. "Randon, come with me. There is something I must show you."

He turned to her, his face clenched. He walked alongside her down a winding corridor until they reached a massive lair. It sprawled under the throne room and opened to reveal her quarters. It was a cave room, the walls built for bookshelves into the stone. She walked around the long table in the middle of the library room and pulled a book from the shelf.

As she opened it, she sighed. "The thousand-year queen means something. It also means something you guard over her."

Randon scoffed. "I was not chosen Brovina. Serimi called me to come. I am not her mate."

Brovina sighed. "Yes, but you are the only male primordial in the world who can handle her right now. Now that Tala is gone, Ashina needs to lean on an equal. That is you."

Randon's face fell to a dull white as his eyes widened.

"Ashina is the first in one thousand years to be born a Primordial and a white wolf. Thirty years ago, she was born under a hunter's moon, and when it came again, the world knew she was ready. Do you have any idea how rare and frightening that is? Every one thousand years, a primordial is born, but they have all been black, like you, Randon."

"Then where did Alaric get his powers from?"

"Those powers are handed down through his bloodline and have been so for thousands of years. Makes sense fate would want him to breed with one to keep it going. After all, the line does weaken in time if a suitable mate is not born."

Randon met her stare.

Brovina sighed. "There has never been a female wolf queen, ever..."

Randon swallowed. "Oh."

"Do you see the terror these kings envision if she does become a wolf queen of her own?"

Chills darted up Randon's spine.

"She was taken when she was little because of it. Look how she is hunted because her power can bring vast prestige to the king who takes her. The power he will have when he bonds to her..."

"She nearly died. She has not tapped her primordial yet." Randon warned.

"Oh yes, true. Once that awakens, then the wolf kings will bleed. That power comes during a great emotional upheaval, which she has not endured yet. It is surprising since Tala is gone. That is where you come in, Randon. We need you to help her."

She opened a page that showed a story and read a passage. Randon closed his eyes and huffed. As he listened to it, he shook his head.

If a female white wolf is born of primordial bloodline on a hunter's moon, the endowment is the power of Biophilia. The one endowed with this power commands even the wind and trees to their will, and kingdoms quake in their fire. The most dreadful wolves are born to this.

Randon noticed the drawing showed a kingdom rendered in half with collapsed towers and walls. The earth broke open like something burst forth from the depths. He held his breath.

Brovina warned him. "You see, that is why Alaric needs her. He can pivot her powers to him and keep his kingdom the most powerful. He will control it as he is also powerful."

Randon huffed. The same power Alaric has. He has rendered whole kingdoms with this power."

"Do we need Alaric to get more of this power, Randon?" Brovina worried.

Randon swallowed. "No."

Brovina shook her head. "I need you to help her. We have a short time, mere days before the Dakitae come. If Alaric takes her, she must know how to use these ancient powers to protect herself. From him. And from all others who seek to exploit her."

Randon huffed.

"You have been a primordial a long time and know your strengths. Ashina does not. You need to help her control them. Tala did what she could, but she was not a primordial."

"We will be under attack, and Conri and Alaric are coming," Randon growled. "They will pull down these walls."

"Yessss. They all come. They come for her. It is up to you to ensure she is strong when you have her because you understand her strength, Randon. You have had lifetimes to hone your powers, she has not. Help her."

Randon crossed his arms, his heart beating his chest to death. He stared at the story and the picture. "I do not have seer bloodline in my wolf blood like Ashina and Alaric do. I can only help her so much, Brovina."

Randon sighed. "I will protect her with all I am. I cannot let her down."

Brovina sighed at him. "Whether we rise or fall, we must help the white wolf queen. She is the only hope we humans must undermine the wolf kings..."

She smiled up at him. "She is your kind's hope as well."

Randon held his breath.

"You see, you will do what is right like Tala did with her, and Ashina desires to do. Ones who fight to do what is right will prevail over the darkness coming to our gates." She patted his arm and then turned away from him to the books again.

"We are both alphas. That poses challenges."

Brovina laughed at him. "Oh, so you see her now, do you? Yes, she is an alpha and the first female primordial white wolf ever born to be an alpha. The kings are terrified. But she can unite us..."

Randon felt his face get flushed. "Damnit."

"She is strong and will be healed by morning. I have clothing and armor coming to her shortly. Our army may be human, but we are mighty or would not have stood so long."

Randon agreed. "That is true. Your kind is very brave."

"And Serimi is coming to flank Conri and Alaric. The wolf kings will war with one another at our gates to get her..."

"They will not get her. I will not fail her again." Randon clenched his teeth, his eyes a fiery blue.

Brovina froze at the table, a book in her hands, her face gawking at him. "Ah. Spoken like a true alpha male."

Silence, and then she continued. "You need to understand that we had Tala raise her to be a warrior, Randon. I intercepted the guardian chosen to raise her, and we killed her..."

Randon's face froze.

Brovina smiled. "Tala was the wisest choice to raise a warrior queen. Alaric's father had a wolf coming to her that would have bent her to their will. We raised a warrior that will not bend to the wolf kings. So, we need your help to help her til war comes."

Randon held his breath, meeting her stare as if something had slapped his face.

"Will you help her, Randon?"

Randon sighed in her face. "You humans give me no choice; I will do what is right."

"Yes, you will because you are of the light." Brovina turned away from him and pulled more books off the shelves.

L ate that evening, Randon stood with Louve on the tower as Falcons lighted upon them. Fifty human warriors held their gloved hands up to accept the birds. The birds had messages to carry to the farthest reaches of the villages to wolves not loyal to Conri or Alaric. Randon wrote the messages himself and signed them. Any wolves questioning would know a primordial was calling them to come.

Louve pressed his arm up with his men and Randon. The Falcons lifted off them. They filled the horizon with their fluttering wings in all directions.

Louve cleared his throat and clenched his face. "We are gravely outnumbered, but that has never stopped us."

Randon watched the commander march away from him. Darkness lingered around them as if a pit of despair screamed out.

Chapter 11
The Calling

Louve overlooked the rolling plain at the back of the city. Mountains rose in the distance as fog lingered through the woodlands. He leaned into his bulky arms, held his breath, and watched a lone figure on the hill. He stood upright when he recognized Ashina in the fog just as the sun emerged.

Randon appeared and stood beside him. He froze at Ashina's half-nakedness upon the hill. He remembered what she told him about her rage and nature. The color drained from his face as he gawked at her.

Ashina wore skin-tight trousers and was barefoot. Her breasts were wrapped, but her stomach showed. Her hair swung down her back like a whip with her movements. Her eyes were closed as she breathed in this new world around her. As the sun kissed her face, Randon got chills. He lunged away from Louve to get to her.

Brovina lingered behind Louve, gripping her staff and watching with him. Louve met her stare and sighed. "I hope this plan of yours works with these primordials."

Brovina swallowed. "We are about to find out."

Louve narrowed his black brows. "About to find out? What? What are you saying." He questioned her.

Brovina cleared her throat and shrugged her shoulders. "Mmmm. Nothing."

Louve gripped the stone in his palm, his spine stiff to watch them. "Nothing is always something with you, seer."

Ashina lunged her leg out and stretched deep into the sun. She swished her arms in a rhythmic dance until the grass bent toward her palms. As she closed her eyes, she saw Tala. She clenched her teeth as she remembered what Conri had done to her. She clenched her jaw and belted out an angry scowl at the pain from him shooting her with arrows twice.

Her mind went to seeing Tala's body on Randon's shoulder. She raged and moaned. She burst her palm open, and the ground cracked at her feet. The crack slithered from the tip of her toes over the hill and toward the rising plateau. Her mind played everything over again and then went to Alaric.

"You are my mate."

"You belong to me and me alone."

"Ashina," Alaric called to her suddenly.

She opened her eyes, and they were fiery golden. "Get out of my head Alaric!" She screamed. "Get out!" She demanded.

She stood upright and belted out a roar from the pits of her soul that echoed over the plain. Randon burst through the fog in his wolf form and grabbed her fist in his palm. He pressed into her and snarled. He grunted with her power as it raged against his strength.

"Ashina! Stop!" Randon commanded her.

Ashina yelled at him, growling in her human form, and clenched her face harder. She ignored him. Randon moaned and fell to his knees, her fist grasped in his paw with all his strength. Her rage filled him with a weakness he could not describe or even begin to understand. A trickle of fear rose within him.

"I will be forced to stop you." He warned. "Please..."

But Ashina only saw Tala dead, Conri forcing her, and Alaric taking her. She saw the women taken by Alaric's commander and his wolves. She saw flashbacks from her childhood as Tala raised her to have a mind of her own, to be free with purpose. Ashina cried as she raged, and Randon became subjected to her pain.

"Do not make me do this..." Randon pleaded with her, but she would not listen.

Ashina only saw horrible things hurting her and raged because of it. She could not stop. From within the wind of her rage, she heard a little trickle of a familiar voice, but she turned a deaf ear anyway.

"Ashina, no! Ashina, come to me..." Alaric beckoned her again.

"You are not the master of meeeee..." She belted out. "You do not control me, Alaric! I will destroy you..." She roared. She wanted to break the world.

From the tower landing, Louve stiffened his shoulders, his eyes wide. Brovina stood there and watched it unfold, her hand nervous over her staff. They watched the ground crack as an opening burst up. It melted to the cavern wall at the plateau as the ground quaked.

"Ummm, Brovina!" Louve feared.

Brovina sighed. "Randon." She hoped. "Come on."

Louve widened his eyes. "She will destroy us, Randon was right."

"I just need him to bite her…" Brovina mumbled.

Louve glared, his face pale. "You want what?!"

"She needs to bond to another primordial to help hone her powers, a good one, and Randon is good. I need her bonded to Randon before Alaric bites her."

"You are mad seer." Louve shook his head at her.

"I am not mad. I am doing this to protect our hope." She swallowed. "Her and Randon are our only hope now as the wolf kings seek to take her for her power. She needs a buffer like Tala was to her…"

Randon saw her eyes filled with rage and hate. He met her eyes as a blue fire lit in his, and then he stood upright and loomed over her. He pressed into her mighty wind, his snout snarling as he glared at her naked neck and shoulders.

"Ashinnnaaaa!" He growled, his snout sneering.

He lunged into her neck, his fangs sinking deep. He tasted her flesh and blood, drowning in the bite of her power. Ashina screamed as he bit her and stopped fighting him, but it was too late. She plunged her fingers against his forearms to push him off and screamed. Randon gripped her naked forearms with his massive paws.

He pulled her in tight against his bulky wolf chest. He tasted her as his eyes lit up to a fiery golden to match hers. He did not want to stop. He needed to keep going and take all of her.

Randon's heartbeat filled her veins as her heart throbbed. She closed her eyes and bent her neck for a moment to let him take more before her fangs burst through. Her loins pulsated with fire, and she pushed him off. She catapulted herself away from him. Her eyes were back to normal, but her face froze in terror at him.

"Noooo!" She screamed. "Randon!" She yelled at him.

She gripped her bleeding neck and shoulder that throbbed. She slid backwards from him on her elbow in the grass. Her eyes met his, but his eyes looked as if the rising sun kissed him inside.

Ashina had never been bitten before. She met Randon's magnificent wolf form and screamed at his snout.

Randon raised his snout high and breathed her in, empowered. His growl echoed through the morning, caressed by the love of his dreams. His whole body flexed as he loomed over her in his wolf form. His eyes met hers again as he wiped her blood from his snout. He crept around her on the hill, his eyes upon her, his body clenched.

He warned her he did not want to do this, and now she had to face the primordial wolf craving her. All of her.

Ashina spit an angry yell at him, her eyes cold as ice. She stood to face him, her body clenched as her fangs burst out. Randon bent down and lunged to get her. Ashina met him in midair in her wolf form. As she met him, she catapulted him away with her broad paws, kicking against his chest. Randon flew backward over the hill and hit the rock wall that was cracked because of her.

Louve and Boldana followed his wolf form with their eyes as he flew over the hill.

Louve burst out in thunderous laughter. "Damn! She is strong." Louve shook his head.

Brovina widened her eyes. "I bet that hurts."

"She kicking his ass." Louve smiled.

When Randon slammed into the wall, he slid down in his human form. He glared at her across the hill with firm eyes and growled at her face. He plunged his fist into the rock, and it cracked under his knuckles. He stood and lunged over the hill to get her.

Ashina bent down to face him off in her wolf form. As Randon reached her, he returned to his wolf in midair and blocked her paw strikes. He wrapped his long wolf arms around her midsection and gripped her back. Randon lunged her up by her waist and slammed her down on her back. He breathed into her snout, growling.

"Ashina!" He roared.

Randon gripped her paws in his paws, pushed her arms out, and held her down, growling in her snout. Ashina lunged around his snout into his shoulder and locked down. She sunk her fangs deep in his flesh.

Her fangs sprayed blood on her white fur. Her eyes shimmered in blue like his and folded back to fiery gold. She sneered in rage, sinking into him harder. Now she wanted him, all of him. She moaned into his blood.

Randon froze as realization dawned she was biting him, and he belted out a moan in terror. His mind froze with her breathing in his soul. "Noooo no!" He pleaded with her.

Randon moaned in rage as her fangs locked into him, and he could not move as she tasted him. Her eyes simmered in gold on fire, and she did not want to let him go. Randon got lost in this surrender of her for endless moments just as she pushed him off her again. Randon rolled head over foot away from her, his whole soul inflamed.

They both lay quietly opposite one another atop the hill for endless moments. Randon moaned in pain and rolled over to face her. His face clenched as he gripped his bleeding shoulder and neck. His heart throbbed through his blood. To make matters worse for him, he had an insidious urge to mate with her. He sneered at her from across the top of the hill, his groin throbbing for her.

He slipped back into his human form, his arms weak, and eyed Ashina. She was back in her human form. They rolled over and glared at one another on the hill, their bodies exhausted. They were bleeding from each other, bitten. They made each other weak and weary. It was always the male that bit, not the females. But Ashina was an alpha, putting Randon into a new territory he had never navigated. He hated it.

Randon pressed his face to the ground and moaned. "Whyyyyy!"

He took a deep breath like fire filled his lungs, and they stood to face each other, bloodied and weak. "Damnit! I did not want to bite you!" Randon moaned.

He crept up on her slowly as she stood to face him. Her face was pale, and her eyes wide at what they had done. There was a hardness in her face, and Randon paused. Her whole shoulder bled down her arm. Randon's was bleeding, too. He closed his eyes and shook his head at her. He gripped his shoulder, pulled back a bloody hand, and sighed at it.

"Do you realize what we have just done?!" He whispered.

Ashina plunged her head into the clouds and closed her eyes. They both fell to their knees as tiredness overtook them.

He bent over as if he was in pain and glared at her. "We bonded!" He screamed at her from across the hill.

"You bit me!" She yelled back, her face clenched at him. "Of course we bonded! Of course, we are." She closed her eyes and leaned her head into the sun again as if she was crying. "I can feel you inside me, raging."

She mumbled; her face clenched. "Your power and virtue…" She got lost in a trance because of his lure. "Augghhhh!" She cried.

"Ashinnnaaa!" Randon raged at her.

"Your raging temper could have destroyed the city! Look at what you have done! The bite of a primordial is the only way to stop your power. Even if for a moment." He pointed to the earth, and she followed his hands to the plateau. The wall cracked as rocks caved in at it. "You gave me no choice. I will not let you destroy the human stronghold. Serkily is all they have left!"

Ashina gazed at the devastation she had caused, and her eyes teared up. "What have I done."

Randon stood up and lingered to her, shaking his head. He rounded her, his eyes on hers. Ashina stood up fast to face him, watching him with her eyes. She melted in a circle as he rounded her like she was prey. Her eyes saw him as the black wolf. The black wolf eyed her in the face as his ears sat upright, his arms and chest muscles flexing at her presence.

"I see you." She whispered in his face, her eyes golden.

As Randon rounded her, he saw her as the white wolf, and his eyes softened. "I see you too." He bellowed.

Randon saw her white wolf form. Her silky curves, muscle-ridden body, and powerful snout pressed into his eyes. Her eyes sparkled in gold, and her presence made his knees quake. They stared into one another in silence until Randon stopped circling her. They met each other's faces, Randon's chest heaving.

"You do not get to lose yourself to your unbridled temper anymore. We are the most powerful wolves, Ashina. Our kingdoms are on a thread of destruction as is." He clenched his fists. "You are a mess. You will bring catastrophe to the humans if you do not control your power! You must control your emotions."

"I was thinking of all the pain..." Ashina bit her lip. She pulled at her shoulder, her palm bloodied. The ache of him burned through her bones. "I heard Alaric calling me again to stop."

"He calls because he was chosen as your mate! He has the same power. Do you think he does not sense when you do it?" Randon complained.

"He will sense we are bonded." Randon sneered at her. "Bonded Ashinnnaaa!"

Ashina gasped.

"You still fail to see his power in these lands. You and him are the only wolves with this power."

Randon eyed her up and down, his loins burning a fire within him to mate with her. "Augh. We are double-bitten! We are both alphas. He belted out a moan as if he was in pain. "Aug-ghhh." He sighed, not believing it.

His voice was deep and echoing. Ashina backed away from him, her eyes wide at his lust. He was bigger, and although she was strong, he wanted her. His whole body was tense and his muscles flexed at her.

He roared into the sky and yelled. "My blood boils with you inside me!" He bellowed, his face clenched. "I have never been this lost before, and it is because of you."

He moaned, gripping his shoulder at her deep bite. He closed his eyes and sighed. His face was as hard as his groin when he opened his eyes again. He swallowed at her face, clenching his fists as if fighting with a force he could not explain.

"You will use me to pivot your anger. We have bonded now, Ashina."

Ashina swallowed at his face, her chest heaving up and down with her deep breathing. "Tala helped me with that, so now you will help me?"

Randon met her face, shaking his head, his jaws clenched. "I will help you. We have a short time."

Then he turned his head and glared at the devastation. "You are powerful." He warned, shaking his head. "You could have destroyed this city. No wonder Alaric and Conri want you. Hunted by every being who craves your power."

"Now you have me." She whispered; her face drawn.

Randon pressed toward her. He stared down into her eyes as she met him there, his powerful body rigid against her. "And you have meeee white wolf."

He sneered at her, his eyes lingering over her body. She backed up from him, her face pale. "Stop it, Randon."

He continued to roam his eyes over her. "If I wanted to bite you and mate, you would not escape me." His voice was hard. "Ashina." He met her eyes, his face clenched. "I have more virtue than most alpha males. You got lucky."

She huffed. "I just kicked your ass! Luck had nothing to do with it. Randon!" Ashina gripped her shoulder. "I am not afraid of you."

Randon closed his eyes and sighed, his groin hard as stone. "You are stronger than I thought." He gawked at her.

She growled at him. "I mate when I am ready! No wolf will force me. Including you." She warned him. "Do you understand that, or must we go again?!"

He shook his head at her face, but his eyes were hard. "Fine."

"Tell me you understand it, Randon." She commanded him.

His fangs burst up. "We do not cower or rule over one another unless the other is willing to submit. I am in your court now. Do you understand?!"

Ashina took a deep breath in his face, as her mouth dropped open. "What have I done."

Randon lunged into her and breathed on her lips. "White wolf queen, you are the most powerful wolf, next to me." He took her face in his bloody palm and smiled in her eyes.

"Forgive me for attacking you." He begged. "I do understand, and I was wrong."

She gripped his bloody palm against her face as her eyes lingered on his lips. "Damn mating drive." She told him, but her heart was racing.

She would have fallen into him, but he stepped away from her. He breathed deep and fell to his knees again, his back to her.

"I will not go long without wanting to be near you. I am patient, but, if this happens again, if given an inch I will take it." His whole body flexed and tense.

He craned his eyes to glare back at her, his face roaming her body again. "I will not regret taking it."

She stepped away from him, her eyes wide. "You will not take me until I want you, Randon."

He rolled his eyes. "You cannot bite me again, Ashina. Understand?! The bites are only for our mates!" He bent his face to the ground, his deep breaths heaving to control his hunger for her.

"You bit me first!" She yelled at him, blaring her nostrils.

"You gave me no choice. You would have destroyed this city." He closed his eyes as her rage burned through his loins, and he thought his lungs would explode. The vibrations of her lingering behind him set his ears on edge. He clenched his teeth and took deep breaths to control it.

"I don't know what to do…" She whispered, her heart racing as she watched him control himself.

He changed the subject. "When the wolf kings come for you, I need you to be able to stand on your own against them." He moaned out, warning her.

"I need you strong in case something happens to me." He finished, exhausted. "I will die to protect you. There is no going back now."

"Even if we never mate?" She questioned.

Randon craned to stare at her, his handsome face still clenched. "Even if we never mate." His voice quivered like his aching heart.

Ashina stared at his back, the side of her face red from his blood. "What do I need to do?"

Randon craned his neck and smiled, but he was in pain. "Right now, I need you to walk away from me." He turned back around and sighed, staring down at his groin.

"Why."

He did not look at her. "Just give me a few moments…" He sounded exasperated. He closed his eyes and moaned, his face in pain. "Damnit Ashina."

She shook her head. "The mating drive is too hard after being bitten."

He took a deep breath and blinked his eyes when she said that, his jaws clenched. "It is…very hard." He moaned.

Ashina did not leave the hill. She stood as a looming shadow at Randon's back for endless moments until he was ready to turn and face her again. Moments later, he realized she was not leaving and stood up to face her. He adjusted his crotch and shook his head at her.

"Ashina," he sighed. He met her face with a stern glare, but his eyes held passion.

Ashina widened her eyes when he did that, noticing his golden eyes. As they gazed upon one another, their eyes matched the passion already on their faces. They bonded. She smiled at him, her face lit up as he loomed over her. Randon smiled at her, his powerful face soft at her beauty.

They bowed to each other, their eyes upon one another. The chills that darted up Randon's spine did not stop there. Something clawed its way deep inside him and grew a forest of hope. He stared at her face, the longing in his eyes evident as Ashina met him there.

"My queen." He swallowed.

They fell to one knee and bent their heads to the ground together, forged from the same fire. They showed each other respect. Something lingered and lit them up from the inside out, ravaging them inside. When they raised their heads back up, they smiled at one another again as their faces lit up in the sunrise.

"Come on, white wolf. Fight me." Randon enticed her.

Ashina smiled. "Fight you here? Like I just did and tossed you across the hill?" She laughed.

Randon laughed at her, his whole face lit up. His laugh was thunderous and echoed. "You think that was funny?" He shook his head at her. "Yea. Sure. Try to toss my ass across the hill again." He laughed. "Since Louve and Brovina are gawking at us in panic, let me work with you on sparring." He added.

Ashina bit her lip. "Okay, but I will kick your ass again."

Ashina flew into him and Randon blocked her strikes. "You won't get me like that again, I can assure you." He laughed.

They sparred with one another in the rising sun atop the hill. Their movements were fluid with one another and their hearts beat as one.

Louve rolled his eyes. "If this is the wolf mating ritual, I hate it! Look what they did to our hillside." He shook his head just as Brovina sighed. "They will bring the whole damn kingdom down mating."

She turned to go. "I am relieved this worked. They are now bonded, just as I hoped. They have chosen one another, and Randon will follow her til death."

Louve gasped, his eyes as wide as melons. "What! You did not know if this would work? You said you planned this."

She sighed. "I needed a primordial to bite her, a good one. And he has. Now, the most powerful wolf will always have her back. The wolf kings will be unable to control her if they take her."

Brovina sighed again and walked off from him, but Louve met her back, his face in terror.

"Now as Randon has called other wolves, they will follow her."

"Brovina! You did not know this would work, did you?!" He followed her to demand an answer but Brovina shooed him off.

"Did you." Louve followed her, his black beard swishing down his chin.

Chapter 12
The Fated Mate Lies

Alaric fell to his knees and gripped his heart as a rage shot through him. He belted out, his fangs pushed up from his gums. "Ashinaaaaa!" He moaned.

He bent his face to the ground and put his fist against his forehead. When he raised back up again, his eyes flamed in gold and his face clenched in agony. He stood up just as his commander Rieka plunged through the forest at him.

"Sire, are you well?" He fretted, his dark eyes wide.

"Another wolf marked my mate." Alaric sneered. "I can feel it. She slips from my grasp. I am running out of time."

Rieka growled. "Hunt her and take her!" He gripped his fists and twisted his face. "You are Alaric! King of the thousand-year realms! We are the strongest wolves in the world."

Alaric bent his neck and clenched his jaws. "We ride upon Serkily and bring down the walls. She has given me no choice."

"Yes, my king. What of the wolves waiting in reserves at the mountain?"

"We have one hundred thousand going to Serkily." Alaric smiled.

"Yes, my king."

"We need the remaining at the mountain. I know Cayden has emptied his lands of wolves to get her. They will march north of us and may come through the mountain. There will be war at the plains of Serkily."

He paused, "Take fifty thousand and split them up over the five kingdoms and seek the wayward wolves. My mate has a primordial who hunted her, and he is not loyal to me. These wolves must be loyal to me, or they will die. I cannot have my mate gathering her army to her side."

"Yes, sire. We ride at dawn to Serkily to pin in Conri and then will take Serkily. The wayward wolves will die or serve."

Alaric smiled, his eyes flowing back to green. "I will kill that wretched wolf Conri for trying to take her. He injured her! She was weak and almost bled out."

Rieka growled. "He will die, his wolves will die. The humans will bleed again. It will all be well, my king. You shall see!" He turned his horse into the camp under the woods and left Alaric standing by the river.

Alaric clenched his fists and closed his eyes. "Ashina, why do you hate me? I am your mate."

He turned away from the river. At dawn, they would head south to Serkily. They would pin Conri and his wolves in between them and the Dakitae. They would be coming upon the gates there within days. Alaric thought back to the field before the river when she disappeared again. She had used her power and killed the wolves, ripping them apart.

"You have a powerful gift. Do not make me use it against you..." His face clenched. "I am coming to the gates of Serkily to take you."

Brovina watched Ashina stand with slumped shoulders as they buried Tala's body in the woods at the base of the mountain. The grove leveled under fronds of evergreens as the forest engulfed them. Delicate white flowers kissed the grass around the grove. The wolves dug the grave for Ashina as they stood around the body on the mound and lowered their heads.

Behind her, the grove filled with King Meltivi and Louve with his warriors. The high court of Serkily joined them in burying Tala and celebrating her life. Ashina cried for her guardian. She swallowed and ignored the pained look Randon and the other wolves gave to her. Brovina stood to the side, picking one of the flowers and dropping it on the grave.

"Tala was a brave guardian. We thank Tala for her sacrifice in protecting the white wolf. We will write Tala into the book of warriors for Serkily."

Ashina closed her eyes, her face wet with tears, her lips quivering. When she opened them again, a wind blew in on them. The evergreen branches swung over them, bending toward her to kiss the grave. Everyone watched. Brovina glared at the wolves standing alongside Randon. Their faces fell to a pale white as their backs grew rigid.

Louve stared into the trees, swallowed, and said nothing. He lingered tall and silent alongside his warriors as they stood as replicas of himself. They were armed and formidable in their attire and stamina.

It was no small gift to have nature's power on your side. The wolves always had some natural powers, their strength and being at one with nature in the wild evident. But this was something ancient, a relic of power so dangerous, it could destroy kingdoms.

The king bowed to the grave, and Louve walked him back to their horses. Ashina stood there for a moment alone as Randon lingered behind her, waiting for her to come.

"Thank you for saving me," Ashina whispered, wiping her face. "I will fight for these kingdoms, human or wolf. I will fight with all I am, Tala. I will get the villagers back..."

Randon turned his face away from her as she said that and closed his eyes. He clenched his jaws, and as she walked by him, her followed her in silence with his eyes.

They had taken horses there because it was five miles in. Serkily was a vast kingdom walled in, even to the mountain passes. The wolf kings had never breached it, but now they would be desperate.

Brovina gathered the last flowering herb she needed to perform the blood spell. She followed Ashina and Randon with the other wolves back to the city. The king and Louve had already gone back. Ashina was silent on the horse, her face solemn. The skies thundered ahead of them, and black clouds billowed in. Ashina stared into the heavens as her hazel eyes sparkled under the daylight left.

Brovina had led them over the rolling plain on the road the city had built toward the mountain. The evergreen woodlands spilled around them like a haven of hope. It was beautiful, expansive, and brilliant. Ashina closed her eyes and took a deep breath. Her heart ached, and her bones ached.

Something was not right in her. She heard Alaric call to her from the deep as a throbbing ache hit her temples.

"I am not your enemy."

"You are mine and mine alone."

"Please come to me. Do not make me come to you, or the city will fall..."

"I will burn the world down to get to you."

She craned her neck and closed her eyes when she heard him say the last warning. Something beckoned her to action and pulled through her veins. His call was so deep it ripped through her heart and echoed in her head. Her mind wandered off to the first time he found her, and she found herself wandering inside his eyes. His deep green eyes screamed his heart was bigger than his brutality.

She could no longer fight it. Alaric's call was strong. She gripped her chest, her heart racing.

She took a deep breath and craned her head back to Brovina. "We must break the bond tonight." The wolves and Randon gawked at her, but Randon agreed. "I need free of this. I cannot help the kingdoms otherwise."

"He will continue calling to you until it breaks," Brovina warned, her voice echoing.

"He will not stop calling me." She gasped, a weariness overcoming her. "He is relentless. He is an endless weariness upon me."

Brovina sighed. "Yes. The alpha males are relentless when fate calls them to their mates. It will get worse. Even his strength is empowered. He will not stop."

Randon gazed at Ashina when she said that, his eyes lighting upon her. Ashina met his stare but did not smile. They rode back together in silence to the city.

Hours later, Brovina concocted the green goo that Randon gagged at. He sat aside Ashina shirtless in his trousers and bare feet and downed it. Ashina lay on an altar in a massive cavern room where Brovina worked. The full moon would fill the window and spread the beams upon the altar.

Ashina laid on her back as her white gown spilled around her ankles. Her white hair spilled to the floor and touched Randon's feet.

Brovina walked in with five women younger than her, all dressed in black. They surrounded them and gazed at the window as the moon began kissing the horizon in it. Brovina pulled out Randon's hand and sliced it open. He sneered and held his breath. She then slit Ashina's hand and tied them together.

"The blood bond of two primordials is what breaks the fated mate bond to the wicked wolf king."

Ashina swallowed as her eyes craned to the window. She watched the moon fill it slowly. Randon's eyes were upon her, his face clenched as he loomed over her. He gripped her hand in his palm as she twisted her bloody fingers into his. She met his stare but was not smiling. Randon felt her grief because breaking the fated bond grieved him. He did not want to be on the receiving end of it.

"The fated mate bond has never broken," Brovina warned them.

Ashina swallowed.

"It has never been challenged."

Randon swallowed as Ashina widened her eyes.

Brovina approached Ashina, her face hard. "Once a fated mate bond severs, you will be free from his control…"

The room fell silent. Randon listened, his brows furrowing.

Ashina scowled. "Why does fate rule in such wicked ways." She pursed her lips. "Fate does not rule me. I rule my fate. You will all see."

Brovina sighed. "Let us begin."

Ashina and Randon closed their eyes as the moon set in the window of this round cavernous room. The five women stood around them and chanted an ancient curse in a language Ashina could not understand. But something happened inside her, and she began to get sleepy and closed her eyes.

Randon watched her close her eyes and relax as her hand grew limp in his, and then the burning started. He sneered at it. Brovina watched his veins burn red under his skin and melt into Ashina's. He clenched his jaw and took a deep breath.

"Your powerful primordial blood is siphoning your strength into her to sever the bond…" Brovina warned him. "It could kill her otherwise."

The women kept chanting and getting louder as Randon found himself getting hot and edgy. His hand became numb, and Brovina watched him grip Ashina's hand harder. She nodded her head and turned to the women. The women followed the runes on the floor.

Brovina stood back as the runes glowed into an ember haze at their feet. The rays pilfered atop Ashina until she lit up in a luminescent glow. The glow hit her chest, and smoky fingers pried themselves out of her. Ashina held her breath like something tore through her heart.

A smoky apparition sloughed off her chest and rose midair like a fog had lived within her this whole time. It twisted and turned as if it was alive and breathing. It rolled into the air above her and rose into the moonbeams. The smoke seemed to have one side stronger in form than the other.

The women stopped marching in a circle, and Brovina entered the circle again with a broad sword. She eyed the smoky apparition.

"We command fate to break the fated mate bond."

Brovina lunged up and sliced it in half. The smoke twisted and melted within itself, writhing in pain. Ashina's eyes flew open to reveal golden pupils. She gasped for breath as her chest lunged into the air atop the altar. She let out a moan in pain and seethed, her insides burning.

"The mated fate bond has been severed." Brovina smiled.

Ashina raised her eyes to see the smoke writhe in pain above her. The half closest to her dissipated, but the piece left lingered above her and stared into her. Brovina froze, her eyes wide at this apparition. Ashina met it with a firm face even as Alaric called to her again. His voice echoed, and everyone heard it.

"I come for you, my beloved."

"You leave me no choice."

A damn of pain opened within Ashina and broke loose. *"Ashina..."* Alaric called. The smoke evaporated, and the room filled with an eerie silence.

Ashina bent her head to the voice as chills darted up her legs. "Alaric! Get out of my head!" She yelled.

Brovina closed her eyes.

Randon lunged up, shaking his head. "He will pursue you and burn the world down to get you."

Randon sighed and glared at her, but Ashina gasped when he said that.

"There is dark magic in this fated bond." Brovina belted out.

Ashina put her free palm in her face and bellowed out in anger. Her heart ached as Alaric continued to beckon her deep inside. Randon stood there with wide eyes, his mouth open at what he witnessed.

"This will not end well for Serkily." Randon spit out. "My wolves do not have enough time to get here."

Randon turned his gaze to Ashina and raked his fingers over her face. He bent up to face the moon, the light and smoke gone. Brovina cut the ropes at their palms as Ashina sat up, glaring into the round window. She took a deep breath, her face clenched.

Ashina stood up and stared at the moon. "He is coming for me." She swallowed. "He wants me in the mountain. There is something there that is dark. Yet, it pulls me to go there."

Brovina sighed. "Yes. Seer magic. Something attaches itself to Alaric, pulling you to him. All the queens have fallen this way..."

The room gasped.

Ashina stared at the moon, her eyes lighting up at it. "For centuries, that mountain has taken primordial queens who never left. There is a great evil there."

Silence.

"Tala wanted me to change the world."

She turned to glare at Brovina, her eyes golden. "Something broke inside me. The piece you cut off was the bond. The piece remaining is not pure. It is dark magic; I can feel it."

Randon met her stare, his brows furrowed. "What does this mean?" He stared at Brovina.

But all Brovina could do was shake her head and sigh. "It means that Ashina must go to the mountain, face whatever is pulling Alaric, and destroy it."

Randon sighed and rubbed his fingers through his hair. "He will bite you, Ashina, and…"

Ashina sighed. "I bite, too. I mate with whom I want. I will go to breach the mountain of Worgen. I will free the women from my village. They are my friends."

The room was very still and fell into a pained silence.

Ashina barked, her voice deep and hard like a two-edged sword. "I cannot see the evil in that mountain unless I am in it. That is the only way to destroy it."

Brovina dropped her head and sighed. "You are either the bravest white wolf queen or quite mad."

Randon sighed, his heart aching.

A laric sat atop his horse, leading his army with his commander, Rieka. Behind them, the wooded plains flooded with his army on their way to flank in Conri. His wolves filled the land with darkness, dreadful to look upon. Their tattoos snaked up their muscle-riddled arms, caressed their chests up their necks to their long beards. They were black and deep and twisted like the branches in the forest of his kingdom.

"*Get out of my head*!" He heard her scream at him, and he froze on his horse. He froze so fast his heart skipped a beat, and he widened his eyes to a shimmering gold when he heard it. His ears rung of her voice as his heart sang in laughter.

"No." He whispered back, laughing.

"Sire?" Rieka wondered.

Alaric smiled, his handsome face beaming, his heart beating wild. He gripped the reigns with powerful tattooed hands and clenched his arms. He turned to Rieka, his face clenched, his eyes sparkling. "The bond will not be broken. The seer has failed. The power of the mountain remains."

"Ah goooooddddd." Rieka laughed. "There is hope yet for the stubborn white wolf, eh."

Alaric smiled and nodded. "Keep the army back from me as we approach."

Rieka eyed him, a smile on his sinister face.

"I will take down the wall to get her, and the city will fall."

Rieka's laugh echoed.

Chapter 13
The Heart that Never Rests

King Meltivi had all new body armor made for Ashina. She stood on the hill and faced Randon, her resolve strong. She wore a long skirt split over tight trousers as a black breastplate kissed her chest. Brovina had an emblem carved in it to look like the moon cycles. It was perfect for Ashina.

Her black pauldrons matched her breastplate. Her greaves and tabard fit tight on her frame like an obsidian goddess breathed her to life. Her long white hair whipped down her back in a ponytail. Her eyes flamed in gold as she bowed to Randon. He had new armor, all black.

They complimented each other as their faces shone in the morning sun together. Randon bowed, his eyes roaring back at her in gold. They bonded, and nothing would change that. She had not bonded to Alaric, but he was her mate. Alaric would have to bite her to force the bonding first.

"Ashina." Randon stood to face her. "You are going to learn to control your temper. Once you hone that in, with your power, you will take out whole armies. Just as Alaric's throne has done for centuries."

"Go." He whispered, and they fell as one and bent into the wind together with Ashina in the lead.

"You will pivot your anger through me, and I will channel it into what you seek to control." He told her. "You will use me as a siphon to your worst fears, and I will bend those fears for good."

Randon closed his eyes and let her guide him to her motions as she whispered in his head, his heart flowing with her power. "From here on out, no matter where you go, I will come to you. I will fight for you..."

Ashina had chills dart up her spine.

"Always." He added.

"Always bend your fears for good, Ashina..." He beckoned her. "Fears are powerful and can be used for good."

Ashina closed her eyes and breathed in the morning air. But then Tala's face appeared, and the ground shook beneath them. Randon breathed deeply and whispered in her heart, *"calm yourself, white wolf"*, and it calmed her. She bent into the sun and focused on breathing as Randon melted behind her. They synched as one.

As she stretched and practiced her defensive moves, the earth rumbled beneath Randon's feet again. He opened his eyes to witness the grass swaying with her movement and froze. He bent his head to see the trees by the plateau flowing toward her. There was no wind. He held his breath, his heart overflowing with this dawning.

Ashina whispered again. "Breathe..."

Randon closed his eyes as his soul followed her. He stretched out to match hers, his legs bent as if they faced a mighty wind together. Ashina pressed a fist out. The hillside blew as if something blasted up from the ground. It lunged the grass from the roots where they stood and catapulted it into the air over their heads. The grass pressed toward the clouds like a hand had pushed it and spilled dirt upon them. Ashina swished her arm out and forward, and the grass became darting arrows bent to her will.

Randon's cheeks tickled as slivers of grass pressed against him, and he opened his eyes. She pressed her fist out again, and the grass darted away from them. It hit the plateau where she had broken the earth, filling the open crack's breadth with grass.

The echo of it hitting sounded like a wall of parchments had spilled.

The round hill was stripped of grass. Randon stood upright, his face clenched. "You have dark magic in your bloodline. Ah, shit." He warned her.

Ashina turned to face him, her face flat. "This is the only thing I have going for me that will defeat the wolf kings."

Randon swallowed. "And you think letting Alaric get you will punish him? We have all fought and bled to get you here, where Tala wanted us to."

"Tala did not know the bond would be with dark magic." Ashina bit back. "Brovina is right. Alaric has some ancient power in that mountain. I must find out what."

"In tens of thousands of years. No one has escaped to tell any tales about that mountain. It is a fortress, Ashina." He warned her.

Randon sighed at her face, shaking her head. "If Alaric gets you, he will keep you. He has enough army in the mountain to do so, and you will be powerless against it."

"I will not be powerless. You are not giving me enough credit."

He bent his head into the sun and rolled his eyes. "I will not be able to come for you. Neither us wolves nor man have enough army to stand against Alaric!"

Ashina breathed in. "I will find a way to get out and take the women his wolves have been taking, rendering his kingdom empty of hope."

Randon swallowed. "Thousands upon thousands of women? This city will not hold them."

"You are afraid." Ashina barked at him.

Randon huffed. "I am not afraid Ashina. I fought in wars with this Alaric years ago. I fought to protect humans from his cruelty before you were born."

She rolled her eyes around the open plain and the stripped hill. Her eyes craned to the tower and the humans who watched them. She noticed the landing became busy with movement, and Randon peered with her, his eyes squinting.

"The wolves have come. I knew they would come." He walked away from her.

"Where are you going?" Ashina asked.

Randon yelled back at her. "To prepare the wolves to protect the city. The women and children are to travel to the caverns beginning today. We have a lot to do!"

Ashina watched him go, her face twisted. They had not finished yet. She sensed Randon's fear for her. She sensed him rising and falling in her presence over and over, and it troubled her. He stayed conflicted with emotions over her and was having a hard time with them. If Ashina did not stop these wolf kings now, everything and everyone she ever loved would die. Tala lost her life for her. She could lose no others.

Ashina bent her head back and closed her eyes. She kept seeing Alaric's eyes bore into her. His tall, muscular body and strong tattoos were intimidating, but she liked them. She had a tattoo on her back that sang like an ancient tree had been carved into her, and she was the main branch. It was not a big tattoo, but it did fill the space between her lower neck and upper back.

She thought of her first encounter with Alaric, and a fire burned through her chest as he called her.

"*Ashina. Come to me.*"

"Stop it, Alaric." She complained.

"*You are my mate. You belong to me, Ashina.*"

A pain in her heart pricked her deep inside about him. Although she had a bond with Randon, Alaric continued to pull her through that and call her. It was so powerful she could hear him breathing in her soul. Something inside her rose, and from the depths of her mind, Alaric called her again, and she answered him.

"I am coming to get you. Now."

"Come and get me, wolf king." She barked back. "Do not hurt the humans." She warned him, her call deep and bellowing.

"Do not destroy this city." She warned him. "I will come with you, Alaric."

He was on his way. But so was Conri. So were the Dakitae humans.

Serimi led the human faction, and they were coming from the west. Conri's horde marched north of Alaric's Mountain kingdom with hundreds of thousands ready. The world would burn at the gates of Serkily anyway, and there was nothing Ashina could do to stop it.

She sighed. She could not let the kingdoms fall because of her. So many thousand-year queens had bent to the will of their fated mates. They did so because the wolf kings were raging and power-hungry. Ashina had no choice at all. Did these kings love their mates?

She closed her eyes in the sun and breathed in deeply. Her heart was steady in her chest as Alaric caressed her deep inside.

He caressed her so deep a pit of passion rose from the depths of her very essence. She bent into the sun and breathed in the hope of its power. She stretched her arms and legs again toward the earth as Tala had taught her.

Wolves were the gods of nature. They lived and breathed with the trees, the earth, and the water. They sensed the layout of the lands like a vicious roar. They felt vibrations from movement on the forest floors. The wolves smelled danger like a hot iron seared in their souls. They could sense when something moved within the trees or on the plains by the breaths in the wind. They knew what moved in the wind and smelled motives in the movements.

Their world rolled inside them like nature had sprouted them and birthed monsters. Instead of monsters, powerful wolf beings formed. The wolves were to guard over nature and the world. But the seers changed that somewhere in time, and the wolves came to hunt man and enslave them. The wolves rose to rule, and with their cruelty came malice and pain.

Ashina's heart burned thinking about the pain her kind had brought upon the lands. For thousands of years, they warred, took, pillaged, and burned. Ashina clenched her face and narrowed her brows, seething inside. She feared for the human women. They knew they would be taken and did not run because they could not outrun the wolves.

A horrid fate for a human woman was to be taken by a wolf for them to bite and then breed for life. Once the wolves bit their woman of choice, they bonded, and the women lured to them. Like a damn spell. A curse. The wolves were loyal to these women until death, but it was wrong.

It was a twisted fate of injustice and evil. For years, even human men and women had taken spouses of wolves too. The world filled with a demise of no end. They all warred with one another, breeding indifference and pain like none other. It was time to end it.

Alaric's throne had bred and built armies of mass proportions for ages this way. Meanwhile, the kingdoms deprived more and more of human men. Yet the ones who lingered were formidable warriors and brave. They had crafted the finest weapons to take the wolves out. They had stood and survived, somehow.

When Ashina opened her eyes, she stared at a chasm toward the plateau. The ground vibrated beneath her. The echo of the demise roared into the clouds. The crack in the earth she made the day before had fallen into the hill. The cave-in shook at her feet. The forest leading to the plateau tipped into the darkness, and boulders rolled into it. The ground vibrated through the rolling plain to the city walls.

Her face fell as weak as her knees. From the hillside behind her, Randon ran up on her again. Behind him, the wolves that had come to help fight filled the hillside, gawking at her. From the tower, Louve arched his back and eyed Brovina, who watched this spectacle for some time.

The warriors on the wall peering over the plain at the back of the city murmured, and some hollered at the catastrophe. Ashina bit her lip as tears came to her eyes.

"I cannot stay here. I will destroy this city." She bellowed. "I am safe nowhere."

Randon stood beside her, his chest heaving. "You took out the whole hillside." He glared down at her. "Now you see why Alaric wants you, right?"

"I see everything." She moaned. "Kingdoms fall to this power."

Alaric plunged his army through the forested plain into Serkily. They would be behind Conri by less than a day.

The Dakitae he sent to Serkily would arrive any day now, but he was desperate.

She was using her power and had to learn to control it. He was her mate for this very reason. The mountains of Worgen are where she needed to be. Every time she bent nature in her fury, Alaric sensed it. A writhing pain filled him with desperation.

She was now enticing him to come, so he bent his head into the horse's mane and chased her. She taunted him as if laughing, *"Come and get me."* Alaric would because she did not realize the extent of his power or wolves.

"Come and get me, wolf king." He heard her smart off.

There was an edge in her. Alaric found himself cautious and weary because of her. Not one had dared challenge the kingdom like her in all the years of his throne taking the primordials. She intrigued him and scared him.

He sighed as she spoke to him again. *"Do not hurt the humans."*

Alaric shook his head. "Stubborn white wolf."

And then he heard, *"Do not destroy this city."*

Alaric narrowed his brows as if she had bent him to her will and he had not yet bitten her. Her luring power was strong for him and he could not understand it. As he focused on the travel ahead, he heard the most beautiful beckoning as she said "*I will come with you, Alaric.*"

He would lunge behind Conri and fight through them to get to her, but the Dakitae he sent would be a buffer. It would pin Conri in, even though his army was vast.

In Worgen, his half a million wolves guarded it with fervor. It would not be breached, and no one had ever escaped. His mountain kingdom was designed that way for a reason. It was one of the reasons his family had reigned so long. As the thousand-year queens were taken, they never left. And it would stay that way. Forever.

Once Alaric had her this last time, she would never leave. She would never leave because he was going to bite the shit out of her to make her bond, no matter how stubborn she was. And then he was going to mate her hard until she bore him an heir.

Chapter 14
The Demise of Hope

Ashina glared from the tower landing to the plain at the damage she had done. She stood there in her new body armor and armed, thinking. She had come an hour before dawn crested the mountain, and now it was rising in her face. All around her, the tower walls melted onto the plateaus and catapults. The Ballistas lined up in the thousands for miles and surrounded the city on the high walls.

Alongside them were piles of silver blades to kill the wolves. Louve had been painstaking in his preparation of the city. Ashina watched the last of the families march up the road toward the mountain cavern. It was a safe place where they could hide.

Ashina lingered her eyes on the human children as she smiled at them, though her heart ached. The father was not with them, but he would be fighting. The children's mother led them, who were only four and five years old. Ashina bent her neck to gaze at them until they climbed into the back of a wagon and disappeared over the hill.

The rolling plain spilled for miles as the plateaus rose on either side and forests kissed in between. The hill she destroyed was now brown and dirty on top instead of pristine green.

"Tala, I need you." She whispered to herself, her heart moaning.

"Why did you take me through the unexplored where your people come from…" Ashina bit her lip as the sun hit her face.

The unexplored lands were east of Alaric's kingdom. Alaric had found her in a matter of days, and Randon tracked her there the day after. Tala told her there were caverns there where Ashina could hide. Ashina took a deep breath and shook her head at the sunrise.

"You wanted me there."

"There was no time to show me anything."

Ashina breathed and closed her eyes. "I must go back."

She turned, and Randon stared at her, the sun lighting his face. He was fully armed and his eyes screamed war. He gripped his broad sword hanging at his side and nodded at her.

"The Dakitae will be here by nightfall."

"And Conri will come, and Alaric." She warned.

Randon nodded. "Yes. They all come."

"Because of me." Ashina scowled, turning her head to face the sunrise again. "Why would Tala bring this upon the humans." She questioned.

Randon met her stare. "Tala wanted to unite the wolves and humans. For far too long, the wolf kings have ruled and oppressed humans."

"What lies past these mountains." She asked as Randon.

Randon glared into the sunrise. "More rivers and lakes, more valleys, and plains. Nothing lives there to our knowledge."

"To your knowledge? Serkily could begin again there if they needed."

Randon knew where she was going with this, and he huffed. "If they had to, I suppose."

"When you tracked me in the falls, do you know of caverns there?" She questioned.

Randon thought a moment. "There is a set of falls in the heart where an ancient kingdom lay thousands of years ago. I do not know where it would be. Why?"

Silence.

"You are not going back there." He chirped at her.

She stared into the horizon. "I will take the women there once I have freed them from Alaric's Mountain, and you will meet me there with the wolf army."

Randon scoffed at her. "No, Ashina." And then he froze. "What wolf army." His eyes were wide.

"The army you will assemble for me. Every wolf not loyal to the wolf kings should be on my side, fighting for what is right."

"Ashina." Randon dropped his mouth at her.

She smiled at him and blinked her eyes. "I bit you. You will summon the wolves to me. We will undermine the wolf kings and save the people."

Randon closed his eyes and breathed in deep. "I see where you are going with this." He clenched his face. "No." He barked at her.

"Yes. We have bonded. I need your help. Did you think I would let a primordial return to the wild while the kingdoms burn?" She stared at him.

Randon dropped his mouth open and widened his eyes. "You are a devious wolf..."

Ashina half smiled at him, as her eyes sparkled.

He shook his head. "It will only work if you can get free of Alaric if he takes you."

"When he takes me." She added.

"He's not taking you." Randon met her face with a stern glare.

Ashina bent back as he barked in her face.

"I did not track you and bleed for you for nothing." He gripped his sword, his arms flexed. "That will not happen on my watch."

Ashina met his face and swallowed. "I have to undermine him, and this is the only way..."

"No," Randon warned her, his face clenched and his eyes hard. "It cannot be the only way."

"What should I do then?" She questioned. "So, we are going to war here and then will never breach his mountain? His reign will never end if we do not get in there to see what evil he is spawning."

"He has hundreds of thousands of wolves waiting. His numbers are so vast, Ashina."

"What should I do then, commander."

Randon leaned away from her face when she said that. "What are you doing? Ashina, no."

"I need a commander, and you are a powerful primordial like me. I am the white wolf queen. I need you to help me build an army of wolves and humans who work together. Men and wolves who fight to do what is right and protect the lands. Together. Tala told me the stories of her kingdom and how it used to be before Alaric came."

Randon sighed and rolled his eyes. "I should've taken you on that hill." He moaned. "I would've gotten something out of all this and probably felt better."

Ashina laughed at him, her face bright and wide. "You are my commander, Randon. I am calling you to my court. Accept it or die." Her smile fell as Randon met her stare, his face clenched.

"I cannot do any of this if Alaric does not take me into that infernal mountain. I am the only one who can do this. Why are you not listening to my gut? I know you hear it."

Randon's voice broke. "My biggest fear with you going is that I will never see you again. I will never know what happened to you in that damn mountain. Once he has you there, he will never let you go. And then I will go in and kill a bunch of them but may not live to get you out."

"I need you to trust me." She paused as her eyes met his. "I need your trust more than anything else in this world."

Randon closed his eyes and then felt her firm grip on his bulging forearm. He opened his eyes and met hers sparkling back at him. "I trust you with my life. I need you in my court. I need you to help me."

He bent away from her, his face soft.

"You have saved me over and over. There is no one else I want by my side to do this. I need you to trust me. I am not some weak wolf craving a mate. If I were, I would have let him take me. I would have stayed in the village waiting on his commander to get me."

And then she laughed. "I would have taken you on that hill and mated you. I don't feel led to do that with you. Trust me, I go after what I want."

Randon burst out in laughter. "Damn alpha."

Randon smiled at her face, his eyes lingering over her. "I know Alaric calls to you, Ashina. Whether it is seer magic or not, you have answered him as your mate." He warned. "A mated bond is powerful. I warned you."

She glared into his eyes. "I am in control of my fate. Nothing can change that. Fate does not rule the wolves. You will see."

Ashina did not believe in fate. Ashina believed she controlled her destiny. They both craned their eyes toward the horizon suddenly. The beaming torch lights from thousands of Dakitae were miles out. They had come, and the war was at the gates of Serkily.

Randon took a deep breath and growled aside his white wolf queen. She gripped her swords with clenched fists and eyes on fire.

"Fate has deemed these human betrayers will die," Randon growled.

King Meltivi joined Brovina and Louve on the towers. They overlooked the rolling wooded plain over the river as the horizon bled in torch lights. The Dakitae humans were coming in tens of thousands. They were but miles away. Meltivi nodded.

"The women and children..."

Louve answered. "In the cavern passes, ready to flee into the south if needed."

"The warriors and guards."

Louve turned and gazed upon the plain behind them filled with human warriors. Their black body armor shimmered in the midday sun. Their silver spikes atop their helmets and pauldrons beamed back at them. The human faction had fifty thousand at Serkily and was considered small. Compared to the Dakitae serving Alaric, they were in trouble.

The warriors gripped long spears and had axes strapped to their backs. The rear lines held ballistas and catapults. The ballistas filled the span of the kingdom walls for miles every fifty feet. The warriors lined the walls and numbered ten thousand. Behind the warriors on the plain in the city were ten thousand archers waiting.

Louve's archers stood on the tower walls beside the ballistas, their human strength a fortitude of power. To beat the wolves in battle, the humans modified their armor with spikes on their sabatons and gauntlets. Their tassets and greaves had silver spikes, their sheaths filled with poison-tipped arrows in wolfsbane. All the warriors held elongated shields in their free hands with spikes to gore the wolves.

The humans looked spawned from silver-spiked demons. The warriors filled the rolling plain behind them in black. The guards awaited Louve's command on the city walls as the Dakitae moved in closer to the river at them.

King Meltivi nodded and turned to see his warriors. Then he gazed at Ashina and Randon standing beside Louve. "If this city falls, get her south into the mountains. Get her as far away as possible."

"I will not run," Ashina told the king, her brows furrowed. "I will fight to protect Serkily. It is because of me your city is in peril now."

The king smiled at her; his gray eyes sparkling. "I knew you would say that, white wolf queen." He patted her on the arm and walked past them with Brovina.

Louve shook his head at the king. "I do not know why he does that. He confuses me many times."

Louve nodded to his guard and bent his head down the wall. He noticed Randon's wolves joined them, ready and armed. They spaced up and down the wall between the human guards and ballistas. The guard blew into the horn, its bellowing shriek aching the skies. The archers on the walls pressed arrows against the knocking joints, ready to pull back.

The Dakitae filled the horizon and then disappeared under the trees in the forest. The sun tilted from midday to late afternoon, and Ashina held her breath thinking of the brutal Conri. The wolves were always stronger at night. The humans would be fighting for their lives then.

The field before the river flooded with Dakitea lunging out of the forest on horseback. Louve bent his head down the wall as the drawbridge was up. The only separation was the white rapids of the raging river. It was wide, deep, and fast, and horses could not cross it.

As the Dakitae cut down the trees, Louve sighed. "Damnit. Not the trees!" He sneered, shaking his head.

Randon watched them cut into the trees, craning his head to pull an arrow from his back sheath. He fired across the river into the Dakitae as he leaned into a tree with his axe. The arrow plunged through his back and out his front, and the human gasped and fell. Louve laughed, and his guard sounded the horn. The space between the wall over the river became consumed with darting arrows. They shot into the Dakitae to keep them from cutting down trees.

Ashina joined them, her face clenched. She fired her arrows aside Randon into the bodies of the humans she could see under the canopy. Her eyes froze as she loaded another arrow. Her eyes met another darkness on the horizon from the plain. Her heart beat faster. She peered into the horizon at a dark-headed rider with a crimson cape. Thousands upon thousands followed behind him, and the earth spilled in red.

"Conri." She bellowed; her face clenched.

Louve sneered. "Conri is coming! He will wipe out the Dak-itae who serve Alaric."

He raised his arms and had the guard blow the horn again to stop firing. "Halt!"

Randon peered at him as Louve shrugged his shoulders. "Saving arrows. Let them kill one another."

Randon shook his head as a smile left his lips, but he was bitter. Conri had come for Ashina again.

Louve hollered. "Ready the silver! Ready the ballistas!" The guards slid the silver blades into the ballistas all along the wall for miles. They needed the silver to cut down the wolves once they transformed. The silver blades gave the humans an edge against the wolves. The blades could decapitate them, cut them in half, or gore them. It gave the human faction time to lunge in and cut off their heads.

Ashina held her breath as Conri's surviving army lunged into the forest. "He has a greater army than any of us realized."

Louve agreed. "He does. His strategy has always been to sac-rifice wolves on the outer rims of his forces to let his real army in. He plots something else; I feel it!"

Randon smirked. "Where is Serimi?"

Louve met his stare, his face stern. "They will be here at nightfall! He has emptied the plain of men to protect us."

"Damnit." Randon scoffed. "If Alaric comes with his army the humans may not survive."

Louve scoffed at him. "You have no faith in your human brothers, eh? No one messes with Serimi and Galin! You shall see."

Randon did not answer him. He sighed and watched the Dakitae emerge from under the canopy and turn to meet Conri's wolves there. The plain flowed like a black river as the Dakitae and Conri's wolves plunged into one another.

Conri's army pressed up on their horses and changed to their wolf forms in midair. The black wolves the kingdoms feared had come. They roared into the Dakitae with obsidian claws and dagger fangs. As they catapulted off their horses in midair, the air became consumed with silver shards.

The humans serving Alaric were no fools. The Dakitae had planned on Conri. The front line continued cutting down trees to make a bridge across the river. The back line pulled their crossbows and shot silver blades into Conri's wolves in midair. The wolves fell as their horses trampled them.

The Dakitae held the wolves at the back lines. The silver blades plunged into their necks or heads or through their chests. The wolves fell in midair, their moaning growls filling the forest for miles in pain.

Conri's archers pressed to the front and gored the Dakitae alive, still in their human form. The wolf arrows hit the humans like speared shafts shoved through them. Conri's archers were in the thousands and bled together in brutality and strength.

The archers pressed through the Dakitae as the forest filled with screaming humans. The wolves roared under the canopy in the darkness. Conri veered around them with another black-headed man riding with him. As they disappeared under the tree line, Louve waited.

They watched the trees sway as shouts of rage and moans of defiance filled the forest with dread. Louve's brown eyes sparkled in the sun as his gauntlet squeaked. He gripped the hilt of his long sword at his side as Conri's army flooded the plain and disappeared under the forest canopy. The human screams echoed to the city wall and over the raging waters.

"Why does my kind serve Alaric? They are now dying for him." Louve sighed.

"Alaric has used them as a buffer," Randon warned, his eyes glowed in blue. "He stalls Conri. Wise."

Then everything fell silent.

"He has sacrificed the whole of his Dakitae human army to get to her." Louve gasped. "Alaric is a cruel king."

Louve watched along with Ashina, Randon, and the thousands of warriors, waiting for endless moments before a roar echoed and the ground shook. A pine tree fell from the banks, landing across the river and sinking in the soil. Another one fell, then another, as if they had been ripped up by the roots.

The burly black wolves burst from the canopy darkness, snarling. They pressed upon the trees to cross the river and climb the wall. They burst out as their numbers seemed to overwhelm even the trees.

Louve rolled his eyes. "Lower the spikes!"

Silver spikes on the walls looked like swords grew out of its stone. The spikes pivoted from the walls, taking three humans to lift them and drop them over the ramparts. The spikes were built into the stone floor of the towers and designed for them to sink into. They gripped the wooden handles and pivoted, turning the spikes upright. They pulled them from the stone and dropped them over the walls.

"Fire!" Louve commanded.

The archers fired their wolfbane-tipped arrows. They hit Conri's wolves, who lunged out of the canopy, reaching the river at them. They lined up along the river banks for miles as they slithered from the woods. The arrows hitting them were thick, hearty, and loud kerthunks echoed as they gored them. The wolves bellowed in pain and writhed on the banks of the raging river. They crawled back under the canopy to pull the arrows out as they got hit.

"I knew we should have cleared this forest. I did tell Meltivi. No one listens to me." Louve sighed.

Randon watched the forest bursting with wolves toward the river banks. They numbered in the thousands upon thousands. Conri had taken the Dakitae within hours, and now the sun was setting. Randon clenched his jaws as the sun set, growling into his wolf form.

Louve felt the burst of wind from his change. His long black beard blew sideways across his neck, but he did not bother to look at Randon. He wiped his fingers through his beard to straighten it and sighed.

"You think you are so damn special," Louve smirked, eying him.

Randon snarled down upon him, his black primordial wolf sneering. "I am."

Ashina laughed at them both and rolled her eyes. Louve shook his head at him, continuing to glare at Conri's army as they filled the fields at the river in blackness.

"Fire!" Louve commanded, and Ashina and Randon joined in shooting the wolfbane arrows. It would injure them and make them weak, but not kill them.

They would be weak til morning because there was enough wolfsbane in each arrow to make them sick for hours. It would take a lot for them to fight the weakness now flooding their veins. Louve was methodical in his warring, and Randon knew it. The human commander weakened the brute wolves. That way, when Serimi and Galin showed up, they would kill them. He hoped.

Conri's wolves continued to pull trees down even though they had gotten struck with arrows. Louve pursed his lips and watched them. These wolves were bigger than Alaric's wolves. If they tried to cross the river, the rapids would pull them away from the castle.

The river was wide, but the trees rose over the breadth of it. The trees they pulled down were tall enough to get them across the rapids. Louve was right. they should have cleared the forest before the river. Conri had a perfect position, even though his wolves were taking wolfsbane hits.

Ashina's spine pricked like a finger poked it. She found herself drawn to the darkness under the canopy. Her eyes craned to watch the trees fall, and a man writhing in black armor slithered out on horseback to face them. Ashina froze at the sight of him, her back rigid.

His ebony armor sang on his bulky body, his long black hair and beard as dark as his whole body armor. His beard trimmed on his face made his passion seethe from his eyes as he clenched his jaws. His eyes were bright and golden, and as he gripped the reigns with his black gauntlets, he smirked up at them. His wolves attracted the arrows away from him, and he did not seem to mind them taking hits for him.

Louve grimaced. "Hardulph! Son of a wolf bitch."

It looked like hell had come to the river to take the white wolf as a blackness followed him.

Ashina gawked at him and his magnificence, shaking her head. "Who is that?" She questioned.

Louve grimaced. "We have always known him to be a commander, aside from Conri. The most powerful one."

This dark wolf craned his eyes, looking for Ashina. He noticed her standing beside from Randon, and his eyes clenched, recognizing her.

His face lit up at her. "The beautiful white wolf."

He pointed a finger at Randon. "Do you think that primordial will protect her?" He warned Louve. "I am coming to get her."

Louve huffed. "Where is your king?" he hollered. "Is he hiding?!"

Hardulph clenched his powerful jaws and smirked, his black tattooed neck singing in rivets down his massive arms as he flexed them. Ashina glared at his tattoos and something lit up inside her at his presence. It scared her to death.

Hardulph huffed and pointed at her, his eyes on fire at her face. "Waiting for herrrrr." His voice was deep and powerful and demanded presence. He watched her as if he could see her wolf form.

Ashina bit her tongue and pulled a wolfsbane arrow from her sheath. She fired it upon his head. As it twirled in the air straight and true, Hardulph grabbed the shaft in midair. His eyes lit up at her, and he shook his head.

He sighed. "That was brave, white wolf." He lowered the arrow from his head, breaking it in half in his palm like a stick. "Very brave." He met her eyes, amused.

But then he smiled at her. Ashina glared at him, chills darting up her spine. Hardulph was striking to look at. He was not with Conri when he attacked her. Something pinged her gut about him, but she did not know what.

His ebony hair spilled down his back in braided ribbons and danced on his armor. It gave him a sinister appearance. His eyes were full of strength like something ancient bred into him. Ashina found herself clawing into a hole deep inside because of him. It dawned on her this wolf coming for her meant something else.

Hardulph pointed at her again, his brows narrowed. "She comes with me, human. She comes with me when we breach the city in a moment." Hardulph's nodded, sure of himself.

Randon met his stare. "I'm going to have to kill him," Randon growled, his snout twisting.

Hardulph sat calmly on his horse as more trees fell around him, the ground rumbling. "I will take her if you send her out now. We will leave Serkily alone. I respect the power of the primordial who protects her. You can come with her, and serve the army of Cayden. You are highly regarded in my court for protecting the white wolf."

Randon belted out a low growl that echoed over the river, his eyes lighting up in fury.

Silence pestered them all as Hardulph demanded presence. Then he put his palm to his heart and bowed. "You have my word. We will leave Serkily and never return if I get the white wolf today. The primordial can accompany her."

Randon flexed his whole body and seethed at him, but Hardulph stared at Ashina again. "If you do not send her to me, I will take this city." He bit. "I will bleed it dry to get her. There will be loss of life."

Hardulph steadied his horse. "I will get her." He belted out, his face hard. "One way or another. I did not come all this way for nothing."

Hardulph glared hard at Ashina, his face firm, his eyes glowing as the night fell around them. "White wolf." He beckoned her, calling her.

Ashina met his stare and swallowed, her heart thumping wild.

His strong face clenched to her eyes. "You belong with me! You belong with me and I am not leaving until I have you."

Ashina met his eyes. She believed him and found herself wavering at his face. "That is their king…" She moaned as realization dawned. "He is the king…" Chills pricked her cheeks.

She believed him with all she was, and it terrified her. He would take the city and her. He smiled, his face soft as he gazed at her. "You are beautiful, white wolf." He beckoned her with his demanding glare. Ashina gawked in awe at his brazenness toward her, her heart raging with fire.

He huffed at Ashina, laughing. His laugh was not sinister and that bothered her more. "Stubborn. Have it your way, white wolf."

He turned his horse, craning his head back to stare at her. "I come for you soon."

He turned away from the wall, his whole backside flexed and broad under the ebony armor of intimidation. He disappeared under the canopy again. Ashina dropped to her knees and pressed her back against the wall, her heart racing. She gripped her hand on her breastplate over her heart and closed her eyes. Her knees grew weak, and when she closed her eyes, she kept seeing the powerful glare from his eyes.

She widened her eyes, sensing something about Hardulph that set her on edge. "What is happening to me?" Her whole insides shook because of him. It was like he had pulled the air from her lungs, and she struggled to breathe because of him. She shook all over, her guts rumbling.

Louve and Randon watched her as Louve gripped her shoulder. "They will not take you, white wolf." He encouraged her.

Ashina was not so sure. All she could think about was the power of Conri and his rage at her when he hurt her. He would have bitten her, and then forced her, and taken her into Cayden. The land of darkness where the sun never rises, and the wolves are raging mad. That is what she knew about them her whole life. She closed her eyes and took a deep breath as fear tore a hole through her.

Randon sneered at where Conri's commander had gone, rage boiling in him. "That wolf is ancient..."

Louve turned and had his guards blow the horns again toward the plains behind them. The human warriors filled the fields before the city and disappeared in its wide streets to defensive positions, ready. Her heart raced with Hardulph's harassment of her.

From the west, a horn blew at Serimi's arrival.

Louve sighed. "Should have cleared the forest."

Conri and Hardulph heard the horns blow as their wolves lunged from the forest canopy, just as darkness began to fall. They surrounded the trees they had pushed down as Louve commanded they keep firing wolfsbane arrows. The wolves of Cayden lifted the trees, their bodies bulging and roaring.

They pivoted them on their shoulders, flinging them back and forth until the trees were midair. The trees melted over the river waters and lodged into the silver spikes. Louve, Ashina, and Randon lunged back from the wall and readied themselves.

The trees lodged into the spikes and lingered over the river waters. They dangled and formed a bridge. The wolves burst from the woods and jumped across the water, their claws digging into the trees. They raged and roared, climbing up the trees to the other side. They slithered upon the wall at the spikes and raised over the humans and wolves fighting to protect the city.

Ashina roared into her wolf form, gripping her broad sword in her paw. She stood back and waited for them to breach the wall. Her eyes lit up like fine gold, her muscles aching to spill blood. She growled and seethed, her heart racing in her chest.

Randon stepped back as everyone readied themselves to face Conri's wolves coming for Ashina. His wolves turned and braced themselves. The tree branches piked into the silver spikes, lunging over the wall and spraying leaves high in the air.

Randon catapulted atop the wall over Ashina's head as a wolf crested it at his face. He was the biggest wolf aside Ashina, his size evident. He swiped its head off with his massive paws. Randon roared and kicked the body off the branches into the river.

The wolves crawled up the walls and met Randon's wolves and human warriors. Arrows filled the air behind them, and the wolves fell into the river. There were too many, and they were relentless as they breached the wall into the humans. The humans plunged into them with their silver spiked armor. They gored them, but the wolves ripped into them. The wall got sprayed with blood and cries of rage as they fell, both wolf and man.

Louve turned to the ballistas and catapults. "Fire!"

The wolves emerged through the forest and the world broke into blackness. They climbed the wall and silver blades flung through the air as they jumped across the river to the trees. It flayed them alive and the waters became blood. Conri's wolves fell roaring. Their eyes were wide with pain as their deaths filled the breadth of the river wideness.

Ashina turned to face two wolves breaching the wall at her. Randon kissed the wall over them and swiped them with his massive paws. He was keeping them from breaching but could not stop them from coming, and Ashina could not help him. The two wolves lunged at her as she roared into them with her blade, gutting one of them. They pressed into her chest and pulled her off the wall into the city streets below.

She landed on her back as her blade slid through its neck and cut its head off at her face. Blood sprayed her cheek as her mouth filled with it. She spit it out and roared, pushing the bodies off her. She had taken a hit, the claw marks up her forearm now bleeding. She gripped her sword and growled at the wall. Randon, with the warriors, and Louve, fought them off one by one.

Conri knew what he was doing. The wolves rushed out from the trees and breached the wall by the thousands. They lunged over the wall atop the trees stuck in the spikes and flew into man and wolf, their eyes on the white wolf. From the plain, archers hit the black wolves atop the wall, and they fell into the streets around Ashina.

As they fell, she flew into them and cut their heads off, the wolfsbane making them sick and weak. She stood in the streets flanked by human warriors and waited. She craned her snout to the gate and gasped as the gate rocked. The wolves of Cayden tipped three massive trees from the spikes into the drawbridge, and it split open at her snout.

Chapter 15
Alaric's Vengeance

Serimi and Galin lunged into Conri's wolves on horseback, filling the breadth of the fields through the forest at the river. Behind Serimi, the archers shot over their heads into them. The silver blade shafts ripped into the lines to make an opening.

Serimi spread his army out to flank the wolves, and they plunged around them. Their body armor pricked with spikes, shadowed the wolves as their horses raged upon them. Serimi pulled his long sword and met the wolves as they turned to face them. The wolves raised on their horses and growled, readying their claws, even as bodies fell around them with silver-shafted arrows.

The humans consumed the left of the river wall with shimmering silver blades as Conri's wolves roared in their darkness.

Serimi shouted to Galin. "They breached the city! Take them down!" He glared as wolves lunged across the river onto the trees lodged into the silver stakes. They kept coming.

Galin plunged through the lines with a fortress of his warriors behind him, and they readied their wolfsbane arrows. The city wall filled with darkness as the arrows hit and wolves fell, even as more breached it. It gave Louve and his men enough of a breath to handle the wolves continuing to climb the wall into the city. Serimi plunged into wolf madness along the river while a sect of his warriors focused on the wolves climbing the wall.

Ashina pulled back along with the human warriors filling the streets behind her. As the wolves lunged over the wall into the streets at her, they met them with swift vengeance. The gate burst open, the roaring fangs of the wolves desperate to pull the wood chunks apart to get in.

She readied herself and gripped her broad sword in her paws as the gate blew apart. Slivers of the wood darted like arrows. Ashina dropped to the road to avoid getting hit, but men behind her were gored and fell into the streets.

She lunged up to face Hardulph as he slithered in with his wolves. They overcame the street around her, avoiding her. She glared at them in shock. The human warriors met the wolves, but the wolves did not touch her. She pushed her sword out, facing Hardulph, and his face lingered upon her.

Ashina held her blade out to him even as wolves continued to breach the city, her arm shaking. She had never feared this way before. He did not pull his sword; he was still in human form. He was tall, intimidating, and magnificent. Ashina growled at him, and as she lunged at him, the human warriors behind her shot arrows around her at the wolves.

A sharp pain bit her arm as an arrow plunged through her shoulder, knocking her sideways away from Hardulph. She fell to her knees, growling in pain. A wolfsbane arrow had catapulted through her shoulder and out her back, and she roared in pain.

Hardulph turned his head and growled at the human who shot her by accident. "No!" He screamed, but it was too late.

She roared her head back and growled in pain, gripping the shaft of the arrow in her shoulder. It was the same shoulder Conri had hit. Burning melted into her arm as she pulled at it. Her head ached, and her knees grew weak.

Hardulph sighed and walked to her calmly, watching her writhe back to her human form. He loomed over her. He gazed at Randon fighting dozens of wolves off and pointed. "Your guardian cannot come to help you now. I am keeping him very busy."

He bent on his knees toward her face and gazed into her eyes. He did not try to touch her. "Hello, beautiful." His face was hard and clenched, but his eyes held truth in them.

"I can pull that wolfbane out for you. If you wish." He whispered.

Ashina gasped as she met his eyes. His voice raked her insides, and shards grew on her backbone like broken glass. She pushed her blade toward his throat and pulled her injured arm at her side.

Hardulph's face clenched upon her. He stood with her as she faced him, her arm bled down to her fingers. "You are the king." She whispered to his face. "I knew there was something about you."

Hardulph froze. His eyes shimmered like the sun had kissed him from the inside. He breathed at her face, recognizing she knew the truth.

"You let Conri harass me!" Her backside hit the road as she fell back again. She closed her eyes as the wolfsbane filled her with dizziness.

Hardulph clenched his teeth. "And he will die for it! They were waiting on me..." He sighed at her. "I would never harm you."

"What do you want with me? I am not your mate!" Ashina belted out, her shoulder throbbing.

Hardulph held his breath and shook his head, meeting her eyes. "Yes, you are." His voice was a sharp edge with passion.

Ashina crawled away as he shook his head down at her. "If not for that treacherous liar Alaric and his wicked mountain seers, you would be in Cayden right now." His face was as hard as his firm body looming at her.

"You use your wolves as pawns!" Ashina belted out, the pain filling her with dread. "You are cruel." She shook her head as he continued to come for her.

"War is cruel, white wolf. It is cruel and spares no one. My kingdom is sacrificing to save you."

"What..." Ashina bellowed. "Saving me from what..." She begged him. "You are coming to take me like Alaric is..."

Hardulph huffed at her, pointing to the arrow in her shoulder. "Yes. I have come to take you, white wolf." He glared at her shoulder and sighed. "You have wolfsbane in you. I can tell you have never been hit with it before. I know it hurts. You will be very weak and sick. Do you want me to pull it out?" His voice beckoned her.

"I will not touch you unless you want me to, white wolf." He sighed.

Ashina scooted back further.

"I cannot talk to you if you are sick from wolfsbane." He sighed. "You will stay sick the longer it is in."

"No, you will bite me." She questioned him.

He stared at her with a strength that made Ashina gasp. He was indeed powerful and persuasive. He sighed. "I will not bite you. There are truths you do not know."

Ashina held her breath when he said that, but her head was pounding. "What truths." She pleaded.

"I have to get you out of here to show you." As wolves continued to filter into the streets and over the wall, he bit his lip. "I need you to come with me."

Ashina scooted back further, her head spinning. She moaned in frustration as her head fell back to the street. She stared into his eyes. His eyes were like hers, so he was also a primordial, and he knew she knew it.

Hardulph shadow cast over her. "You feel my power in your bones. I can see it in your eyes as a primordial. You know what I am."

"I see you." But she denied it still.

"You know what I am to you, white wolf." He whispered. "Don't you."

"You are ancient." She moaned. "You are strong and power-ful. I can feel your power."

Hardulph belted out a growl. "You have been taken from me by those wicked seers serving Alaric! I am fighting to pull you out of it."

Ashina thrust her sword out to him and pressed further down the street away from him on her elbows. She moaned, her eyes rolling open again. "Who are you..." She begged.

He did not flinch at her sword. He continued to watch his wolves taking the city and killing humans, even as they died themselves. "I am your mate! You have been living a life of lies, white wolf." He warned her.

"Alaric is coming..." She moaned.

He growled. "I hope you never see the truth of that wretched mountain."

Ashina felt her temperature rise. Shouts of rage echoed harder in her ears, and her head hurt. All around her, the humans fought for their lives and the city, and Louve and Randon stayed together. Randon was not getting a chance to protect her because every time he dispatched a dozen, a dozen more would throttle him. He was strong as they pummeled him atop the wall to keep him occupied.

She heard a familiar voice, and the forest shook. Vibrations filled the air like something opened from the deep of the world and lingered.

"I am here to get you, white wolf."

Louve caught Ashina scooting back on the road in her human form. She had a wolfsbane arrow in her shoulder. She closed her eyes in and out of consciousness as a shadow loomed upon her. Louve hollered at Randon.

"Randon! Ashina!" Randon turned away from the wolves and catapulted down the wall into the street.

He rose over Hardulph and snarled as Louve hit the wolves coming into the street with his warriors. Behind him, Galin plunged into the forest, and Serimi pummeled the wolves to the river waters. They kept the wolves from breaching the walls further, but now they were coming in at the gate.

Randon rose over Hardulph and belted a growl at him as the wolves around him fell to the human warriors. "Ah, the primordial guarding my white wolf!" He sneered.

Hardulph laughed in his face, but then a wind pressed over him. He grew to tower over Randon, his bulky black form ribbed to perfection. He was broader and ancient, and Randon saw another primordial. Hardulph looked as if he had been carved from the beginning of the wolves.

Ashina gasped at him, her eyes wide with terror. "No!" She screamed. She knew he was a primordial. She knew it because his presence pricked her spine and warned her.

Hardulph loomed over Randon, his black fur shining and brilliant. He twisted his neck and took a deep breath in his transformation. He belted out a low rumble and growled at Randon's snout, his eyes a pristine gold. "Did you think you were the only one, great wolf? There are only a few of us left."

Randon seethed at him and hunkered down to attack. "You betray our kind."

"I was there at the beginning of us. I liberate our kind." He growled.

Randon leaned his snout back and growled at him. "You will not take her."

Hardulph's laugh was thunderous. "She is the white wolf queen. Fate does not dictate her to Alaric if he used dark magic to bend it. She needs to be free."

Randon pulled away from him. "What..."

Ashina bellowed out, desperate.

Randon flew into him, and they raged into one another in the street at the gates, even as a lone rider plunged over the plain toward the forest.

Ashina grew weak in the knees and watched the primordials rage. Randon lunged into Hardulph's shoulder, but he blocked it with his long claws. Randon spiked his claws into his shoulder instead, pivoting off him. Hardulph belted out a screaming roar in pain and pushed Randon off him by his legs. He picked Randon up by his waist and tossed him across the street. Randon hit the wall across from Ashina but landed on his feet and lunged at him again, going midair.

Ashina bent her head against the street and closed her eyes as her heart raced from the wolfsbane. To make matters worse, she was so disoriented she could not pull the arrow out. She was helpless.

On the plain at the forest line, Alaric was in his human form, but behind him were a hundred thousand wolves on horseback. They gripped their bows ready and pulled their long swords. Their growls filled the night air like a solemn curse had bled out. Alaric bent his head down into his horse's mane, his blonde braid whipping the air behind him. His naked, long arms flexed like his firm face, and he roared into the woods.

As he neared the forest, he raised on his stallion and bent his arm by his leg. As he lunged it up and out, the trees bent away from him. They blew apart like a mighty wind throttled through them. They split, and the ground rumbled from the forest over the river beneath the city. Alaric clenched his face, his eyes hard pressed into the wind, and belted out a growl. His fangs stuck up in his mouth. His roar echoed.

All along the wall, the human warriors and wolves fighting screamed in the air: "Alaric is coming! Ready yourselves!"

The ground shook on either side of the trees where Alaric split them. The earth cracked in the forest and split open as a deep chasm kissed it. A quake pummeled up a wave of dirt and rock, and the wall belted up to the tree lines. Alaric pressed his strong arm down at his leg again and lunged it forward.

He belted another raging roar that shook the air, and the earth moved over the river bed. The wall from his power hit the wolves at the drawbridge like a flood had come upon them. But the flood was rock and earth. The echo of the devastation rolled in the air throughout the kingdom. The drawbridge the wolves split open burst off, and the stone wall cracked at the foundation. The city street buckled like a mountain had hit it as the blow undermined the wall.

Ashina felt the street beneath her flow like she was on water. She witnessed the wall over the drawbridge sever off and collapse into the river. Randon and Hardulph slammed into the tower walls opposite of one another. The wolves still coming into the city were flayed open with the rock, and their bodies were flung high into the air over the river.

The sudden wave of Alaric split the armies away from each other and pivoted the humans off the wolves. It saved more human lives as it divided the wolf army away from Alaric. His wolves pressed in right behind him, and they took the forest.

Randon growled as the earth wall pummeled through the city around them, leaving Ashina unscathed. The main wall of the tower at the gate fell as a big chunk over the raging waters. The watchtower over the bridge collapsed into the river and rolled into the rapids. The weight of the tower collapse pulled the trees off the walls and spikes.

The stone from the wall aside the watchtower laid flat atop the river. It changed the current toward the city, and the street flowed with water and flooded to the hill. Ashina chilled as the frigid waters hit her. The water rolled around the streets against the walls. The force of it pushed the human army to the hill, but they were still alive.

Alaric had taken down the wall to get to her. The ballista and guards atop that wall fell, and dozens blew into the waters. Alaric lunged through the clear path he had created while his army filled the span around him, his eyes on her past the gate. He used the collapsed wall into the river as a bridge to get her.

Ashina stood and dropped to her knees again. Her eyes met Alaric's as he soared into her. He pressed his strong fist through the leather straps at her chest and yanked her up against him hard. He pulled her into his lap, her hip into him tight. Then he gripped his strong arms around her and turned around. His eyes lit up like a fire breathed in him.

He looked at her, his mission clear. He got her. He clenched his face hard and rode back through the wave he had created to protect her from Hardulph, leaving the city street behind them.

Ashina felt his strong arms against her as if she weighed nothing. His face clenched hard, and his eyes lit in golden fire. She melted into his lap and held on for dear life. She closed her eyes, gasping through the pain in her shoulder.

He rode back across the river, where they met his general Rieka, who commanded the wolves to surround them. Alaric pressed the stallion hard back through the forest and the devastation he had made, giving his army a buffer between the humans and wolves. Behind him, his wolves filled the woods and hit the wolves' lines, but they had what they needed now and were retreating.

Alaric gripped Ashina hard in his lap as she held onto him, bleeding and aching. As they cleared the forest again, Conri met Alaric on horseback as if he had waited for him. Conri readied his arrow and fired. Alaric's eyes caught Conri, and Ashina witnessed Alaric grab it midair. Alaric stopped the horse suddenly, growling. He snapped the arrow in half, and it fell from his fingers.

He turned his horse to face Conri and slid off, letting Ashina bend over the saddle. Rieka lunged into them with his wolves from the woods following their king. Conri met Alaric with a dozen wolves surrounding him to get Ashina as Reika came behind them.

Conri laughed. "We will be taking her today." And then he turned to see Rieka come up behind them.

Alaric approached him closer and pulled both his long swords. Ashina watched as he did not turn into a wolf. He calmly gripped his swords and waited. Conri's wolves began taking blows from Reika behind him, and it was then just Conri and Alaric. Conri lunged up from his horse into his wolf, and Ashina watched Alaric meet him in the field.

She watched him bend into Conri. His swords sliced into him and made him bleed. Alaric moved as the earth breathed through him, and the ground seemed to move with him as he fought. His whole body clenched and on fire, and nothing else was going to take her.

As Conri melted back, he bled and rounded Alaric. Alaric dropped his swords and lunged into Conri in his magnificent wolf form. Ashina watched Alaric pummel into him as if Conri weighed nothing. He grabbed him by his chest hair and lunged him up over his head. Conri's arms and legs splayed out like he was a rag doll. Alaric slammed him down on his back and made an indentation in the ground. The echo from his landing vibrated the hillside. Alaric roared into his face; his growl echoed. He pressed his fist through his chest and ripped his heart out.

"No one touches my mate!" Alaric growled. He flung the heart down by Conri's body.

Rieka met him in the field and rushed around the chaos to follow his king. Alaric jerked around and changed into his human form. He climbed back on the horse, grabbing Ashina into him. He pushed his steed with his army further west to his mountain until his army had effectively blocked the wolves from following them.

Ashina moaned in pain in Alaric's lap. He slowed down as Rieka lunged up to them with the wolves, eying her. "Injured again." He belted out.

"Pull it out!" Alaric demanded and lifted Ashina higher in his lap.

She held her breath at Rieka as he approached them on horseback. He eyed her with great caution and grit his teeth. "Hold on, white wolf."

Alaric snapped the tip off in his hands at her back, and Rieka gripped the shaft. Ashina met his dark eyes and swallowed. He yanked it out of her. Ashina clenched her teeth and moaned, her arm shaking in pain. As she fell back into Alaric's chest, he sighed. She remembered looking into a determined face before she blacked out again, the wolfsbane poisoning her.

He held her tight against him and rode hard toward Worgen. He put as much space between him and the humans and wolves as possible. Behind his army, the raging river spilled into the city streets. It spilled into the city streets because Alaric had used his power to bring down the city wall at the gates. Alaric was a powerful wolf king for a reason.

Alaric bent his head into Ashina's and pressed his face into the wind. He raced to get her out of there. He was right. He told her he would come for her, and he did.

Hours later and well past midnight, Rieka had the army stop for a brief rest. Ashina ran a fever and was in and out of consciousness. They had no choice but to stop. Alaric let her slip into Rieka's arms while he melted off his horse. Rieka looked at her as she dangled in his arms.

"She needs medicine. And she is heavier than she looks." He grunted.

Alaric pulled a leather bag off his horse and sat down. Rieka laid her in his lap. Alaric gripped the buckles on her shoulder and under her arm and undid them. He pulled her armor off and ripped her tunic off her shoulder. He poured water over the wound, pulled out a salve, and pressed it into her wound.

Ashina gasped in pain, and her eyes flew open. As she met Alaric's eyes, she froze. He had been successful in taking her, after all. She knew it. She pressed away from him, inching her butt off his lap. Alaric grabbed her tighter around her waist and pulled her back on him. He stared into her face, pulling her hands down to subdue her against him.

"You are injured. I will not bite you like this. You are in pain."

She took a deep breath as he pressed a cloth against her wound and put a salve on it to make it stick, the calming soothing her aches. "Wolfbane will make you very sick and weak. You will be better in a few hours."

He stopped touching her and stared at her face. Then he spread his legs so she fell between him to prop her up against his chest. He sighed in her face as his body loomed into her. His bulky tallness and muscles clenched around her. His body armor was hard against her weak body and smeared with blood.

She gazed at his face as he held her there; blood splattered across his forehead. His beard shaped his face on high cheekbones, and his eyes lit up in perseverance. His blonde hair kissed his powerful face, and he caught her admiring him. He huffed; a half-smile lit up on his face.

"You are stubborn." He whispered in her face.

Ashina sighed against his face. "I know." She belted out, non-apologetic.

Alaric's heart beat wildly with her against him, and Ashina felt it thumping against her. She pressed her good arm into his hand at her waist, and Alaric held his breath. She gripped his hand hard, the blood from Conri still sticky on it. He killed Conri for her.

"You killed Conri." She whispered, her eyes closed.

"He hurt you. He had to die."

She opened her eyes and stared at him. Alaric grazed her face with his fingers and breathed into her. "I told you I was coming for you."

She swallowed. "The humans..."

He shook his head. "I spared them."

She sighed, thankful.

Alaric took a deep breath and shook his head, his face flat. His face was stern, but a softness lingered in his eyes as he stared at her. He did not answer her. Ashina lifted her fingers to his face and swallowed, meeting his eyes. She ran her fingers over his soft beard and stopped at his lips. He closed his eyes, and she heard his breath like a soft wind had bled into him.

"Thank you." She whispered.

Alaric breathed in her face against her lips. "You are my mate. We belong together. There is nothing that will break it."

Ashina closed her eyes against him but could not answer. Rieka approached them from the darkness of the wood as his army filtered through the trees on horseback. "My king, we must go. We have five days to reach the mountain. Hardulph is regrouping to follow us."

Alaric huffed and pulled Ashina up with him. "He dares come into my kingdom."

Alaric bent her into his arms and carried her to his horse. She stared up at him, her head still bleeding and in pain, and her head fuzzy from the poison. She found herself pressed against his chest by her backside in the saddle. He wrapped a long arm around her waist. He bent over her shoulder and kissed her cheek, his lips pressed hard into her.

His kiss was one of passion but of relief. Ashina closed her eyes when he did that. His gaze lingered upon her naked shoulder, and he found himself closing his eyes and holding his breath at it. He wanted to bite her, but she was too weak to withstand his bite right now. He had to wait.

Ashina held her breath. "You want to bite me." She whispered.

Alaric pressed his forehead against her face instead and breathed her in. "I am not a monster, Ashina."

She felt his breath on her face, leaned into him, and closed her eyes. "You better not be." It was a warning.

"I will bite you soon enough." He warned her, his voice strong and determined. "We must bond soon."

Ashina took a deep breath, acknowledging the inevitable now that he had her. She moaned, the desperateness in Alaric's tone filling her guts with dread, but butterflies on fire also lingered there.

Alaric lunged with her through the forest into the west. His army surrounded them, their numbers filling the journey with protection. Once they reached his kingdom, they would go north. Alaric's heart soared. The white wolf queen was coming home.

Chapter 16
The Call of the Wolves

Randon stood aside Serimi and Galin while Louve surveyed the damage with the king and Brovina in the street.

He kept hearing what the primordial Hardulph had told him. *Fate does not dictate the white wolf queen to Alaric if he used dark magic to bend it.* Randon found himself questioning Hardulph and the kingdom of Cayden. The powerful wolf had disappeared in the rubble when Alaric hit the wall, and it tumbled. But Randon knew he was still alive and chasing Ashina.

Outside the gate, bodies of wolves were piled up and burning. The rushing river waters had taken many of them downstream. The birds were already circling the air outside the forest.

His heart ached, thinking of how he failed Ashina. The bonding between him and Ashina burned through him like an aching sorrow. He needed Ashina with him. He needed to protect her and fight for her. He gripped his broad sword in his fist and glared at the devastation Alaric had done to the city. He knew this would happen. Alaric was powerful, and now he had a powerful white wolf queen.

The watchtower that collapsed over the gate had sunken into the deep river, but now the raging waters had formed a dam at the shoreline because of it. The rubble sunk into the earth around the damaged walls. Alaric had brought the wall down like Randon warned the humans he would do. Humans had a deep hope inside them that sprung from a vat somewhere, and Randon was always amazed at them.

He surveyed the damage with them and his wolves as the seers emerged to help the injured. They had not sustained losses like they could have. Alaric did not want them all dead; he just wanted his queen. Which he now had.

"It will take months to fix this breach in the main wall," Louve warned the king.

Meltivi eyed his sister, and Brovina agreed. "Yes, this was a catastrophic hit to the foundation of our city. Alaric is strong."

"He saved us in a way also." Louve nodded. "He split the ground and kept the wolves from Serimi. He divided the armies and still got Ashina."

Meltivi sighed. Then he gazed at the back plain and the hillside with the chasm Ashina had made. "He takes her to hone her powers. She will be strong, but he will force her to bend to him using her powers. She will essentially be his power slave, among other things."

Randon approached them from the wall, stepping over the rubble. "Conri is dead. His heart ripped out." He pointed to the plain past the forest. "My wolves just got back."

The king scoffed. "Alaric killed him, no doubt."

"And Hardulph? I noticed the coward disappeared after Alaric's dramatic entrance." Louve sneered.

Randon agreed. "Gone. The remnants of his survivors are gone, but tracks show west. He still has thousands upon thousands that survived. His army is strong. They are tracking Alaric to get Ashina. Also, we have a problem..."

Serimi and Galin joined them from the wall, watching Randon, their faces bloodied.

"Hardulph is a primordial. An old one, bigger than me." Randon warned them. "He is one of the first. I did not know they were still living."

Serimi rolled his eyes. "Damnit."

"That also means the fact he is after Ashina means he will more than likely get her, and we will be warring with Cayden. No army has ever breached Cayden or Worgen..." Randon pondered.

Galin nodded his head, wiping sweat off his brow. "That means he is the true king, not Conri."

"That is a problem." Serimi wondered. "That explains his armies, the black wolves, being so vicious. It takes three of my men to kill one. Alaric did us a service by coming."

The king glared over the river and back to his warriors spilling around him to clean up the rubble. "Ashina wanted to go to the wild, where Tala had taken her."

Randon shook his head. "There is an ancient city there, under the central falls. I realized Tala had not gotten Ashina there because Alaric had come for her so fast."

"What are you saying, my king?" Serimi questioned.

The king eyed Brovina and then pointed a long finger past the trees and the rolling plains. "She is our white wolf queen and led to go there. Let us find the city, take it, reinhabit it, and ready ourselves to face Alaric when the time comes."

Galin huffed, standing aside from Louve. "How big is it? Is it fortified?"

Randon thought a moment. "It is Tala's people's city."

The king smiled, and Brovina joined him. "It is perfect then." He turned to go and then turned back to them all. "Pick your builders to repair this wall, and we travel to the heart. When Ashina is successful in bringing the women out of that mountain, she will go there. We need to be ready."

As he left them, Serimi gawked at his back. "Why does he do these things to me."

Brovina patted his arm and smiled, turning to follow her brother. "Because you are the best. And your warriors are the best. And we have always succeeded."

Serimi crossed his arms over his chest, eying Galin. Randon held his breath when the king gave the order. He was going to go back into that damn wilderness, closer to his queen. He closed his eyes and pried into her heart, giving her hope.

"We are coming, Ashina." He belted out.

Serimi eyed Randon. "You have wolves coming?"

Randon nodded. "From the farthest reaches."

"How many, do you think?" Louve asked.

"Tens of thousands, if they all come. We will have an army of them."

"Goooddd. We will begin preparations to vacate the city within days. Then we will go and ready the city at the falls."

Louve patted Randon on his arm. "Do not fear Randon; we will get her back."

Randon growled, his moan filling the air around them. "I am going to get her back. I'll be damned if these wolf kings are going to exploit her."

Serimi stared up at him. The air became silent before the king belted out. "Of course, you will get her back. She has called you to her court. Impressive."

"I am not the beginning of her court." Randon griped.

Louve and Brovina laughed. "You did not see what we saw as she was kicking your ass on that hill..." Louve smiled.

Randon glared at him. "I held my own with her."

"Sure, you did. Sure." Louve rolled his eyes. "Did it hurt when she kicked you so hard you went flying over the hill? Because I laughed."

Serimi laughed with them.

"Alaric is in for a reckoning if he pisses her off..." Louve added.

Brovina interrupted. "It has been questioned for some time if Alaric has seers in that mountain changing fate. For thousands of years, his kingdom has taken the primordial wolf queens. I think there is darkness there, and Ashina will find it. She will also be drawn to them as she has seer in her bloodline..."

"What does that mean?" Louve asked.

Brovina sighed. "She will bring that mountain down, and Alaric's kingdom will fall if she discovers what I fear is there."

"What if he bites her, and they mate..." Serimi questioned, noticing Randon becoming stiff. "Alaric will be able to control her then."

Brovina smiled. "He may be able to control her power, but Ashina chooses who she mates with, even if it is not by fate. We did break a bond for her during the ritual. It was the bond pulling her into fate unwillingly. That is considered the weaker part. The strong part of her defiance remained, and I think Alaric will find that out."

Randon huffed, his whole body flexed. "He better not hurt her. I will kill him."

Louve raked his fingers through his long black beard. "She will kick his ass. I mean, she kicked yours."

The men laughed, but Randon shook his head at them. "She did not kick my ass..."

Brovina turned to go. "That is not what I saw."

Randon turned to walk back to the damage on the walls and ignored their laughter. A low rolling roar beckoned him from the forest, and he craned his neck toward it. Everyone else heard it, too, for the ground vibrated like thunder erupted from the earth. Everyone followed Randon out as wolves emerged from the darkness around the humans.

Randon's heart soared. Thousands coming, just as he had hoped. These wolves were big and burly and had walked in. They nodded at Randon from across the river and hiked over the fallen wall to them, the raging waters lapping at their boots. Randon swung his arm out to meet the wolf, Kylo.

He pulled his cloak hood off his head, his red hair flowing around his face in ribbony curls. His face was clean-shaven, his jawline hard and strong. He met Randon's hand, and they shook, his brown body armor leathers squeaking over his muscular body.

"Got your warning, brother. We have thirty thousand so far. We have all come from the great northeast. More will come."

Randon gasped. "Good!"

"We have our human wives and families heading into the eastern mountains for safety, just in case." He added.

Randon agreed. There was always a sect of wolves who desired human wives, treated them well, and had children with them. The children would be half-breeds, but many chose not to turn when they began to grow in their adolescence.

"What the hell has happened here?" Kylo glared around with the wolves who followed him.

"Alaric has the white wolf. He brought down the wall to get her. Hardulph, the king of Cayden, tried to take her also. He is an ancient primordial, one of the originals..."

Kylo widened his eyes. "Damn. You know Hardulph will go to war at Alaric's Mountain to get her then."

Another wolf approached, and more came, and they stood around Randon and waited. The breadth of them filled the banks along the river at the walls.

"What is your command, Randon." Kylo blurted out.

Randon turned to Serimi and Louve with the others who had joined them outside. The humans' faces were wide and pale but ready. Serimi nodded to Randon. "You have the command of the wolves, Randon. I am relieved."

Randon growled in the direction Alaric had taken her. "I will track her and get her back. I need a pack to stay here and help rebuild the wall and protect the humans. We must find the city at the falls in the wilderness and ready it for our queen."

"It is an ancient fortified city. That is where Tala wanted Ashina to go, and that is where Ashina will rule."

Kylo smiled. "Indeed. Alright then. We have a lot to do. Let's get to it."

Randon turned to guide the wolves, and the humans reveled in their glory.

By dawn, he had tracked northeast to get Ashina back.

Chapter 17
Where the Command Calls

Ashina awoke to the sun calling her gently like the trickling of water flowing in the stream where she had slept. Alaric made her sleep against him in the night, and he wrapped his arm around her and breathed on her neck until her exhaustion took her. He did not bite her still. He had shown great restraint so far, but Ashina knew it was coming.

She prepared herself for that moment when she could no longer deny him because her insides burned as he stayed in her presence. She sat up from the fur bed he made and pulled at her naked shoulder. He brought her armor, but she did not wear it. The wound was still fresh but healing fast. She stood up, craning her neck to see a lone figure on a hill, and followed it.

Alaric's army swooned around her, watching her viciously. She knew she could go nowhere. She pressed toward an incline through the trees, and the sun blasted her with crimson glory.

She melted into it against Alaric's chest just as he turned to face her. His face lit up in the sunlight.

She let him touch her shoulder and gaze at her wound. "You are better. Good."

Then he took her face in his palms and stared into her eyes. "How do you feel?"

Ashina met his eyes and found herself smiling. "I am well."

He released her and turned back to the sun. "You are bending into the sun." Ashina confronted him.

Alaric smiled in her face. "Do this with me. I want to show you something."

She gazed into it as he lingered behind her and pressed against her back. "You are born of the light," She whispered. Something inside her broke open and she realized Alaric was hiding something.

Alaric bent over her shoulder, his eyes into the sun, and pulled her hand out in his palm. He stretched her arm against his and laid her hand into his palm. His strong hand was warm, and Ashina relaxed her palm in his. Then he leaned into the side of her face and breathed.

"Close your eyes."

Ashina closed her eyes as the sun kissed her face. Alaric craned his head to stare at her long, naked arm. "Move with me."

She followed his movement with his arm, her hand in his palm. They moved their arm up and down into the sun, and the trees swayed on the hill to touch them. Ashina breathed deeper as chills darted up her arms. The trees swayed with their movements like a gentle dance.

He pressed harder against her backside, and Ashina held her breath. His powerful body lingered against her as if he pressed inside her. His whispers sang in her soul. They became one in their power, even as he whispered in her head. She froze, her stomach twisted in knots.

Ashina opened her eyes. "Stop it. I hear you in my head. Inside me."

He smiled on the side of her face. "Not inside you. Yet." He whispered; his whole face lit up in anticipation.

She smiled too and turned to face him, her face firm. "Our power is not the equivalent of lovemaking, Alaric."

He met her eyes and whispered, "Yes, it is..." She held her breath at him.

He was still smiling. "You are bending nature just as I. You have been losing control. You could have taken Serkily to the ground." He warned her. "Our seer bloodline demands we have control of this power, or the world falls. It is up to the wolves who have this power to use it right."

"And you will help me with this? Or you will control it." She inquired.

Alaric swallowed.

She leaned away from him and sighed. "Of course you will."

Alaric put his palms on her hips and made her turn around and twist back into the sun. He pressed into her back again, his body bulk and tallness overshadowing her. He pulled her naked arm out in his palm, but this time kept their eyes open. She followed his movements and watched the forest below them split like a wind had blasted through it.

She had done this before but with less power. The wind roared up over the trees, melted back down, and blew over them as if Alaric controlled the breath of the whole world. Her movement was fluid with his as he controlled her. A force from his strength pried her arm into his, and demanded she bend to him. And she became empowered with him and fearful of him.

The power in his arm cradled her palm and made her knees weak. He bent into her ear and whispered, and she craned her head into his lips. "This is with one hand, with me commanding you. You will learn to use all of you to bring cities down at my command."

Ashina watched the trees finger back together and shake, her eyes lighting up in the sunrise. He stared into the sunrise with her, his eyes golden. She fingered his palm with her fingers and held her breath in his grasp. His lure was strong. He commanded her arm, and it would not be released until he commanded it to.

She leaned harder against him until her head was leaning into his chest. He breathed deeply behind her, his body a formidable power of strength. His eyes bent from the rising sun and met her naked shoulder again. She heard him sigh heavily, even as his fingers cradled her palm. An echoing sorrow filled her guts.

Ashina sighed. "You want to bite me so badly. I can feel your rage for me burning you up inside."

Alaric froze when she said that and clenched his jaws.

"You will not control it when you do bite me, so you are in pain wanting it." She taunted him. "Alaric." She tested him.

Ashina bent her head away from him and pulled her tunic off her shoulders to the top of her breasts. "Bite me, Alaric. I crave you biting me." She waited. "I know your bite will be strong, and it will fill my blood with your strength. I am ready for it."

Alaric's face clenched, and he closed his eyes, his mouth shivering at her neck. Ashina breathed deeply, waiting. She lunged her neck more, her chest heaving up and down. Alaric bent his lips to her skin, and she felt his hot breath on her. She heard a low growl rumble up from deep inside him.

"Go on, Alaric." She beckoned him, her voice sweet and soft. Her whisper was soft and beckoning, and shivers raced up his spine as she said it.

He stared at her naked shoulder and pulled both her arms out either side of her. He stretched them wide into the sun in his palms and clasped her fingers in his. He bent into the skin at her neck and kissed her there slowly, taking his time. His lips were like flowers blowing against her, wild and soft. His mouth was open as he kissed her neck at her shoulder, and she closed her eyes, hearing the breath of his moans against her.

He melted up to the side of her neck and kissed her harder, his whole body tense. She leaned her head back and found herself holding her breath at the luring power of his lips. He stopped one time, and his lips quivered against her skin. And then she heard him moan through his breath.

She breathed him in; a part of her wanted him to bite her. He pulled away from her, his face in agony. She turned around to face him. He gazed at her naked skin. As his fangs slithered up, he stepped back and shook his head. He growled at her, his chest heaving up and down as his eyes rolled over her.

"You taunt me on purpose." He met her eyes. "You know we cannot do this here now as we flee into Worgen."

He moaned. "Why do you taunt me."

Ashina pulled her tunic back up to cover her shoulder. "Just as you are taunting me with honing my powers. This power is not yours to control me."

He sneered in her face, his eyes golden. "You cannot lure me this way, Ashina." He warned her.

She leaned into his lips, breathing in his face. "You taunt me with freedom cloaked in oppression, Alaric of Worgen." She craned over his handsome face. "I do not bend to oppression. You will find this out the hard way."

He took deep breaths to control his burning rage for her. His eyes met hers as if she had slapped him. He watched her storm away from him back to camp and followed her with his eyes. His chest heaved desperately. His groin was on fire, too, like the one she had lit within him from her seduction. She had done this on purpose.

"Stubborn white wolf." He bellowed after her.

He followed her back down and met her at the spring as she picked up her armor. The army around them readied their horses to ride. He loomed behind her and grabbed her waist tight in his palm. He breathed against her face; his palm gripped hard like his grip on her heart.

"You taunt me with your beauty," he warned her as his fangs burst up. "You taunt me with your bravery."

She lunged around to face him. "You taunt me with freedom, but that is a lie."

She pulled her armor on before him and eyed his expression, her face flat. Alaric held his breath at her boldness, perplexed at her defiance. He froze at her demanding presence in his face. Her eyes were firm and as adamant as her courage.

"I bite hard, king Alaric." She kissed his cheek, soft as a gentle rain, to taunt him further.

He leaned into her kiss until she walked away from him to the horses. Alaric narrowed his brows as he followed her. As she stood there strapping her armor back on, she eyed him with a determination that made his stomach shiver. Alaric watched her, his eyes narrowed at her defiance.

His chest beat wild as he climbed on the horse behind her. He pulled his arm around and pressed her hard against him. She held her breath at his strong arms. He breathed against her skin, his breath hot on her neck again. Her whole body was tense against him, and so was his. His breath against her neck was like a storm, his mouth open.

He leaned into her ear. "I'm going to fuck you hard when I finally get you home." He whispered. "I don't give a shit you are an alpha."

Ashina felt his breath ravage her deep inside. He did not wait for her to respond. He lunged into Worgen with her.

Chapter 18

When the King Hunts

Hardulph sat atop his stallion and peered through the morning fog as the survivors of his wolves lingered around him on the open plains. They were taking their time following Alaric into Worgen. He knew Alaric would know they were tracking him. Hardulph wanted Alaric to know this.

His third in command, Cole, sat horseback beside him and clutched the reigns as they watched the skies. They had found Conri's body in the field outside the woods and knew Alaric killed him because of the white wolf. Conri was brutal, and his tactics questionable, but to touch his queen put him in treasonous territory. He was going to die anyway. No one touches the mate of another without paying the price.

Hardulph sighed and shook his head. He heard a cawing in the sky and pressed his arm up, and an Eagle lighted upon him. Hardulph smiled at the magnificent bird, meeting its eyes with golden hues of his own.

"Have Kira meet us on the mountain. Our white wolf will need her guidance once I get her, and we go to Cayden."

Cole agreed. "She travels as we speak, my king." He raked his long fingers through his red beard, his red hair in a ponytail down his back.

Around him for miles spilled his survivors galloping full speed at him and stopped in the plain for his orders. They would ride the Worgen kingdom line to draw Alarci's wolves to them and away from their king soon.

"When I get her, I need the remaining to divert attention. That is the only way we are going to save our queen."

Cole nodded. "The losses have been grievous, my king."

Hardulph sighed. "They will not be forgotten. The losses will always be grievous until I have my queen, and we deliver her from Alaric."

Then he narrowed his black brows, clenching his fists, his ebony gauntlets shining. "It is time to have the wolves turn south into Worgen." The eagle belted out a shrieking scream and lighted up off him. "Go, my friend."

Cole huffed, his long red beard and hair flowing over his shoulders. Hardulph met his stare and then turned to the heads filling the space behind him. "We have taken many losses sacrificing to get our queen! We will take the white wolf and bring these kingdoms back to glory! Alaric and his wolves will die!"

He raised a fist, and his thousands left did the same and shouted. "For the white wolf!"

They followed him, slithering through the fog to track Alaric's trail. And then they turned northwest suddenly, the ground shaking beneath them.

"You talked to the white wolf." Cole wondered.

Hardulph huffed. "Briefly. She had wolfsbane in her. She was shot on accident by a human warrior. She was not herself. I will call her soon. I will pull her through the lies. Once I have her at Cayden, then she shall see everything."

"Alaric's mountain wolves will be formidable."

Hardulph nodded. "Yes, but we must get her out. It is the only way. Not one primordial wolf queen has ever left that mountain, but not this time. This time, the queen comes home."

"We attack in a week," Cole confirmed.

Hardulph smiled. "Goooooooddd. The wolfsbane will be out of her system by then, and she will be free soon. I will call her once I know her head is clear of that poison."

Cole bowed and lunged away from him to lead the survivors. "See you at Cayden, my king! With the white wolf!"

Hardulph nodded, his face clenched and his eyes on fire. "I am not leaving until I have you in my arms, white wolf. My beautiful mate."

A day behind Hardulph, Randon tracked the remnants of his army through the rolling plains and wilderness toward Worgen. He bent on his knee into the fog, his eyes piercing the darkness of the eerie morning before dawn. He pressed his fingers into the dirt and smelled the horse hooves.

He noticed the army tracks heading northwest to the Worgen line while one kept going west. He narrowed his brows and sighed. It became apparent this king had plans, and he was meticulous. Randon moved forward silently, ever watchful, as his rage filled him with a piercing hunger.

Chapter 19
The Bite of Passionate Lies

Alaric stormed through a mountain pass wide enough for one horse at a time. Ashina found herself in awe of the evergreen canopy that lingered over them. Bursts of sunlight blasted upon them through the darkness, and she craned her head into Alaric's chest to gaze up at it. He pressed his chin on her head and smiled as he watched her.

He had fallen for her, and there was no going back now, no matter how stubborn she was. The pass went on for miles, and Alaric slowed the stallion to a gentle walk. Rock walls rose all around them. They were steep and stretched into the clouds, it seemed. A sultry flowering vine grew in the rocks, and she smelled a sweet aroma from them.

"Welcome home." Alaric breathed.

The pass craned open, and she held her breath. She rose on the saddle, her back tense. They stopped on a plateau as a path was worn down and open to the mountain. It looked like a hollowed-out volcano. A rolling plain spilled in emerald green rock walls surrounded this plain. Stone houses and flaming lights beamed back at them.

Horses galloped alongside the road built to go down there. The mountain rose into the clouds, and a forest shrouded around it as the trees stretched into the heavens. Ashina gasped at the beauty. It looked like the mountain hollowed out, but another rose in the distance.

They were going there. This kingdom was a fortress, and Ashina held her breath at its magnificence. Alaric turned the horse right and followed the road off the plateau.

"Nervous." He whispered.

Ashina's heart beat wildly. "Yes." Her eyes were terrified of this place.

Alaric pressed his mouth against her neck again and kissed her, his moan hard. "We are home." His anticipation grew as she leaned harder into him.

"This is beautiful." She whispered.

For five miles, they traveled over the road through the horse fields. The road melted under rising stone homes built into this mountain. Ashina caught the stares of women and children.

Alaric met their stares, and they nodded at him and went on about their duties.

"How many families are here." Ashina wondered, smiling at the beautiful children walking along the road with their mothers.

She gazed at the women, and they smiled back at her, their long tunics draped in cloaks. Some of them wore leather breastplates and carried swords as they pulled their children along with them. Ashina found herself smiling back at them.

"Every male wolf has a family here. They are proud of their wives and children." Alaric told her, his voice firm.

"Where are the women of my village." She demanded.

Alaric sighed. "They are being taken care of until they are ready for their mates."

"What if they do not want a mate." She craned her eyes to stare at him. "What if they want to go home? What if your wolves scare the hell out of them."

He laughed out loud, and it took her by surprise. "My wolves are vigorous. They are fine specimens. They are veracious protectors of their mates, and they provide for them. Trust me, the women are happy. There is nothing for them to go back for once they come into my kingdom."

He galloped with her over the plain behind the rock houses, and Ashina saw his fortress. They melted into a forest, and the mountain facing them had a castle built into it. A wide opening was carved for a look-out. She determined that to be the throne room. Her eyes went from the forest to the stone fortress that loomed over them.

Alaric lunged the horse under the mountain into an expansive cavern with halls and corridors lit by torchlights. It lit up like daylight. Rieka lunged in behind them with the army, and the cavern filled with the wolves and their horses. Alaric lighted off the stallion and pulled Ashina off with him, his grip firm.

Alaric ignored the army and pulled her through the cavern to the end, where daylight pestered through. Ashina gawked at the magnitude of this mountain fortress. She had never been in a mountain before, let alone a fortress. He pulled her up winding stone steps carved in the cavern to a well-lit corridor. Beams of light surrounded her and kissed the stone at her feet.

Alaric watched her face as he led her on through. Her eyes craned up to a carved stone ceiling and a wall carved to form a wide breadth of windows open to the forest. She froze, her mouth open. The forest rose in her face as the leaves bent into her. She touched the oak leaves, and they were wet from dew.

Alaric stepped back and watched the leaves bend into her palm, and he smiled.

"Come." He pulled her past the wall of windows into a royal cavern suite.

"Ohhhhh." She walked to the edge of the walled opening, and it looked as if the room melted into the tops of the forest. A wind blew, and she closed her eyes.

She craned around to see a room off to the left, where the large bed sat against the wall. It jutted out to enjoy the views of the forest. She smelled roses and walked into the room. A stone basin filled with water and roses adorned the quaint washroom, and she breathed it in.

Ashina turned to glare at him as he turned to go. "Alaric."

He turned and stared at her.

"Why are there no female wolves in your kingdom." Ashina's face was firm.

He sighed. He leaned away and narrowed his brows. "I will be back for you after I wash up."

Ashina's insides burned when he said that, but before she could say anything more, he pressed his palm on her face. He leaned into her lips and kissed her. He stared in her face and smiled. "You are my mate, Ashina. We secure our bond tonight." He turned away from her and marched down the hall.

She watched him go and shook her head. Then she disrobed and lunged into the water, dunking her head under the roses. She closed her eyes and breathed in the perfume, eying the fortress suite. When she finished, she dried off with the cloth hanging. She slipped into the long flowing gown she found in there. She stepped over her dirty clothing and bloody armor and marched out of the room with wet hair to stare at the forest.

Ashina stood at the fortress wall and peered out. Her face lit up in the light blasting down through it that seemed to grow all around them. She smelled Alaric lingering behind her but did not stare back at him. He joined her there and stared out, his naked chest ribbed on his tall frame. His blonde hair was loose down his back.

Ashina turned to stare at him. He was a fine specimen for a wolf, down to his ribbed arms and chest and intricate tattoos. His long blonde hair was wet, and kissed his back to his buttocks. He turned to gaze at her, but she turned to stare at the forest again, ignoring him.

"This is beautiful." She closed her eyes and breathed it in.

Alaric rolled his eyes up and down her body. Her long white hair had waves in it, and her olive-toned skin glistened against her hair. She had strong arms and long legs, and the gown stretched loosely over her shoulders. Her hips were slender and tight, and he grew excited and walked to her.

When she opened her eyes again, her face met his. He eyed her up and down and settled on her lips, his face clenched. His chest and arms flexed at her face. The tattoos kissed the spaces she wanted to touch. She raked her fingers on the tattoos on his chest, exploring his muscles. Her eyes lingered up and down his ribbed chest and arms until her mouth watered at the perfection that was Alaric.

He held his breath and let her fondle his arms and chest again, her fingers lingering up and down his tattoos. He closed his eyes as his heart shook his chest to death, but now it was his turn.

He whispered. "Ashina."

Ashina let the fire inside her burn and bent up to meet the inevitable with this wolf king. He pressed her toward the bed. He took her face in his palm and leaned into her lips. She swallowed him whole in her soul as he blasted into her lips with a desperate passion.

Alaric pulled her gown off her shoulders, it slid to her feet, and he stood there stunned at her curvy perfection. He jerked his trousers off, his body flexed and stiff and perfect. He rolled his eyes upon her with anticipation and moaned in her mouth as he melted into her kisses.

Their kisses melted into a raging wind through their souls. He pressed between her legs as an anxious fire lit and would not go out. He lingered his open-mouthed kisses from her lips to her neck and caressed her nakedness on her shoulder. She bent her head back, her body shaking at his perfection. As his fangs burst up, he bit into her neck and lunged deep inside her.

He gripped his strong arms around her shoulders and pulled her tighter into his mouth as he thrust hard inside her. His aching throb was a thunderous heartbeat as their moans filled the expanse of their cavern room. Ashina bent her head back further to let him take her harder in his mouth even as he roared into her blood.

Her hands slid down his powerful back while his face clenched in agonizing surrender, his eyes lit in flaming gold. He rolled into her back and forth while his fangs sunk into her, their bodies a sweet release of pain and pleasure.

Ashina gripped his muscular back, sinking her fingers into his beautiful tattoos. When he finished biting her, he raised over her and belted out a moaning roar. He raised higher over her, lunging harder inside her, his arms flexed at her sides. His face clenched in unbridled passion.

He moaned over her head as a growl rumbled deep inside him, closing his eyes. He took in a deep breath as blood dripped down his chin, and his breath sounded like a gentle wind kissed them both.

Ashina kissed his neck with a wide-open mouth. She froze in sweet surrender as his lunging made her body fluid with his thrusts. Her head fell back and she moaned as Alaric licked her neck to her breasts and lingered there. He took her breasts in his mouth and sucked her.

He clasped her tight in his palms and dug into her back and hips with his fingers. He raised his lips back up and met her moans with his bloody tongue in her mouth. His heart raced against her breasts as he moaned, exploding inside her. He held her there as his face clenched and continued to stretch out inside her as his seed erupted a hot release.

Their breaths filled the silence in the room as Alaric bent his head into her neck and closed his eyes. Ashina gripped the back of his head, his blonde hair spilling over her arms. He breathed deeply, his fingers stretching out her white hair to the side of the bed.

Ashina closed her eyes, with him still over her and inside her. After hours of this passion, they melted into the comfort of solitude together, their heartbeats the only thumping left to their exhaustion.

Alaric closed his eyes against her face, pressing his forehead against hers. "Ashinaaaa." He moaned, exasperated.

She met his smile as he dug into her lips again with desperate open-mouthed kisses. He opened his eyes to face her, his hands exploring places on her body again as another raging fire lit. Her guts twirled to her knees at his touch. She wanted more of him. There was no going back now.

Ashina felt his hardness bulging against her groin again and rolled him over. She straddled him, and he held his breath. She bent into his lips as he met her in anticipation again. He pressed his palm against her head as her hair strung over his chest. Her tongue rolled in his mouth. She breathed on his chin to his neck and lunged in and bit him. She bit him so hard his throbbing veins filled her heart with desperate beating.

He belted out a roaring moan, pressing his head back to let her. He gripped her hips in his palms and began thrusting inside her again, arching his back under her. When she finished biting him, she raised and arched her back. She let her head fall back and closed her eyes as her long hair draped over his legs.

Alaric gripped her breasts in his palms as his head fled back while thrusting her. She grabbed his forearms to hold on, lunging up and down as he pushed deeper inside her.

Ashina melted on him as their moan echoed through the trees, their bodies one rhythm. She thrust atop him so deep until his whole body clenched under her, and he was growling, moaning between breaths. He belted out deep-throated screams.

As he moaned cries of passion, Alaric exploded inside her again. He found himself broken. He found himself dying. He found himself for the first time in his life. And he was breathing.

His white wolf queen would never leave this mountain.

Chapter 20
The Commanding Power

Ashina woke up with Alaric caressing the side of her face with his fingers, their bodies still naked and lingering into one another. They had made love all night as if years of unbridled tension they had pent up exploded. Alaric was now exhausted and love-struck with her. She watched him sleep for endless moments, still inflamed with his touch. She smiled in his face.

She had done this one time to a human man in her early twenties. She had unlimited energy as a primordial and a veracious appetite for sensual desires. She knew it was forbidden, but she had taken that human anyway. It did not end well for the human, and Tala had scolded her for months and told her she could not have intimate relations with human men.

The human got very sick and rundown after she had quite literally drained him. She could not help it. So last night, she let everything go and enjoyed every moment with Alaric. At one time, Alaric had fallen asleep inside her, and she fell asleep with him on top of her. When they woke up again, Alaric took her.

She opened her eyes as his fingers fell off her face, and he breathed loudly. Dawn had not risen yet, but it was coming. She stared at Alaric; he was very handsome. He was brave to have saved her the way he did. He brought down the city wall to get her. The wolf king would not allow any other to take her.

She slid out of the bed to wash up and find food. Moments later, she was slithering down the hall in trousers and a long tunic, her boots clunking the stone at her feet. She braided her long hair in sloppy knots and craned her ears toward movement in the forest. She had found a cloak in the washroom and pulled that over her as a brisk wind pelted in from the forest.

It smelled like storms were coming. Something else was coming, and as Ashina followed the smells and sounds to the cavern where they had come in, it dawned on her. She had sensed a presence since coming into the kingdom. The presence pricked her spine and whispered, but a wall kept those voices secret. They were still there, and it bothered her.

Vibrations filled the bottom of her feet and pricked her backbone, but she could not find them. It gnawed at her deep inside, like fingers sprouted vines and pulled something apart.

She walked outside to a brisk wind roaring around the open plain, her eyes drawn deeper into the forest toward the mountain. A whisper called her, and she froze. It was ancient and chilled her bones. She glared through the woods to a path, her eyes craning behind her to see the army and Rieka lunge up on horses. They filled the rolling plain in blackness like they had when they had taken her.

She rolled her eyes. They would wake Alaric, and he would find she was gone. Oh well. She was not trying to escape yet. She followed the path through the woods as the dawn kissed her face through the trees. The Sycamore and Oak bent around her and whispered into her soul.

Follow me, please! Hurry. Follow me please.

"What do you try to tell me..." She was perplexed.

This way, white wolf. And it led her west.

The path led to a big stone house built into the mountain, and she heard women talking. She recognized Anna's voice, and her heart screamed. Wooded hills rose around it as the mountain loomed like a shadow over them. A rage roared within her as she belted over the field to it. The spindly yellow grass was high, and round seeds clung to her hips.

It had double doors made from thick oak planks, so she knew it was heavy and strong. It was locked from the outside, so that meant they were prisoners. As she neared closer, she heard wolves talking. She dropped into the tall grass and disappeared, her eyes watching them. These two men were big and tall, burly and strong.

As she watched them, a wind blew through the woods and kissed her cheek. She touched her cheek as if something had grazed a finger on her face. It prodded her and raked over her cheek. It wanted to pull her away from the field to go west.

"What magic is in this mountain..." She questioned.

The two wolves lingered by the door. They were in human form and armed. They were protecting the women in that house. Ashina rolled her eyes. She closed her eyes, breathed, and talked to the wind. She bent her wrist at her face and commanded the trees to move on the hill, and the wolves followed the motion. The trees rustled and sounded like footsteps, and the wolves followed it north.

She ran through the grass, lifted the heavy plank on the door, and burst it open. She raged in hate. The women of her village huddled among straw. They had given up. She closed the door and glared at them, and the women recognized her and gasped.

"You are alive!" Ashina bellowed.

The women rushed to her, and Ashina hugged them, her eyes teared up. There were fourteen of them.

"We feared Alaric had taken you!" Anna hugged her.

Ashina sighed. "Oh, he took me."

The women gasped, but Ashina smiled at them. "Who has been bitten?" She glared at their shoulders. They shook their heads.

The women confirmed. "We are not bitten yet. We fear Alaric was waiting on you."

Ashina growled. "Damn them."

Their faces wide were and pale, and they looked hungry.

"Are they feeding you? It looks like you still have the same clothes on." Ashina complained.

They shook their heads. They were not getting fed well and still had the same clothes on. Ashina sneered, her eyes lighting up. "He is a liar. A damn liar like they all are."

She craned her ear toward voices again and put her fingers to her lips. "Did they bring you in through a slim pass?"

They nodded, silent.

"Of course they did."

The same two wolves approached the door and noticed it was moved and unlocked, and Ashina waited until they both opened it fully to glare at the women. Her fists met their faces, and they fell back, knocked out cold.

"Assholes." Ashina bit out.

Anna giggled. "We see you still take no nonsense with wolves..."

Ashina smiled at them as she pulled their bodies into the house and took their weapons. She closed the door and put the wooden plank over it so it looked locked. Then she bent down and touched the earth, feeling the vibrations from the army looming by the fortress and up the hill.

Ashina led them in the opposite direction, east into the forest. She led them away from the mountain, letting the rising dawn and forest guide her away. When she felt vibrations, she made the women hunker down and be silent. She was primordial and had better senses than the wolves, but they would still sense something off.

By now, Alaric would know she was gone and be on the hunt for her. Hours later they met a river that trickled between sloping plateaus. Ashina bent her head into the rising sun and breathed in deep. She pulled the weapons she had stolen from the wolves and handed them to the women, with Anna leading them. They took them and sighed. They were not fools for humans. After all, Tala had raised them together.

"You were brave against the wolves, but they know your defiance," Ashina warned them, hugging Anna with the others again.

"Follow this plateau. You will go to the unexplored forest where Tala's wolves come from. There will be humans there also and more wolves, but good ones. They will not harm you. They will know I sent you."

The women gasped, shaking their heads no.

"Ashina, you cannot go back. Alaric will bite you..."

"I have already been with him."

Anna gasped, meeting the women's faces with disdain. "Oh, Ashina."

Ashina smiled, her face lit up. "I enjoyed it. It was beautiful, I cannot lie." She laughed.

Anna widened her eyes and smiled. "Oh my."

Ashina swallowed. "I must go back. That gives you enough time til nightfall. I need you to stay together and follow this plateau, follow the rising sun. You will be traveling two days east, and then you will see the falls. The humans will have warriors monitoring the forest by now. I know that Alaric's Dakitae are all dead."

They nodded at her, their faces tired and weary. They were hungry and exhausted and missed their families. The women could forage for food until they made it safely.

"Something more comes to these lands, and I need you all safe. I love you all." A tear fell as they hugged her in groups. "But I need you with my wolves, who can protect your people too."

She pushed them over the river in knee-deep water and watched them rush up the incline to climb the plateau. She watched them until they disappeared over the horizon. Her heart weighed like a heavy burden pressed inside her. Alaric would be furious, but he lied to her. He said they were taken care of. No, they were not.

She turned her head to hike back to the mountain, and a fire rose in her. Anger sifted her pride, and it raged. It raged in her heart as her fangs burst out. Her eyes glowed golden, but she did not turn. The hair on her neck stood up as she glared through the woods again toward the mountain. By going back to Alaric, she hoped it would stall the wolves hunting the women.

Alaric did not have wolves all over the woods as she had feared. He ensured his wolves stayed together in packs on horseback for his army. It became clear of that as she neared closer to the house again where they had kept the women. Vibrations roared throughout the city, and the echoes filled in her ears.

Hours later, as she neared the field again, Rieka burst up from the high grass and met her with a blade to her throat. He glared at her face, his dark eyes disappointed. Ashina froze, not surprised.

"Should have kept wolfsbane in you." He bit. Ashina froze, sighing at his face.

"Do you have any idea what you have done?" His bald head swimming in tattoos accentuated his dark eyes. He gripped his long sword at her throat, his face clenched, shaking his head.

Ashina craned her eyes to see other wolves pulling the two out of the house. The fields through the woods had erupted in wolves on horseback or foot, tracking her. The wolves she had punched had bloody and broken noses. It was apparent they had just found them. They were confused and rattled still. She huffed.

"I broke their noses." Ashina rolled her eyes back to him, her hazel eyes kissed by the sun and the forest. "Looks like they just woke up."

Rieka noticed her eyes glimmering and he scoffed at her. "You have a lot of nerve. You may command the trees and the wind, white wolf, but you do not command the women we have taken." He sneered at her. "You have crossed a line."

Ashina met his sneer with her fangs. "You do not command women. We bend not to the will of wolves nor man."

Rieka growled at her, and then Alaric lunged in on his horse to confront her. His face was as hard as his eyes at her, and he growled at what she had done. He slid from his horse, his body armor hugging his body. His face still held the passion from their all-night love-making as he met her face. Rieka still pressed his blade to her throat as she held her breath.

Alaric loomed in her face. "I gave you my whole soul all night, and you betrayed me in the morning."

Ashina stared at him, her eyes craning up his magnificent muscle-ridden body. "And I enjoyed it..." Her voice had an edge to it.

Rieka gawked at her, his face pale, his eyes wide. He dropped his mouth open as if he wanted to say something but could not. He almost dropped his sword at her throat when she said it.

She added. "Immensely." Her voice was passionate as her hazel eyes glowed at him.

Alaric pulled back when she said that, and a smile lingered on his face. "Damnit Ashina." He rolled his eyes.

He turned to Rieka and sighed. "Hunt the women. Bring them back."

Rieka rolled his eyes. "Damnit."

He turned to her again. "You used the wind to hide you taking them out. You used the trees to cover them from us." He sighed.

Ashina scoffed. "They are fast hikers. You will not find them."

"Yes, we know. These human women have your stubbornness all over them." Rieka shook his head.

"You will leave them alone and let them go!" Ashina warned.

Alaric lunged into her face, his eyes lit up golden, his fangs out at her. "You do not tell me what to do, white wolf. You do not control the methods we use in my kingdom. If you betray me again, there will be consequences."

Ashina growled in his face. "You do not get to keep women as hostages. You did not feed them, clothe them, or make them comfortable. You lied to me." She bit back at him. "You treated them as chattel!"

Alaric pulled back and turned to Rieka again. "When you find them, ensure they have food and new clothing. Ensure they have beds and are comfortable. The wolves chosen to guard them failed." His voice was edgy.

Rieka pulled the blade from her throat, but his face was wide and shocked at her. Ashina glared at him, but Rieka shook his head and pointed his blade toward her again, even as he backed away.

"I am watching you, white wolf." He widened his eyes and bolted away from her.

"It's obvious you are not." She whispered.

Rieka heard that and turned his scowling face back to her, his eyes hard. He shook his head, and Ashina watched him whistle. A pack of twenty wolves roared in on horseback to hunt the women.

Ashina growled. "They just want to go home." She closed her eyes, her breathing heavy.

Alaric pressed into her face, his eyes roaming her lips. "They are free Ashina…" He breathed in her face. "There is nothing for them to go back to."

Ashina glared into his eyes.

"You were free all night to be yourself, and you did. I did not imprison you or force you to lie with me as we mated over and over." He bent into her face. "You exhausted me all night. You enjoyed it. I enjoyed it." He whispered against her neck and met her lips. "You crept out as I was sleeping..."

She held her breath as that fire that burned through her loins all night met his lips. She kissed him back. Her heart raced. She wanted to taste him again.

He breathed in her face. "Now that you are here, you failed to realize something about me." His voice was like a crack of lightning had hit her and set her on edge. "Something your guardian could not train you see..."

Ashina met his eyes, and as they lit up golden, he raised higher over her, his tallness a looming shadow. "You are not the only primordial white wolf."

She froze, her face wide as he glared at her. "There are only you..."

He paused, his face hard. "...and me." He took her face in his palms, his jaws clenched at her, his eyes hard.

She widened her eyes at him. "What." She gasped. "No." Her heart raced. She gripped his palms on her face.

That would explain his power over her. That explained his strength and prowess. She sighed in his face. "You lied to me."

Alaric did not care because anything she said did not faze him. She closed her eyes but it was too late. He had bitten and mated her. The world did not know the male heirs of Worgen were all primordials. They would never know because the primordial wolves taken every thousand years could not leave. No wonder the kingdom was the most powerful.

Alaric met her face and kissed her lips with an inviting passion, his hands clasped against her face. "You do not need to know everything..." He kissed her and sighed.

He pulled back and stared her in the eyes, his eyes cold and calculating. Ashina had not seen that before. He doted lovingly on her but with an underlying maliciousness.

"You will never leave the mountain...." His voice was sharp like a dagger, his face hard.

He bent down, pulled her over his shoulder, and marched with her to his horse. He climbed into the saddle with her over his shoulder and dropped her into his lap. "You will not be turning to your wolf here. That stopped yesterday as we arrived, and I mated you."

Ashina gasped at him, which explained why she could not change to her wolf in the woods. Brovina was right, dark powers lingered here. She must find out what.

She rode on his lap and held on to him, his bulging muscles flexed around her waist. His eyes lingered up and down her, and he bent into the side of her face and kissed her. They trotted away from the house and the field, and he led her to a rolling plain away from the fortress. He stopped the horse on a flat-topped hill where vast views of this plain spilled from the mountain. To the west, Ashina noticed snow-capped peaks and sighed at their beauty.

Miles below them, Alaric's wolves bled out from a cavern under the mountain in their wolf forms. They wore full body armor, and golden breastplates shimmered under the morning sun. Their pauldrons on their shoulders were leather, and their vambraces sang in the same design as the tattoos she had seen. They were mighty wolves and roared into the plain from the mountain as pitch black and terrifying.

They filled the breadth of the plain and dispersed through the valley. They looked like bugs compared to where they were sitting. Ashina froze against Alaric's chest as she noticed the magnitude of his army. They flooded the land in perfect formation as if they had been bred their whole lives to serve and be mighty war machines.

Ashina's knees grew weak. Alaric had hundreds upon thousands. Alaric felt her tense up against him and she heard him huff out a slight laugh. "Now you see the power of Alaric." His eyes sparkled at his army.

"Why do you show me this? I already know you are powerful." Ashina taunted him.

Alaric smiled in her ear. "To show you there is no escape from my mountain. You are mine, white wolf."

"Have you found the women I freed?" She smarted off.

Alaric sighed. "Human women are of little value compared to you."

She shook her head. "I could have kept going myself."

Alaric laughed at her.

Ashina leaned into him, her whole body relaxed. She blinked when he said that, and a slight smile erupted from her lips, but he did not see it. Power-hungry wolves always fall the hardest. He fondled her neck with his lips and breathed hard against her skin. Alaric's passion burned her insides for him. She would be lying if she did not have feelings for him because she did. She enjoyed the passion in the bed.

Alaric turned away from the hill and led her to a trail in the forest on a sloping knoll. Evergreen trees surrounded it with an expansive view of the mountains to the west. He slid from his horse and pulled her down off it. She let him lead her through the glen to face the mountain and then pressed in behind her.

He pulled her arms out to either side and breathed in her neck again. "You see that snow on the mountain?"

Ashina sighed and closed her eyes. "Yes."

"I want to see you bring it down." He smiled.

"What if there are villages there?"

Alaric huffed. "Bring it down." He commanded her arms against his. The ground shook and vibrated over the forest. As Ashina refused him, he bent harder and sneered in her ear. She struggled with him. Her arms were not her own.

"Do not fight me, white wolf. I am the alpha here."

Ashina bent her tongue and clenched her face as Alaric bent her arms anyway, and she could not control them.

He bent into her ear and whispered. "The beauty of bonding to your mate with our seer lineage is seeing one command the other..."

She belted out a frustrating growl at him.

Alaric laughed. "You will bend to me, Ashina." He smiled.

The air roared over their heads as the snow spilled down the side of the mountain before them. The massive avalanche drenched the sky around the peak in a powdery white. The snow rolled down the side of the mountain and took the forest with it.

Alaric released her arms. Ashina turned around and slapped his face. He pulled back from her, his eyes hard and cold. He took a deep breath in her face and then growled, his fangs showing. As his eyes glowed golden at her, she held her breath at his face, scowling.

"You have no right to control my gift to use as demise. You do not know if you killed innocent people on that mountain." She lunged away from him.

Alaric pulled her back by her forearm to face him. He jerked her body against his and glared into her face. She slammed into his chest, their glares hard at one another. He clenched his face, his cheek red.

"If I give a command for you to follow, you will obey it." He warned her. "You will obey it because I am your king."

Ashina sighed in his face. "I am your mate. Or did you lie about that also?"

"You are my mate. You are also a warrior. That was clear when I found you to claim you at the falls. You will use your powers to keep our kingdom strong. There will be no further discussion of this."

Ashina shook her head at him. "Why."

"We have powerful seer blood in our veins, Ashina!" He yelled at her. "We are the most powerful mates in the world! There will always be one to dominate the other."

"You are controlling me! You are not teaching me to control it. Why?" She bit.

Alaric stepped away from her, his cheek red. He rubbed it and growled at her. He shook his head and then stood in her face again. "You will hone your gift to me when I say so."

"This is my gift, not yours." She demanded, her eyes falling to his bulging arms flexed at her. She found herself roving over him and her stomach ached. She wanted him again.

Alaric pursed his lips at her. "It is your gift for me. You were given to me by fate." He turned to the horse, and she followed him.

Then he turned to face her again. He bent in and kissed her lips ferociously, and Ashina met him back. "It is my turn to exhaust you." He whispered in her lips.

She found herself pulling him closer to her, her fingers digging into his breastplate. He gripped her bottom and pulled her up to straddle him, his fingers clutched into her thighs. She wrapped her legs around him as he kissed her aggressively, her loins throbbing against him to have him inside her again.

"I want you." Ashina moaned on his lips.

Alaric moaned, his mouth open to her kisses. "My turn."

"Yes." She breathed in his mouth.

When they reached the cavern fortress, he pulled her off and slung her over his shoulder again as if he had found a prize. He had food brought in while she crept off that morning.

A table pressed against the wall had a wooden bowl full of big red apples. There were loaves of hot bread and a bowl filled with butter and honey. Alaric had rare chunks of venison on a platter and her mouth watered. A vat of spring water and hot herbal tea in a pot with bone cups enticed her senses.

Ashina had not realized how hungry she was until then. He sat down with her to eat, and they ate their hearts full. When she finished, she walked into the wash room to clean up, and Alaric met her there. He bent into her neck as she pulled off her tunic. She faced him and undid the buckles to his armor. As they disrobed one another, he pressed her against the stone wall as she straddled him. He lunged inside her under the cascading falls trickling down the wall from the mountain spring.

And then he pulled her back to bed. He kept her in the bed for three more days and ravished her. He ravished her so hard Ashina lost track of the time or the day. She lost track of time and dove into the passion, her loins aflame like her emotions. But her emotions were all over the place, like a flickering flame with no hope. And if a wind had blasted through them, the flame would blow out.

As the days lingered into the nights, Ashina's moans echoed Alaric's passion. He filled her up with his desire and met her moans with unbridled power. She had never experienced this raging passion before. His power thrummed through her bones.

He had done well hiding that he was a primordial. The primordials were the strongest most powerful wolves. Primordials had the most persuasive power and glory. They were the biggest wolves.

The strongest wolves always win.

Chapter 21
Where Fate Calls

Ashina awoke in the bed to the sun beaming in on her and Alaric from the open cavern wall. The warm beams kissed their bodies and faces and warmed her heart. She turned her head as a whisper called her from her deep sleep.

It called to her and tickled her insides like a finger poked her awake. She craned her neck toward it and opened her eyes.

"Ashina."

The trees swayed softly as a whisper thrummed in her head again. She sat up naked in the bed and turned to Alaric. He was on his stomach with his arm around her waist. His whole backside was exposed, and she lingered on his magnificence for endless moments until it called again. But this time, it made her freeze. She glared into the trees.

"White wolf."

She pulled Alaric's arm off her, and he opened his eyes. He smiled at her, his face lit up and satisfied. She smiled back at him, bent down, and kissed his face. Then she lingered into the washroom and pulled on a thick wool robe. The whisper tickled her ears again, but something else pulled at her heart.

Something pulled her through the darkness like she had been living with a veil thrust upon her. A light trickle flowed from that darkness and burst open. She walked back out to the trees at her face and stared in at the forest. It was powerful and riveting and called to her. She could not deny it.

She stared into the forest as the leaves bellowed in silence at her. The oak and sycamore leaves twisted toward her face, singing in agony. They swam into a wind that howled, but there was no wind. The leaves bent and sounded like parchment crunching at her face. It was silent and eerie. Whatever this was drew itself out from the earth and beckoned Ashina into it.

Darkness shrouded within the forest. It bellowed from something ancient and burst forth. Her soul lit on fire. She found herself breathing hard, even as Alaric turned to watch her. His body tensed up as he rose from the bed. It dawned on him something was calling his mate.

A whisper came again, and a vibration in the earth tickled her feet. Darkness spread through the forest at her face, and the trees swayed as something moved through them to get her.

An unseen force rolled toward her face, seething against the branches.

Alaric lunged straight up, his eyes on her. Ashina stepped closer to the ledge to hear the whisper.

"*Ashina.*"

She jerked back, her eyes wide. The voice sounded at her face as if the trees called her. Chills rushed up her arms.

She heard it as clear as day, and Alaric heard it too. As chills darted up her spine, Alaric lunged out of the bed. He slipped into his trousers and met her at the opening, glaring out. He stood before her as if guarding her, his hand pressed to hold her back. His eyes changed to a fiery gold as his whole body tensed up. He glared into the forest, clenching his fists.

He stared at the stone floor to acknowledge vibrations coming into the mountain. He held his breath and belted out a low growl, his whole face clenched.

"Cayden." His fangs burst up.

"Something is coming." Ashina belted out, her whole arms in shivers. "It is coming..." She warned. "Now..."

She pulled her robe tighter around her and eyed Alaric. He met her stare and ran a finger down her chin. He bent in and kissed her lips gently, his whole body flexed. She met his kiss.

He turned away from her. "Stay here."

He marched down the corridor, and Rieka met him there with a slew of wolves. Ashina heard the men, and her spine stiffened.

"Sire, Cayden has an army marching from the north. Two hundred thousand strong." Rieka belted out. "They are turning south to come into the kingdom. They will be at our borders by dawn."

Ashina heard Alaric growl, and it rumbled through the halls. "Ready the wolves. We meet him there with double. Prepare the wolves to guard the south..."

Ashina heard Alaric growl. "I know he followed her. He comes to take her from me."

As the wolves prepared for war, it dawned on her that Alaric already knew Hardulph would come. Yesterday, the magnitude of his mighty army was evident. He already had them prepared for war. He had hundreds of thousands ready and waiting for his command.

It dawned on her that Alaric would use her powers to kill them. She closed her eyes into the trees and leaned her head into the whispers.

"Why do you come for me again, wolf king." Ashina held her breath as she pondered this, her mind retracing what Hardulph had told her at Serkily.

"If not for that treacherous liar Alaric and his wicked mountain seers, you would be in Cayden right now!"

"My kingdom is sacrificing to save you."

"There are truths you do not know, white wolf."

"You have been taken from me by those wicked seers serving Alaric!"

"I am your mate!"

As Ashina pondered these, Hardulph answered from within her whispers.

"Go west into the snowy mountain, white wolf."

Ashina stepped back. The voice was a resounding echo and strong. It was him. When she opened her eyes, the leaves in the forest craned at her face like fingers lunging in at her. They pushed her. Ashina lifted her head, her heart pounding in her head.

As tears filled her eyes, he called again. *"By dawn, white wolf. Unless you prefer to die in that mountain."*

Ashina lunged back again, her face pale, her eyes shimmering in gold as if his voice had filled her up and pulled her wolf outside her. The chills from the recognition of his voice touched her face and lit her heart up.

"This is not possible. I am with my mate already…" She questioned everything. "What are you doing, wolf king?"

And then she heard him whisper, *"I'm saving you."*

Alaric had Ashina bathe and get dressed within the hour. He had wolves bring her new armor but no weapons. It became clear he was not going to let her fight. She was enraged inside at him for that. He lunged with her in his lap over the hill past the fortress to the rolling plain under the mountain cavern. He belted under the cavern around his wolves marching north.

He pulled her into a dark ravine that opened into a cavernous space engorged with flickering torch lights. A sinking feeling hit her chest as she realized what he was doing.

"No, Alaric!" She pleaded. "Do not leave me here."

But it was too late. Alaric pulled her into a round dungeon room where five elderly women stood around an altar and glared at her. They were seers. Ashina was powerless, and it became apparent why. They controlled her through Alaric.

"What is this, Alaric!" She demanded. The truth hit her heart as her gut churned.

He turned to go and nodded at her. "These are my seers, Ashina. They are powerful and will keep you safe until I come for you."

"I cannot help the wolves this way." She complained. "I cannot help you with the army like this."

Alaric did not care. "Once the mountain is safe, I will come for you." He kissed her and turned and left.

Ashina craned her neck and stared at them. They wore long gray robes that kissed their toes. Their faces were wrinkled as if they had sucked on soured lemons for far too long. She grimaced her lip at them, her eyes meeting the walls. They stood at the altar and watched her but said nothing. The hoods on their heads covered their hair, and Ashina wondered if they had any.

She gazed at their eyes and saw nothing but darkness. As she melted around the cavernous space, she realized why. The whole wall of the cavern had open graves carved into it, and every space had bones. The names above the graves were all women. The wolf queens of Worgen. The wolf queens of old.

Ashina raised her eyes to the ceiling where darkness lingered. A loathing anger rose within her. She turned to stare at the altar, and the women turned to watch her. Before she could say anything to them, she heard muffled voices. She followed the voices around the room to a bend in the cavern. It opened to a vast dungeon cavern room, and she noticed humans. They were warriors for Serkily, and there were upwards of one hundred of them.

The men raised their faces as they noticed her, and they stood up. They pressed their faces into the bars, gasping at her. She lunged toward the bars to release them.

The seers watched her and bent their hands at her. As they lunged toward her, their fingers erupted into vines. The vines wrapped around her chest and arms like fingers and engorged her frame. They were strong and vicious, and they pulled her onto the altar. Ashina roared at them, but she was powerless.

It was a controlling power, and her body sunk against it. They controlled her as Alaric had done. The women held her atop the altar with their vine fingers, lingering their gaze over her body. They pressed her head back and glared into her face with black eyes.

"This will be over soon, white wolf, once Alaric is successful." Ashina heard one of them say. "And you will be reunited with your mate."

Ashina breathed deeply, her heart racing wildly, desperate. "Many queens have been here. And died here…"

The seers smiled, their black mouths as dark as their eyes. The oldest one breathed in her face. "Yesssss. Many have come, many have been called. The mountain is powerful. The fate bond is strong."

"Is it." Ashina wondered. "Is it fate or seer magic?" Silence pestered her. She struggled against the vines and held her breath.

"Tell me, where are the female wolves in this kingdom of Worgen?"

The seers scoffed at her as one of them answered. "We have no female wolves. You are the only one. That is how it has been for ages."

"I will be the only one to escape." Ashina belted out, anger rising within her.

The seer glared at her. "You will never leave this mountain white wolf."

Alaric was keeping her prisoner, using her for mating and keeping the kingdom strong. What happened to the old primordial wolf queens became apparent. She raised her eyes to the ceiling, the room round and vast. Moon emblems carved into the rock danced around her into the darkness. A grief she could not describe filled her bones as chills darted up her spine.

"What will you do with me?" Ashina pondered.

The women did not look at her, but one responded. "Wait for you to bring Alaric's heir into the kingdom."

Ashina's spine tingled. "And then what, after I have birthed an heir?"

The women laughed. "Then you join the primordial queens under the mountain once we consecrate your bones, your power forever ingrained into our kingdom."

"But Alaric loves me." Ashina blurted out, testing them. "I am his mate for life."

The seers scoffed at her. "Alaric keeps you busy in his loins til you birth his heir."

Ashina took a deep breath as something from deep inside her broke loose, and rage lingered there. She had found the evil under the mountain and had to sleep with the enemy to do it.

The seer laughed. "Once the heir of Alaric is born, it will be raised to be king and prepare for the next thousand-year queen. That is the way of it. Worgen will always be the most powerful."

The seers lingered at her belly, and one pressed against it. "You are not with wolf yet. You will be soon." They advised. "Very soon, Alaric will have his heir the more he mates with you."

Ashina roared deep inside. A rage she had never felt sprouted like daggers had grown on her spine and catapulted out of her. Her eyes lit up in crimson, and fangs burst out that were not ones she always knew. They burst out from a deep chasm inside her, and something never unleashed before broke open. Her back pressed up on the altar, and the vines burned on fire to the seers' fingers.

The seers screamed and pulled their hands back, their palms burning. They bent over Ashina and glared into a face of retribution. They noticed her eyes change and loomed over her to inspect, confused. Ashina sat up from the altar as a wind had pressed under her and lifted her from the dark powers.

It twisted her spine as white hair grew, and a ridgeline of spikes burst down her back to a long tail. Her ears laid back on her broad snout over firm eyes. Her fangs burst through like daggers.

She pressed into them with her claws as her body transformed into a nine-foot primordial white wolf. She transformed within seconds, the wind in her soul bursting the air of the cavern room. Her snout gaped open and roared into their heads. With a blow from her claws, she snapped their heads off or slashed them into chunks. Her roar echoed out of the cavern to the rolling plain.

She ripped them apart in her rage as their blood sprayed the bones in the walls. Then she turned and galloped down the cavern and pulled the barred doors off for the humans. They glared at her, from her paws to her snout, their eyes wide.

"The white wolf." She heard them shout.

"Who sent you?" She roared at them.

One man approached and bowed to her. "Serimi sent us over the mountain weeks ago. The wolves found us holed up in a cave and took us."

"I need you to go east to the falls and meet my commander, Randon. Serkily will be there securing the ancient city. Tell them I am bringing down this mountain."

The men gawked at her. She turned to them again. "There are fourteen human women from my village of Hildenia. They are tracking in the wilderness. If you come across them, help them. They are good women."

The men agreed, following her out to the bloody altar. The seers' bodies were ripped up and beheaded, and their blood spilled upon the runes carved into the stone floor.

"Evil. There is great evil here." Ashina growled.

As they followed her, she stopped at the altar again. The warriors watched her seethe into it and cracked the stone with her fists. She pulled the slab off where it cracked and broke into chunks around her. Then she gazed at all the bones of the lost primordial queens, and her eyes teared up. Thousands of them. She raised high on her haunches and craned her snout in the air at them, moaning.

"I am sorry." She moaned. "I am sorry you never got a chance to breathe and live." She roared in defiance.

And then she turned her snout away from them and seethed in pain inside. The warriors followed her out of the cavern, the plain now empty of wolves. Alaric led them to the border of his mountain kingdom to face Hardulph's wolves. Ashina stayed primordial, ensuring the warriors got on horses and headed east. They lunged through the forest away from her, and Ashina retuned to the mountain.

"I am taking down this mountain kingdom..." She whispered, thinking of Hardulph.

As whispers tickled her ears, she put up a wall inside her, and ignored the voices. She rolled a thick stone over her heart and pushed Alaric out, too. She pushed him so far away from her soul that a bridge burned in her guts, and something else burst up from her seething, breathing fire. It fed her from the inside out and would not stop.

"This mountain is evil." She raged.

She purged Alaric from her mind and galloped to a rolling plateau ten miles out. She glared back at Alaric's Mountain. It rose into the clouds as the forests kissed it.

She had only saved the fourteen women of her village. She had not seen any other women there except for the few families at the entrance to the city. But they looked happy and cared for. Ashina hated how Alaric's wolves took human women. It was wrong not to romance them or give them a choice of men or wolves. They were not even trying to woo or find wolf women. They were lazy.

Her eyes glistened in crimson. She craned her wolf neck to glare over the trees and noted Alaric's wolf army filling the plains at the kingdom territory. They would be there by nightfall. Blackness filled the rolling plains outside, and it looked like the depths of darkness had come to face each other.

"Evil kingdom." She belted out, her voice deep and bellowing through the woods.

She clenched her paws and took in a deep breath. She had never used her powers in her wolf form before. But now she had tapped her primordial, and she filled with a raging fire of menace. It ate through her heart as she roared at Alaric's Mountain. She lunged her paw to her side and out as the earth shook to the plains where the wolf armies gathered to wipe each other out.

The earth ripped from the hill she stood upon, and a crevasse opened to the cavern where the seers had been. Their bodies torn up against the stone spilled more of their blood around the bones as the earth shook there.

Ashina's eyes lit up like crimson fire and breathed within her, and she roared. Her snout stretched wide as her ears laid flat on a broad square head. Her eyes grimaced as wrinkles from her snout bent her gums wide. She clenched her muscle-riddled body as she leaned into the wind. She roared toward the mountain.

A crevasse burst open from the earth and cracked the mountain's cavern wall. She roared from the pits of her soul and watched the cavern cave in. The kingdom shook as it pulled that side of the mountain down. The whole side slid as the forest fell into the darkness with it.

As the rumble echoed in the sky and the earth shook, she sighed, her heart aching for the old primordial queens. She turned and galloped into the wilderness from Alaric, away from her pain and the lies. Instead, she lunged south through the forest.

She would not listen to any wolf kings again. She would not bow to them. She would not fill their loins with pleasure. The rage she had in her would not go away, ever.

She traveled south further from Worgen, and a veil lifted from her mind. It lifted off her heart, as she had been swooned with seer magic. He had controlled her power and her body. He controlled her emotions as the magic there had been powerful.

No wonder so many primordial queens had been taken and never left. Ashina was the first white wolf primordial ever born. Her primordial strength helped her escape. The seers were dead under the mountain, and the queens of old could rest.

She defied authority. Tala raised her to be a warrior. Alaric was surprised and disappointed she was a warrior when he met her. That is because his male primordial ancestors never wanted one. They wanted a subservient queen to birth them heirs. They endowed the mountain with their powers then, and Worgen stayed the most powerful because of it.

When the mountainside collapsed onto the plain, Alaric and Rieka turned with their wolf army to acknowledge something dreadful had happened. They craned their eyes, their bodies stiff. They were already miles out and nearing the borders of his lands.

A roar set them on edge as it loomed through the heavens. It echoed like something ancient had breathed it to life and was coming for them. The roar filled the space of heaven and screamed as if spawned by malice.

The collapse was evident from the plain, and Alaric's dread filled him with a fear he thought would never exist. A heaviness tossed over his heart, and he could not sense Ashina. A desperate realization hit him.

"Ashina!" He belted out, his eyes as hard as ice.

Rieka glared alongside him and witnessed the sky behind them fill with a black haze. It roared into the heavens above the city for miles. The earth shook as if they were on uneven ground and thundered through the sky.

Alaric lunged his horse back around and raced to the city to meet the destruction. He thought the seers would control Ashina, but now his heart had been rendered in half, so something happened to them. Something happened because his mate did not like it. He knew when Ashina did not like something, she was not afraid to fight it.

"Ashina." He bellowed, his face hard.

Alaric closed his eyes and pressed his head into his horse's mane, even as the whole of his army turned to face the black tide of Cayden lunging in at them from the plain. They would be warring them by dawn.

As he neared the plain and saw the breadth of the collapse, he knew she had killed the seers and released the prisoners. As the catastrophe breathed before his face, he burst out in sudden laughter. And then he lunged up off his horse and transformed into the primordial Ashina nor the kingdoms had ever seen yet.

Ashina galloped south, pausing every few miles to lunge her snout into the air to smell. She pressed toward the ground, closed her eyes, and did not feel vibrations from Alarik's wolves coming for her. They were preparing to face Hardulph's wolves that had come to Worgen to take her. She was sick of the wolf kings.

The forest was thick and silent. A canopy formed a hovering darkness that lingered over her. She rose to the trees and stood tall, taking in the deep breaths of the forest. She craned her powerful neck and closed her eyes to enjoy the silence.

It was always in the silence where she was strong. The forest was silent at her presence. The woodland creatures had holed up and disappeared when she approached. The birds had stopped chirping. The leaves bent on the trees toward the sky, warning her of rain.

In this silence, she breathed deeply and roared inside. Her heart cried. She screamed inside of retribution, but all it did was spread the empty hole wide that had grown there since Alaric took her. She missed Tala. She missed her village. So many things plagued her she could not describe the hurt filling her up.

The wolf king had taken her and mated her. He had lied to her over and over. Her first impressions of him were correct. His words were like honey, but his eyes told the truth. Alaric could not be trusted to do what was right, for he had challenged her and justified his wickedness from the beginning.

It would do no good for Alaric to pursue her again. She destroyed his seers and the mountain of bones holding the ancient queens' powers. Alaric could not force her to bend or fill her emotions with lies to continue mating with him. The mountain was evil and deserved punishment.

She found herself washed in grief deep inside as a shadow raised over her from the darkness of the woods. She stepped away from it and turned to see the white wolf king had found her after all. Alaric stepped under the beaming streams of light, towering over her. His ears perked high atop his broad head, and his golden eyes glistened back at her.

He walked toward her, his body flexed and moaning in muscles. He swished his long white tail like a whip and sighed at her face. He did not snarl; he did not growl at her. A resonating hum burst from him deep inside, and when he spoke, Ashina thought the sun had kissed his soul.

She stepped back from him and lifted her snout to snarl, warning him. Alaric's chest was heaving with his deep breathing, and his eyes followed her breaths. He stopped in the glen as they stood facing one another off. He was bigger than her. He was stronger than her, and she knew it. He knew it, too.

"You flee me." His voice echoed, dark and deep. He eyed her, and Ashina noticed a hurt within him. "You cast me from your heart."

"You want an heir only and then will consecrate my powers to that infernal mountain." She bellowed back at him, arching her back. "I will die out here and not in that mountain."

He gazed up and down her magnificent body, and she found herself lingering upon his. His primordial wolf form exuded power and strength. He towered over Randon, even. His eyes sparkled back at her as if the dawning of understanding hit him, and he agreed with her. He gazed into the sunlight and sighed.

"You are an impressive and strong primordial. You have killed the seers of my forefathers and brought down that side of the mountain..." He stepped closer. "I am relieved of them, yet in pain."

Ashina stepped back. "What..."

"You have done what no wolf queen has been able to do, ever." He rose taller and swallowed, his chest rising at her. "You will not be tamed nor controlled, my love."

The silence filled her with dread as he paused to stare at her.

"You will not be silenced or stopped. You have brought me to glory." He shook his snout. "What do you want, white wolf." Alaric breathed at her. "I will give you the world."

"What are you doing, Alaric?" She feared him.

Alaric moaned at her, his passion for her adamant. "What do you desire, my queen."

She glared at him. "I am not going back with you."

He flexed his massive forearms.

"I will rule my kingdom." She demanded. "You have bent fate to your will and used me."

Alaric froze, his wolf form tense. "I will not let you go, Ashina. I will give you everything else you desire, but that. I need you at the mountain."

"But not by your side. But not as your wife." She growled. "You just crave my power and loins..."

Alaric sneered, showing his fangs.

"You just want an heir." Ashina raised her eyes to the sunbeams and sighed. He stepped back and held his breath, his eyes meeting hers in a glare that set her on edge.

Ashina bellowed. "You do not love me..."

Alaric breathed in deep and scowled at her. "You presume to know how I feel about you..."

"You have used seers to alter fate for centuries and denied wolf kings their mates. Now I have Hardulph calling to me, the ancient primordial who hunts me and is at your doorstep. The king of Cayden! Why does he call me Alaric?!"

Alaric glared. He let the silence eat at them again before Ashina spoke up. "This is the last year you fulfill the oath of your wicked fathers. You will no longer take queens bent by the seers to control fate. You have twisted my fate, and I do not know which direction to go…"

Alaric twisted his neck, and Ashina heard a growl erupt from within him. He closed his eyes and clenched his paws at his sides. When he opened them again, his eyes bled in crimson and roared. It was then she saw the hard primordial side of the feared Alaric. He snarled.

"His name is not Hardulph." He warned her. "For centuries, he has waited for you to come and hid in the shadows, but I am the one who took you. I am the one who found you first."

"I was not yours to take." She bit. "Was I?"

He growled. "Worgen is the most powerful wolf kingdom…"

Ashina's heart raced because Alaric pressed toward her anyway. She backed up and prepared herself to run from him.

"It will stay that way, white wolf. You **will** stay with me." He warned her. "Love and power are two different things…"

"You just want power." She moaned.

He stepped closer. "You will come back with me. I am your king. I have bitten and mated you. I have chosen you as mine."

Ashina growled at him, her hackles standing up from her tail to her thick neck. "You do not get to control my life."

Alaric growled. "You will get to live, which the queens of old did not get to do. We will raise our offspring. Our powers will keep my kingdom the most powerful..."

Ashina held her breath and seethed when he said that. "I will not."

"You killing the seers have done me a great service, white wolf. I have all the power now without them bending meeee..." He laughed. "For ages, they bent my forefathers too. You have broken that and freed me."

His snarl was deep and euphoric. "I am freeeeee." He bellowed. "I knew when the moon called me to you, that you would be the one to free me. And you have. You are my beautiful mate."

He rose and breathed the forest air in like he sucked the soul of the world inside him, and the trees bent toward him. "You will stay at the mountain."

Ashina felt the ground vibrate beneath her as a crack opened at her paws. She turned to lunge away from him to run. He bent into the air as the wind pressed him atop her. He lunged a long arm out, his strength empowered. He yanked her body against him. He lunged atop her and pushed her down on the forest floor. He forced her on her back and held her there, his long legs pushed into hers.

He breathed into her snout. "You are mine. All of you." He licked the side of her snout. "Our offspring will be powerful and beautiful. And now that I have you in your primordial form..."

Ashina squirmed and growled in his face, but it was no use.

Alaric breathed her in again, his muscles flexed on top of her. "I will taste you, and you will continue being my mate and drawn to me and me alone..."

He lunged into her shoulder. He bit into her, his whole wolf form hard, and flexed against her. Ashina roared in his face, writhing back into her human form. He raised off her and closed his eyes, letting her crawl away from him. He breathed her blood in his snout, his chest heaving. Then he turned to glare at her, his loins inflamed.

"I feel your strength in my blood. It is so powerful. It makes me ache." He moaned. "Our power together and our offspring will rule the world..."

Ashina bent her bloody shoulder into herself and hollered in pain, the blood drizzling down her arm. He bent down and circled her, his wolf form engulfing her size. Ashina twisted to keep her eyes on him, digging her elbows into the dirt. She bent

her arm as he raised to her again, and the trees lashed out at
Alaric.

The branches became like arms as Ashina watched him catapult back away from her in the darkness. She stood up and ran.
Alaric roared after her, plunging back through the branches and
snapping them like twigs. The wood darted around him like the
woods had sprouted arrows.

Ashina's desperate breathing lit her chest on fire. She lunged
away from his claws downhill and jumped into an abyss to get
away from him. Alaric followed her over the cliff, his long white
arm stretching to grab her. His mouth was open and snarling
retribution as they fell together, and his roar vibrated off the
cavern walls.

Ashina screamed while falling, her anger eating her up inside.
Just as she thought Alaric would grab her and they would fall
into the rapids together, a black shadow loomed at her face. She
froze midair, the sudden lurch of her body making her head
spin. She found herself suspended in the air against the cliffs.
She watched Alaric continue falling into the gorge toward the
raging rapids, even as wolfsbane arrows plunged into his chest
and shoulders.

Ashina twisted in the arms of this wolf, her heart freezing as Hardulph pulled her up on his shoulder. He pulled her up and sneered, but his eyes were firm and glistened. He watched Alaric fall and growled at him as he fell. He had one strong arm and claws planked into the rock wall, and his powerful legs pivoted him safely with her in his arms.

He flung her over his shoulder and climbed back up, a paw gripping her backside. "I said meet at the Western Mountain." He breathed. His voice gave her chills, even as relief flooded her. "This is headed south, white wolf."

Ashina froze atop his massive shoulder and hung on, even as her arm ached and she bled down his powerful backside. He lunged up with her, his broad wolf form pulling her to safety. When he reached the top, Ashina met the faces of female wolves. They had fired upon Alaric as they were falling.

The three female wolves had unbridled passion. Their eyes glowed amber, and their bodies were fully adorned with black armor. They bowed and smiled. They were just as intimidating to look upon as Hardulph, and their eyes breathed fierceness but with a solitude of hope.

"I am Kira, your majesty." One of them smiled, pulling her long blonde hair in a ponytail down her back. The other two bowed and smiled. "I am chosen as your protector for Cayden. It is good to meet you."

Ashina questioned. "What..."

Another one spoke up and sighed, twisting her brown hair over her shoulder. "Considering the circumstances..." She rolled back to the horses and jumped on. "We must go. Alaric's army is moving to meet us for war."

Ashina froze at the sight of them, acknowledging a looming shadow behind her. Hardulph raised tall, cracked his neck, and flexed his pecs and forearms. Ashina recognized those fervent golden eyes of his. He was the ancient primordial.

As he reared up, Randon lunged at him from the cliff wall as his wolf. He pressed himself between Hardulph and Ashina. He growled at them, flexing his body, his eyes golden and enraged.

"You will not take her." Randon scowled. He bent down to attack them as the women aimed their bows and arrows.

Ashina yelled. "No! Do not hurt him. He is my commander!"

Hardulph perked his ears atop his head and nodded to the women. They lowered their bows and Kira rolled her eyes.

Hardulph inspected Randon and huffed. "An expert tracker, too, I see. Impressive to come all this way to track our queen. I did smell you twenty miles back."

Randon growled. "What the hell do you think you are doing, Hardulph?! She just escaped from Alaric, and now you take her?" He rose to Hardulph's snout, even as the women eyed him. "She will not be imprisoned again."

Kira belted out. "Two primordial males. Never thought I would see the day."

Hardulph agreed with Randon. "Come and see for yourself brave wolf. If I offend you in any way with your queen, you can kill me. I will free her, but we are short on time."

Hardulph turned back into a human, like a mighty wind had bred him. Ashina stepped back from his grandeur, even in his human form. His armor was as intimidating as his strong face and black beard.

Randon bent to glare at the women and raised his wolf brows in confusion. His ears perked atop his broad head. "Female wolves."

Hardulph pulled at his gauntlets and pressed into them, pointing toward their horses. "The questions can wait. We must go, white wolf."

Randon turned to his human form as the women glared at him, not moving. Finally, Kira rolled her eyes. "Fine! He can ride with me."

Randon smirked at her and lunged on behind her, clasping into her waist. Kira sighed against his back. "Just because you are riding with me does not mean you can command my horse."

Randon laughed at her. "Oh, how I have missed you wolves." His face lit up.

Hardulph jumped on his stallion and lunged a long arm down to Ashina. She let him pull her on the horse behind him, and they raced out of the wilderness west into the mountains. She pressed her head into his back and closed her eyes. She gripped her arms tight around his midsection and held on for dear life.

Hardulph took a deep breath when she squeezed him and craned his head to stare at her from the side. She raised to look at him, her eyes wide, her long braid disheveled around her head. He clenched his jaw as his eyes roamed her face. His beard accentuated his strong jawline.

"I have you." He clasped her hands in his palm. They lunged off the plateau out of the forest to the snowy mountains. As they trotted off at a desperate pace, Hardulph whispered. "Finally."

Alaric writhed into the freezing waters of the rapids and waterfalls encompassing his southern border. He yanked the arrows out of his chest and shoulders in the water. He got shot multiple times. He rose from the water in his human form and took a deep breath. He let the current pull him into a shoreline headed east to his mountain. The current pulled him further away from Ashina. He growled in rage as he pulled himself up, his long blonde hair spilling around his shoulders to the dirt.

"*You don't love me...*" He heard her say. He bellowed out as he climbed to the shore. "I need you for my kingdom." He pained inside. "I need you to give me an heir..."

He raised his eyes to his mountain Ashina destroyed, his eyes still crimson. He stood upright, cracked his neck, and breathed deep, his body armor soaked. He bent his head back and raised his arms out either side as a great wind blew him up through the forest as if he flew. He already had seer blood in his veins, but this was more powerful.

He commanded the wind and woods. He had all the power now that Ashina had killed the seers, which he could never do.

The seers had given specific bloodlines of wolves these powers in ancient times. He had done the right thing by taking Ashina there to meet them. He knew her temper would get the best of her, which was one of the things he loved about her.

She was defiant. It turned him on. It was way past time that his throne had a defiant queen. She was perfect.

Now Cayden had her. That was a problem. Cayden was the original primordial and the most powerful, but he did not have Alaric's power. Ashina would be the only one who could stifle him now. Ashina belonged to him. He had mated her and chosen her for him. He still wanted her. That would never go away.

Alaric was no different from his wolves. Once they had found their mates, they were loyal to them to death. That would never change.

Alaric met Rieka on the battlefield just moments before dawn. He walked through his wolves, now dry, his wounds healed fast. He stiffened his spine and raised his head as they admired his glory. His long blonde hair rolled down to his buttocks in ribbons of curls. He pressed through them into the rising sun and breathed deeply as their king.

He had summoned three hundred thousand, more than enough to destroy Cayden's wolves. But Cayden was not here to wage a war. He had come to avert Alaric away from Ashina, and it worked. Now he had her.

Alaric's eyes were on fire as he slithered to the front lines. Before him, the plain roared in black wolves from Cayden. Two hundred thousand of them. They snarled in retribution and loathing hate upon his wolves. These wolves were big and fierce. Cayden's wolves were precision war instruments.

It was then Alaric met them with the force of his commanding power, and the earth opened to swallow them whole into chasms of pain. A raging wind opened from his mountain and belted onto the plain, and the ground cracked before the armies. The chasm writhed the earth and rolled like thunder as Cayden's wolves fell into the abyss.

His heart was on Ashina as he destroyed them. His heart writhed in pain, and he missed her. His loins burned and ached for her still. He would not live without her. She belonged to him and him alone.

He would sacrifice no more of his wolves for this war. He was bringing war to the world with his unbridled power now. Cayden was next. Alaric would burn the whole world to get her back. Ashina had freed him, and there was no going back.

Chapter 22
The Deep City of the Falls

Serimi led his army into the deep wilderness along the rolling plateaus, following Kylo and his wolves. They pulled their horses over ravines and through caverns bled out by the raging river waters. Behind him, Galin pulled his horse and craned his head to acknowledge wolves and human warriors tracking deeper. The king and Louve stayed back with the survivors of his army and two hundred wolves. They would repair and re-fortify the city wall Alaric had demolished.

To make matters worse for them, word had gotten back by other packs of wolves coming in that Ashina had taken down Alaric's Mountain and killed the seers. Cayden had come to the border to fight against Alaric. But something happened because the battle was swift, and every wolf of Cayden died. Alaric was now enraged at Cayden. Serimi and the others knew that meant Cayden had taken her.

Brovina sat atop her horse as Galin pulled her behind him, his horse lingering aside hers. Serimi was an expert tracker like Galin, and they spread out at the falls where Alaric had found Ashina. The wolf prints from Ashina, Alaric, and Randon sunk at the shoreline, and Serimi bent upon his knees to stare at them.

Behind him for miles, his army of thousands filtered through the forest. They were searching for the lost city of Tala's wolves. They trickled through the forest, rolling plateaus, and along the river, their eyes ever watchful. Galin loomed over the paw prints Serimi was inspecting and huffed.

He pulled his horse and turned the army and wolves northeast from the lagoon. Tala had sent Ashina to these falls to hide, but Alaric had already found her. Serimi figured Alaric had tracked her for a day at least before making himself known to her. Ashina would not have had a good chance to run from him as she had not come into her full primordial at that time.

He pulled the wolves and men another six hours northeast until they came upon a rising gorge where the raging river fell into a chasm. The chasm was a mountain that looked like it had caved in upon itself. But it hadn't. Brovina lingered behind them on her horse and sighed as they stood there.

"This is it." She slid down and walked to the edge, her eyes taking in the roaring falls plummeting miles into a dark ravine.

Rainbows flittered within the falls, and the spray roamed high into the air around them, dousing their faces with coolness and a reprieve. Serimi glared down at it, noticing circular rock formations jutted out. The falls raged over them and roared in the air, the echo from their power shaking the ground.

"There is a path..." Galin tied his horse up as the others followed.

They ventured down the wide path along the ravine, following it until it disappeared into a tunnel under the falls. They were wet but found themselves in an abyss of another cavern, and Serimi widened his eyes at its breadth.

"This is a throne room." He turned his eyes to the falls spilling before their eyes on the vast expanse of opened wall to the elements.

They meandered around the room, the luminescent light from the falls cascading ribbons of shadows upon them and lighting up the space. Galin slithered toward the back of this room and froze as steps loomed into the darkness. But Serimi turned back to the wall and noticed a circular pivot of stone built into the floor.

"Help me turn this."

Galin and Kylo joined him, pressing against the stone pivots until it turned. And then the light burst in. As glory filled the truth of this place, they shivered in the aura of this terror. The ceiling craned open, and light burst upon the throne. The falls stopped flowing, and the river diverted.

The throne steps rose high, and rows of carved stone seats adorned the platform at the top. Pillars carved from the stone showed wolves and men dancing upon them. As magnificent as the throne was, Serimi turned to the falls that stopped flowing at their faces. Kylo's eyes lit up bright in the dark.

The roaring water in the chasm stopped flowing, but the formations carved into the mountain jutted out and became apparent to the army. The formations were carved with wolves holding broad swords. Aside from them were human warriors, and kings of ancient times. The wolves were primordials, brave and vicious, and crowns sat upon their broad heads. They were carved into the rocks like they were brothers.

The wall behind the throne room suddenly burst alive with the roaring falls, and the river flowed along the altar on both sides underneath the rock in a deep ravine. It spilled from underneath the throne room and catapulted across the cavernous mountain space. The wolves of this city engineered it so the falls split and moved as needed. It was brilliant and frightening.

Brovina stood amidst the wolves and men, their faces gawking at this ancient wolf city that had been a hidden gem. "This, gentlemen and wolves, is Tala's city of the falls."

Tunnels and passageways carved into this massive mountain cavernous space flowed to paths and stone railings into the abyss below them. There were windows and doors. There were pathways and ancient gardens. The ravine filled the space of this world in this vast wilderness, and they were but dots upon its splendor and magnitude.

They turned as the light beamed bright behind them and froze at the sight of it. The ceiling craned open and pivoted wide as bursts of sunbeams lit up the great expanse of the cavern. The darkness fled away as the massive power of this space became apparent.

The stone seat in the middle of the throne was the biggest and carved with an emblem. It was similar to Ashina's flaming tree tattoo on her back. Serimi took a deep breath. The light hit the cavern behind the chairs, and carvings showed a hunter's moon every thousand years. The moon bled in red as the wall lit up with mother of pearl and rubies.

"This is not just any city, Brovina..." Serimi blurted out, meeting Galin's gawking gaze.

"No, it is not..." Brovina smiled. "This is the ancient city of the primordials. Where they ruled for centuries before the mountain took them..."

The steps to the throne rose into the ceiling and showed human warriors warring alongside the wolves. They were warring alongside one another because they were brother warriors. They were fighting an evil power from the mountain that rose upon them in the west.

The mountain loomed upon the lands, and darkness spilled from it. From that darkness came a treacherous king wreaking havoc in the lands. They craned their necks to see it, their faces frozen in fear. The king was ancient and wise. He was sinister and malicious.

"That is not Alaric's Mountain," Serimi noted, chills darting up his spine.

Brovina sighed. "No..." She gazed up with them. "That is Cayden."

Galin moaned. "Shit!"

They continued to gaze upon the carved-out war scene above them, their faces drained of color and their hearts empty of hope.

Kylo gasped. "This whole time, we thought it was Alaric's Mountain…"

Galin turned to them and shook his head. "Let's go get our queen…"

Serimi seethed. "Ashina envisioned a world where her city here was alive and thriving still. It is because of Tala she has this vision."

Silence overtook them.

"We cannot let the white wolf queen down." Serimi's face was firm, like his courage. "We must ride upon Cayden."

Brovina sighed.

Galin joined her, his eyes still craning upon the ceiling.

"We must ready this city for the white wolf queen," Serimi determined.

Chapter 23
The Dawning of Alaric's Rage

The world burned around the mountain. It did not matter that Ashina destroyed part of it or killed his seers. Alaric was endowed with the power of the mountain within him now, and nothing would stop him. He would remain the most vicious wolf king in the world forever. It was Ashina's fault for leaving him.

He was content to let her live and have his offspring. After all, she did bring him much pleasure in the bed. He would get her back, and she would fulfill her duties to him and the kingdom, and he would continue to be a mighty power.

Alaric had divided one hundred thousand wolves and split them up to go in all directions hunting humans, especially women. Only now, he began taking the men too. He took them all and had his armies bring them into his mountain kingdom. He needed more bladesmiths. He needed more servants and cooks.

He needed more women for his wolves. He would continue building his glorious blood-filled empire, and Ashina would grovel back to his power. She would because she knew she belonged to him and no other. She belonged to his loins and his aching heart.

Alaric prepared to march upon Cayden in the coming weeks. He would rip Ashina from Cayden's arms and his heart. Alaric's army numbered in the hundreds of thousands. He destroyed Cayden's two hundred thousand with his power. Any human warlord coming to get her would be met with swift retribution by him.

Alaric sat aside Rieka on horseback, his eyes crimson. His human form was still magnificent to look upon. He craned his neck on the rolling plateau and watched his wolves drag humans in. They could not fight back. They were weak beings. They had no powers or strengths and would work for breeding. Since the lands had been bankrupt of female wolves for centuries, he had no choice.

Rieka turned his head to his king and huffed, a smile across his tattooed face. "Beautiful!"

Alaric smiled at him, nodding. "Power is beauty."

They loomed over the plains as human screams and hollers echoed over the mountain. Fires loomed in the distance as the skies filled with black ragelike fingers prodding a cavern of deep despairs.

Chapter 24
The King Saves

They rode west for three days and rested in a cave on a snow-covered mountain. The snow blasted in at them sideways as Hardulph led them inside a small cavern with the horses. Straw and grain were already in the cave for them, and it became apparent this wolf king had prepared for this journey.

They did not talk while fleeing Alaric. The women lunged aside their king, ever watchful as Ashina pressed into his back on horseback. Randon let Kira lead him, his eyes watchful upon them and their mannerisms. They were no threat to his queen and he began questioning everything.

As they lit a fire and pulled apples and grains out to eat, Ashina stood staring at the entrance blasted in white. It was a whiteout as the roaring wind battered the cave. Randon met the women at the fire, and she turned to see he was helping them with the horses.

Hardulph pressed a thick fur cloak on Ashina's shoulders, and she turned to face him. "It is cold. Even wolves as strong as you get cold."

She stared into his eyes, and he met her there. They stood before the opening as the world blasted white around them, and Ashina breathed him in. His strong jawline accentuated his black beard and his eyes screamed his spirit was virtuous.

"What is your real name? I know it is not Hardulph."

He bent away from her, holding his breath. "How did you know."

Ashina smiled at him, her insides tingling still. "What is it."

He shook his face at her. "I am Cayden." He whispered. "I am the first primordial bred of seer lineage." His stare was powerful and firm.

Ashina smiled at him, acknowledging his secret. "You are very old and powerful."

He huffed at her face. "I am old."

"Your kingdom..."

"Everything told about me and my kingdom is lies. Alaric's throne always bred lies to keep the lands in fear."

She found him lingering into her face, his eyes roving over her. She had seen that look before from Alaric. Her mind went back to him, and her heart filled with rage. She thrust that from her mind and sighed, turning to the fire. Hardulph watched her roam away from him, and he smiled at her.

"I am hungry." She turned away from him and joined Randon and the other wolves by the fire.

Kira smiled as Ashina sat down next to her and Randon. She handed her a plate of white fish, roasted carrots, and apples, along with a chunk of rye bread. Ashina dug in, famished.

"My queen, tell us of your childhood," Kira asked her, and the other two wolves rose from their plates to join in the conversation. Randon stopped eating to listen, his eyes craning from them to Hardulph at the entrance.

"My guardian raised me in Hildenia, a beautiful river village northeast of Worgen."

"Ah. So close to that evil mountain! No wonder Alaric tracked you so quickly." Kira smirked and poured hot tea for her in a bone cup.

She turned her glare to Randon and sighed. "I guess you would like some?"

Randon smiled at her. She sighed and poured him some and their eyes met. Ashina smiled at them.

Ashina sipped the tea. "I love this tea. Makes me miss my village."

The women watched her drink it as Ashina narrowed her brows. "You know I have never seen other female wolves besides my guardian. Are there many at Cayden?"

Randon huffed. "What happened to you all to have fled these lands?" He swallowed.

Hardulph turned his head to stare at them from the darkness, listening. He stared at Ashina for endless moments and then turned his eyes back to the cold, keeping watch.

Kira glared at the other two and cleared her throat. "Alaric's father began hunting us to breed with his wolves. He succeeded for many years, and he bred a formidable army. They outnumbered us. So, we fled, and Cayden took us and protected us. Since then, Alaric's realm has taken poor humans to breed, but they are not purebloods."

Randon growled. "Damnit."

Kira nodded. "There are many of us, yes. We are not like humans and interbreed. We breed with our wolf mates, and the humans breed with their kind. All us female wolves learn to fight, and some fight in the army."

Ashina gasped. "Oh. You have humans there?"

The women laughed at her. "Yes, we have whole villages and mountains filled with them west of us behind the valleys. You will see! They are beautiful. I enjoy shopping there on Sundays."

The other wolves spoke up. "Yes, I like the cobblers. My husband and I often go there for a meal."

Ashina dropped her mouth and narrowed her brows. "You intermingle with them? And live peacefully?"

Kira smiled. "Yes, we have done this for many years now, thanks to our king."

Ashina bit her tongue and turned her stare toward Hardulph, but he was already looking at her.

"I have heard things..." Randon whispered to Kira.

Kira sighed. "Yes. Alaric's wicked father twisted the kingdom's stories. You have my word. Cayden is virtuous. You will see."

Randon smiled at her and turned his stare to Ashina, but she knew what he was thinking because his eyes sparkled with hope.

"What of the deep city of the falls?" He asked.

Hardulph lunged his glare toward him, his eyes narrowed.

Kira widened her eyes. "The ancient wolf city? That was abandoned centuries ago because of Alaric's father and the seers of his mountain. He drove the ancient wolves out of that mountain."

"To Cayden?" Ashina gawked.

"Yes. The lands fell to darkness as Worgen outnumbered us all, and with his seers, it left us powerless." Kira nodded.

"Wow." As Randon conversed with the the wolves, Ashina sipped her hot tea.

She leaned against the rock wall, stretched her legs, and warmed them by the fire. She found herself questioning things. She lunged up and marched back over to Hardulph. He watched her come to him, his face soft at her. His eyes lit up in the dark.

"What are you doing?" She demanded.

"What do you think I am doing."

"I do not know, wolf king." She questioned him.

He stared into her eyes. "I think you know what I am doing." He whispered in her face.

"I called you in that mountain to keep you from the seers. They have bent fate to their will for centuries. That is why Worgen has been so powerful. That is why Alaric found you first."

"You did."

"And you got out, the first queen to ever escape that wretched mountain because you experienced a painful event there and tapped your primordial."

She bent back as he said that, but he smiled. "I see it in your eyes, just as you saw it in my eyes at Serkily."

"You saved me from the fall." Ashina smiled.

"I saved you from Alaric sinking his claws into you further." He sighed. "He has bitten you numerous times, and it continues to draw you to him. I can smell his bite upon you still. It will take time to heal from the trauma he has inflicted upon you."

Ashina reached up and felt her shoulder. It had healed but was still sore. "And you?"

He froze.

"Have you taken a mate in all these years?"

He sighed, craning his eyes to the cavern ceiling and then back down to face her. His boldness was powerful. "I have never taken a mate."

Ashina sighed inside and watched his eyes.

He glared into hers. "I have been and always will be the one destined for the only primordial white wolf queen. You."

"You will not force me." Ashina bit at him, her eyes glowing golden.

His face lit up. "No, I will not. You shall live, rest, and enjoy life until you are ready for me."

"What if I am never ready."

"Then you will still be free." He expressed.

He looked at Randon and smiled, noting they enjoyed their fireside chats. "Besides, he is a powerful guardian for you. I would hate to get on his bad side."

Then he gazed lovingly into her face and sighed. "You will be my wife, Ashina. You will not be just a mate, not to me. You will be my wife, my equal. You shall stand by my side, and in time, we shall strive to be best friends."

She swallowed. "Oh." She clenched her face, her eyes wide. She roved her eyes over his face and a calmness kissed her inside.

"I am patient." He leaned into her face and whispered. "...white wolf. You do not bend unless you want to." He turned to the fire to eat.

She watched him march to the fire, his long black hair braided sloppy down his back. He plopped down beside Randon and talked to him. She followed him, joining them for more tea. She watched his mannerisms and the way he spoke to everyone. He seemed easy to talk to. She was drawn to him, and it refreshed her.

Ashina caught him staring at her more throughout the evening, his face soft every time she spoke. After Hardulph had eaten, he walked back to the opening and glared out. He was ever watchful, ever protective.

He was giving Ashina space to get to know everyone and time to rest. She craned to stare at him again, and Kira caught her. She prodded Ashina's elbow and smiled at her face, and Ashina laughed at her. The wolves had a strong camaraderie. It made Ashina miss Tala even more. Even Randon seemed to have found his element among them. Her heart soared.

"He is a fierce protector, my queen. He is a noble king. You will see." She smiled and turned to press against the stone to sleep by the fire.

"I hope so," Ashina whispered.

"He does what is right. You will see."

As Ashina turned to sleep, Hardulph leaned against the rock wall. His black furs encompassed his broad frame. He stared at her from the darkness and clenched his face, his eyes relieved. Ashina knew his eyes watched her, but she put what she was thinking far from her mind.

She was going to Cayden anyway. He called her from inside that mountain, his voice a resounding echo through her soul.

He saved her from the fall. She decided not tell them what she had done in Worgen. She would bring his kingdom down too, if she had to.

She did not let him take her for nothing. Ashina had a way of doing things that scared Tala at times. Everything she did burst from a deep-rooted pit inside her that roared. This perseverance had been bred into her and would never go away.

Hardulph was not without powers. When she thought these things, he craned his eyes to her again. Then he turned to the raging snowstorm and the brutal wind, his golden eyes glorifying his magnificent splendor.

Chapter 25
The Tides of Fate

The black plains glittered in obsidian as a haze drenched the sky toward the mountain kingdom. Ashina was edgy on the back of the horse behind Cayden. That was his name. He was the original primordial, ancient, and powerful.

He had kept a gentle hand atop hers on the way as she wrapped her arms around him. Her eyes craned around this dark land, her heart thumping into his back. They rode ten miles through it until the sun burst upon them, and black pillars chased the skies on a rolling plain. She peered around Cayden, the sun lighting on her face, and gawked.

She gawked at Randon too, for Kira was now riding behind him. They gawked together at this city for endless moments before Kira prodded him to move on. She noticed Randon liked her and they seemed to be well-rounded friends already. Ashina could not help herself but smile at them.

The blackness ended on a hill, and a mountain valley spilled onto plains that rolled into forests. The road opened to an expansive cobblestone through the valley. It was a magnificent city as wide as the mountain. The mountain rose behind it into the clouds, and she could not see the snowy tip.

The walls were black and deep and tall as the plateau. A keep rose in the center with a forebuilding higher than the city. Watchtowers adorned every curtain wall, and the round mural towers kissed the city with shadows to the plains. The city's defenses were magnificent and terrifying, and Ashina gripped Cayden's stomach.

He gasped and turned to look at her. "You have a ferocious grip." He smiled at her.

"Sorry." Ashina released her grip but then laughed.

"Grip me all you want." He laughed.

Another plain rose past the city's defenses to the mountain, and smoke from cooking fires rose with them. A village sprawled atop that plain, and spread out on a ridge where a road twisted from the city. To the right was an arsenal tower at the end it. The black rock plummeted into an abyss. Steam rose and filled that side in a white haze, and Ashina realized there were raging falls.

Her back grew rigid, and her eyes were wide as they neared the watch tower and the gatehouse. A river flowed under the drawbridge, and it reminded her of Serkily. Her gut panged again, even as they rode over the drawbridge as wide as three roads. The walls loomed over her, and a flowering white vine cascaded up the stone. The smell of honeysuckle calmed her nerves.

Atop the guard house and watch towers, wolves stood in full body armor watching them. They strode atop the walls and glared down, hopeful. They raised their snouts and howled into the air. Their roars echoed over the plain. Their bellowing calls beckoned Randon to gaze at their ferociousness as his eyes raged golden.

Cayden led them through the city streets to the keep. Ashina peered around to see the wolf forms of Cayden's kingdom. There were women with their wolf children. There were male wolves moving boxes of supplies. They were all in their wolf forms and splendid and powerful. They were talking in the streets and dining at restaurants, the lingering aromas of fresh meats filling their taste buds.

The city came to a freezing halt as Cayden rode in, and a horn sounded from the top of the watchtower. It was deep, bellowed, and welcomed them. It pierced the howling calls of the wolves on the towers. Their king was home with his queen. Behind them, the streets filled behind them with wolves of all colors to the gates. They were strong and Ashina sensed their curiosity.

Randon froze on the horse, Kira clinging tight to him, and he held his breath. "Holy shit." He moaned.

When they stopped at the keep, Cayden gently tugged at her arm, and she slid off. She narrowed her brows and turned to the wolves. The street filled to the gates, and Cayden watched them as he stood behind her. They came and bowed. They came and put their snouts to the ground and roared solid hums in reverence of her.

Randon slid off the horse and stood aside from Kira. She took his hand in her own and smiled up at him. He gazed into her eyes and swallowed. "Welcome to Cayden."

Chills darted up Ashina's arms as her eyes simmered golden at them. Cayden loomed behind her and bent his lips to her ear. "Welcome home, my queen." She leaned into his lips and smiled as a fire burned from the tips of her toes to her soul.

Then he took her hand and pulled her into the keep. Light glistened in eternal glory in streams from rectangular windows rising to the ceilings. Cayden led her hand in hand, and he gazed upon her as she craned her eyes and neck to this throne room. He admired her, and the whole court of wolves saw it. The isle was long, and all along the pillars stood wolves. They bowed their snouts to her as she entered.

She could not count the number of them. Her eyes flew to the end of this articulate place, where ten wolves stood on the throne, waiting for her. They were black, and there were only two grays. Cayden pulled her to his throne, his face relieved, and it showed as his eyes sparkled at her.

"Our court, my queen. The wisest wolves in the world. The wolves of the ancient city of the falls..."

Ashina froze as she gazed upon them, chills darting up her cheeks. They perked their ears straight up to acknowledge her as the white wolf primordial, and she heard low rolling moans from their breaths. Their eyes sparkled back at her as their regal stances overshadowed the pillars adorning this space.

Ashina found herself tearing up. "Oh." She gasped.

Cayden pulled her hand to his lips and kissed it as his eyes met hers. He bowed on one knee to her in front of the court and all the wolves. She swallowed as he sighed at her and met her eyes with fire in his. Her knees shook.

"You are my queen, Ashina." His voice was broken and powerful. "This is your home. Cayden has always been and will forever be your home." His eyes teared up.

He pressed a palm on his heart. "I have spent years seeking you. We have taken grave losses doing so. My heart is breathing alive again as you are here and safe. Finally!"

The court and wolves erupted in roaring hollers; their moans filled her ears like they did her heart. Cayden bowed his head to her while still clutching her hand.

Ashina's tears slipped down her face, and she turned to Randon, who smiled in awe. She craned her head to the court of wolves, who nodded at her, smiling. She craned her head to the massive room full of wolves standing, watching her, adoring her. She craned her eyes to Kira and the other two wolves, who were still in their human form but no less formidable. Their eyes drowned in hope and perseverance.

Cayden stood to face her again, his hand still clasped to hers, and his eyes devoured her face. "Take all the time you need to heal. I am going nowhere, I promise you. I have been and always will be here for you."

Ashina's heart skipped a beat as chills froze her spine.

"You have fought this whole time to pull me out of there."
She cried.

Her face met the light rays bursting on the court. Her heart breathed in this beauty. She pressed her palm against his face and dove into his eyes. Her hand clasped to him in a desperate hope. He wiped her tears with his fingers as he held her face.

"You have given me hope." Her voice broke as her tears fell.

They stood there holding one another's faces and stared into each other's eyes, the light shining upon them. She smiled through the tears at him. He dove into her smile and met hers with a powerful stare breathed in a formidable fire. They drenched each other in their fire as the light blasted down upon them, and the wolves filled the whole breadth of their world.

Cayden smiled into her as the world around them erupted in cheers. "You are my hope." His eyes lingered over her face.

That night, Kira led Ashina to a suite with views of the rolling valleys. Randon had a suite next to hers. The enticing aroma of food pulled her to a table as she entered. The steaming Peppermint tea calmed her nerves, and fresh flowers sprinkled the room in color. Honeycomb and breads spread out on a wooden platter. There was dried fish and roasted lamb.

There was a king-size bed and a cabinet with new clothing of her choosing, cloaks, and extra blankets. The room opened to a wall of double doors that led to an open balcony. Kira pointed to a side room and a stone basin filled with hot water, and she had a choice of oils or salts to put in it.

Ashina stared at all this warmth and coziness she never had and turned and hugged her. She found herself crying into Kira's arms. It took Kira by surprise at first, but she met her hugs with fierce arms and held her.

"You are home, my queen. You are safe now." Her eyes teared as she hugged her back.

Kira cleared her throat. "I am your protector, my queen. Rest. Eat. Take a bath, lay in your bed, and breathe. Just breathe and be."

As Kira turned to go, she bowed to her. Ashina watched her turn and close the double doors. Ashina turned to this beautiful room, fell to her knees, and cried against the bed. She cried aching sorrows from the pits of her soul until her bones ached. She cried until her eyes hurt and her knees were sore on the stone floor, but her heart felt lighter, and her shoulders lingered higher.

Kira pressed into the wall outside the suite as tears filled her face. She gripped her heart and sighed in relief. As she closed her eyes, she noticed a looming shadow upon her and turned to see Randon. He froze in the massive corridor, his eyes upon her, concerned.

"Hey, you okay?" He came to her.

Kira wiped her face and cleared her throat again. "I am now." She sniffled.

Randon turned to go to his suite, and then she called after him. "Hey, you hungry?"

Randon turned and nodded, his face lit up in a wide smile as she led him out. "I'm always hungry." He joked.

Kira grabbed his forearm and pulled him along with her. "Good! You can tell me more about yourself."

Randon let her pull him, his stomach hungry and his heart intrigued.

S ometime late in the night, Ashina awoke to vibrations. She walked to the balcony as her world lit up in flaming lanterns filling the night sky. She recognized the lamps burning for the dead, hundreds of thousands of them. Their losses had been significant just getting her out of Worgen.

Ashina stood there wrapped in a cozy wool robe, her eyes brimming in gold, and seethed inside. Many losses to get her. This whole time, all she needed was someone to tell her the truth. No one ever did, and she had been taken as a small child and plopped in a desolate, lonely village with poor humans. Tala knew what she was, but it was not enough.

The lamps soared into the heavens over the rolling plains, and Ashina's heart broke. She stood there in the silence of her space, her lips quivering, watching them float into the heavens. Something broke inside her. She turned away from the balcony, changed into trousers and a long tunic, and lunged out of the room.

Kira and Randon met her at the hall and led her outside past the road to the valley. The lake filled the bottom of the plain and glistened in the night, sparkling in the reflections of the lamps filling the sky. As they neared the shore, Ashina froze at Cayden's presence as he lit a lamp. His wolves surrounded him, and they split as they acknowledged her through the crowds.

He turned to her; his eyes lit up. His face was tired, but his passion for her was adamant in his smile. He held out a hand to her, and she took it. "Come, light one with me."

Ashina took the lamp he gave her as he handed her a stick with a burning flame eating it up. She lit it up, and they lifted it together. Their eyes met as they lifted it, and Ashina drowned in the strength he exuded on his face. She craned her eyes and watched it float into the sky, her heart bursting. Cayden stared at her.

"You have not rested," He moaned.

The roaming hillsides over the plain burst alive with flaming lanterns, their faces lit up like the night had burst into dawn.

Cayden's voice broke. "The humans grieve our loss with us."

They watched the night sky illuminate with pain. Cayden stood with her and watched the lanterns, their faces grieved and their hearts broken. Ashina sighed deeply, and Cayden gazed down at her.

"My heart is broken too." His eyes craned back into the sky.

Ashina stared up at him. He was intense, passionate, and empathetic. He breathed leadership and it bled into her soul.

Ashina lunged into his chest and hugged him tight, her head pressed under his neck. Cayden gasped at first but then enveloped her in his arms and closed his eyes atop her head. They stood there clutching into one another. Their faces lit up with the devastation of the losses, even as a fire lingered within them of each other. All around, the plain filled with wolves and their children upon the lake waters lighting lanterns.

Ashina heard him sigh, and it was deep and raced against her heart. She leaned up to stare at him and he met her eyes, his face grieving and clenched.

"So strong." She told him. "You are a strong king."

He swallowed when she said that and breathed on her lips. "You are strong." His eyes lingered over her face. He held his breath as she kissed his cheek.

He leaned into her kiss, wanting more, but waited. "You can heal here." He swallowed in her face. "You can find yourself here, white wolf."

She raised her chin and gazed upon the glorious sky lit up. "I already am, great wolf king."

His eyes were bright and filled with fire as she lowered her face to him. She smiled at him, and Cayden bent into the side of her face and kissed her temple softly. She closed her eyes and wrapped her arms tighter around his bulky chest. She let his strength empower her as if he were a haven of hope. Cayden clutched her tight against him, and breathed her in.

Randon stood beside Kira and watched Cayden and Ashina. He held his breath and smiled, even as Kira gazed at his face. "What is it?"

Randon cleared his throat, his voice breaking. "That is her true mate."

He pointed at them. "You see how he listens to her and talks to her. Look at how patient he is with her. He loves her already."

Kira smiled. "He has waited for his true love. He will never let her go."

Randon swallowed. "He will not need to worry about letting her go. They are made for one another."

Kira agreed with him. "Yes, that is what a true mate does."

They stood together, their hearts lighting up fervently as the night bled in flickering flames.

Chapter 26

The Ties that Bind

Ashina had gotten to rest for two more weeks. Cayden had been a relentless protector of her by giving her space and rest. Sometimes, during the days, he would linger up to her and start a conversation. She opened up to him more by the day, and he began to pursue her daily to walk and talk with her between kingdom affairs.

Yesterday evening, Cayden asked her out for dinner. She said yes. He always kissed her hand and bowed to her, and Ashina found herself shocked at his courting her. The wolves took what they wanted, and that was the way of it. But this king was wooing her. He wanted a connection, not a prize.

Ashina was not sleeping the best, but that part of her that died in Worgen was sparking back to life and calling her. She awoke before sunrise and ventured to the rolling plain. She looked forward to bending in the sun.

She wrapped her breasts tight and slipped into her form-fitting trousers. She marched down the street barefoot and breathed in the city of silence. She stood on the hill and the sun kissed her naked skin. She closed her eyes and rolled her head back as chills rushed up her arms.

She breathed in deep and stretched into the sun, her soul alive. A symphony of power sang to her heart as she rolled into the light. She flexed her muscles even as a shadow watched her from behind. When she opened her eyes again, Randon stood there with Kira, and the hill filled up with women and men wolves.

"Looks like it's not just us today, Ashina." Randon nodded at her.

She gazed at them to see if she had caused any devastation, but there was none. As they split apart, Cayden walked up to her, half-naked too. He was only wearing trousers, and barefoot. He was ripped in sculpting muscles and adorned with raging tattoos and sleeves up his arms. His eyes pressed upon her as he smiled, his black beard shining orange in the sun.

"We are of the light, too. We bend together. It keeps us strong." He stood with her and joined her in the sunrise. "It breathes hope."

"You will not control me." Ashina belted out.

Cayden turned away from her to face the sun and stretched his shoulders. "No one controls you, my queen."

He craned his head to her. "We stretch in the sun at dawn, daily. The stretching keeps us limber. Your power is your own."

"Really." She questioned.

Cayden smiled into her eyes. "Really."

Ashina met him and stood side by side with him, her eyes staring at his face. "Ready then?"

He nodded and flexed his arms. "Been ready."

Ashina closed her eyes and breathed again as the sunlight kissed her soul. Cayden followed her movements in rhythm as if she were leading him. Behind her, the wolves alongside Randon bent to her will. Her power raged a deep forge in them and pulled the warriors together.

A burning fire rose from a deep vat she had never explored before, but it had always been there, calling her, like nature calling her. She listened this time. As she realized what she was doing, she froze, her heart racing.

"What..." She swallowed.

Cayden met her there, and his face lit up in a smile, his whole body flexed. The wolves all around her followed her movements, stretching into the dawn. Their power filled her soul with a reckoning she could not describe. Her body shivered.

"The white wolf queen pulls her kingdoms together, both wolves and human. We sense your movements, your pain, your power. It makes us strong. It makes us formidable in battle."

Cayden raised his face to the dawn and breathed in deeply. "Your virtue is strong. You will lead our kingdom in this power. The wolves will never fail in battle because of it."

Ashina turned to the sun, her eyes glowing. She stood beside Cayden, his powerful body complimenting hers. His black hair braided down his back glistened in the sun, and her white hair was a stark contrast to his. But they blended as one and turned to bend into the sun again, their eyes upon one another.

"Beautiful white wolf." He smiled, enticing her.

"Yes, brave wolf king." She smiled back.

He did not take her hand or control her power. He let her lead. He gave her space to lead. Ashina let the whispers of his hope fill her heart in the sunlight, and she drowned in his love for her. She found herself smiling at his face and lingering her eyes over his sculpted body. As he noticed her gazing over him, he cleared his throat and stood up.

He told her, "I am taking you to a fine restaurant tonight. I hope you will like it."

"I am looking forward to it." She smiled.

Cayden laughed. "Good. I must go. I have matters to attend to. But I will call on you at dusk."

They stared at each other for a moment before he pressed into her. He leaned to kiss her cheek, but Ashina met his lips instead. His kiss was soft, and as he realized her lips touched his, he roared into her. As their lips touched, a fire lingered in them. She met him with open-mouthed kisses. He got lost in her for a moment, pulled away, and let his eyes explore her face.

He grazed a finger down her chin. "You are beautiful." He whispered against her lips.

He turned as the wolves watched them, and cleared his throat. He faced Randon and Kira, who smiled at him from ear to ear. Kira let out a giggle. "How romantic." She smiled, and it left Cayden's face blushing.

"Romantic indeed." Randon smiled down at Kira.

Cayden let a laugh slip out and then pointed at them. "You two are commanders and will work together. War comes still. Begin sparring tomorrow at dawn." He marched away from them, smiling. He craned his neck back to stare at Ashina again. She smiled and watched him go, her guts aching.

Kira froze and huffed, but Randon laughed in her face. "This is going to be so much fun kicking your ass."

Kira scoffed at him. "Will you bite me after you've kicked it?"

Randon widened his eyes, but Kira continued stretching. He gazed at her blue eyes, blonde hair glistening in the sun, and her glorious backside. "And if not, why not?" She questioned him, her eyes sparkling over his body.

"I'm beginning to remember the boldness of the female wolves now..." Randon gawked at her. "Damn." He laughed. "I like it."

As the sun began to set, Cayden knocked on Ashina's door. She met the most handsome black headed man she had ever seen. He wore trousers and a tunic and adorned his chest with a fancy leather breastplate. He had pulled his hair into a long ponytail, and his golden eyes accentuated his regalness.

He gazed upon her, and his mouth dropped when she answered the door. Ashina wore a burgundy gown that danced at her feet. She slipped into sandals and let her hair cascade down to her buttocks. She met a bouquet of roses as she answered the door, it took her by surprise. He pressed the flowers out to her.

"You are courting me." She smiled.

Cayden nodded. "Yes, I am."

She laughed and took the flowers, pushing them into a pitcher on the table. "Beautiful." She sighed at them.

"Beautiful indeed." He watched her.

"You have been courting me for weeks while giving me space." She confronted him.

"I have enjoyed talking to you during the times I could." His eyes lingered over her, and he held his breath.

He led her down the corridor, holding his arm out for her. "I hope you are hungry."

"I am hungry."

"I have been hungry for a long time." He smiled and held his arm out for her as he walked her to their horses.

They rode their horses on the plain past the lake to the village on the plateau. Ashina was excited because she had wanted to see this human village. These were stone houses, two and three stories. They were cottage-style homes. Families filled them, and roaring laughter echoed in the wide cobblestone street.

Sycamore trees lingered over them as big pots of colorful flowers adorned the homes.

He led her past a street of homes to another hill. A stone house built in it accentuated the coziness of the village street. The aromas of seared meats and vegetables made her stomach roar. The breadth of windows stretched from one side of the hill to the other. From outside, Ashina saw wolves and humans laughing and eating together. She thought she was going to cry.

Cayden held the door open for her, and Ashina gawked. "You have never been courted before." He told her.

"No, I haven't." She sighed, her eyes lighting upon this splendid place with tables everywhere.

As Cayden entered with her, the room grew silent. Ashina froze for a moment, and then someone cheered from the back. The cheering erupted again loudly, and whole restaurant was awash in praise. Humans and wolves cheered for them. Ashina's face turned red. Cayden smiled at them all, pulling her by her hand through the masses of them to the back of the restaurant. They were sat at a private table as flowering vines kissed them overhead.

The room was wide, and there was a dance floor, which some wolves and human couples already filled. Ashina was met with a human waiter, who bowed to her. She smiled at him while he told her the specials.

"Ladies first." He whispered.

"I will have the seared salmon." She stared at Cayden and held her breath.

They sat there for an hour and ate their food, and he asked her questions about herself. She asked him questions as if they had not spent days traveling and talking, getting to know one another, or kissing.

"You are a primordial from the ancient city of the falls, aren't you." Ashina confronted him.

Cayden nodded, meeting her eyes. "I am. And so is the council. We are all left of that wonderful city."

"What happened?"

"Alaric's father used the seers of his mountain to begin hunting us. All in all, twelve fell. Female wolves began fleeing the lands, as he desired to build an army of wolves to take the world."

Ashina gasped. "I am sorry."

He smiled at her. "No, I am sorry. We should have stayed and fought harder, you would not have been running your whole life."

"What happened to his father?"

"I killed him. He marched upon Cayden after the female wolves fled those lands. He wanted the wolves to breed his armies."

He paused, picking at his plate. "We never did go back after I killed him. I regret that. The humans who survived those wars became proficient in weapons; it kept them alive."

"You called me in that mountain. Even after Alaric bit me and we..."

She froze as it dawned on her. "You are my true mate. It was always you."

Cayden nodded. "Yes, Ashina." His eyes stared at her.

"Even though Alaric and I..."

He huffed. "Irrelevant. He is an illegitimate mate. Used seer power to woo you to him. Plus, you had wolfsbane in you, it made your mind weak."

"You broke through that and called me. You saved me." She whispered.

"You saved yourself. You pulled down that mountain and killed those seers..."

She gasped.

"I know you did, even though you did not want to tell me. Otherwise, you would not have escaped that mountain." He smiled at her. "I can sense things about you. I am not without powers. I am sorry you endured pain there."

They sat in silence and enjoyed the ambiance for endless moments.

Cayden stood up. "Will you dance with me?" He held out his hand.

She smiled, let him pull her up by her hand, and led her to the dance floor. His grip was gentle but firm. Cayden put his palm on her waist, and she clutched his hand as he pulled her into him. He pressed into her face, and they swayed and breathed into one another.

"When I came to the gates of Serkily and told you that you belong with me, that was true." He whispered.

Ashina swallowed, holding her breath.

"But you do not belong to me as if you are a prize, and I want you to see I understand the difference, Ashina." He encouraged her.

"I know you understand the difference." She roved her eyes up and down his face.

Ashina's heart beat wild as he lunged into her lips. She met his passion back. He wrapped his arms around her tight and kissed her soul, and she let him. She gripped his forearms and found herself caressing his face with her palm, stroking his beard.

"Will you marry me, white wolf?" He whispered. "I promise I will be a good husband to you. I will love you with all I am."

She kissed him with a ferocious hunger.

He smiled against her lips, breathing through her kiss. "Is this a yes?"

She nodded. "Yes."

He smiled into her face as they bent into one another in a swaying dance, their hearts gripping a passion of united fates. Ashina remembered when Alaric told her he would give her the world, but all he did was bite her and give her unending pain and sorrow. She pressed her head into Cayden's shoulder and closed her eyes as he enthralled her heart in a union of true mates.

"I've fallen for you." She swallowed, her heart racing.

Cayden smiled. "Good, this would never work otherwise."

Ashina raised from his chest and laughed, and Cayden joined her. They laughed together. He touched her face with his fingers, leaned into her lips again, and they smiled into each other's breaths.

When Cayden walked her back to her suite, he stopped at her door. He lifted her hand again and kissed it. His eyes never left hers, but Ashina was breathless. He lunged into her lips again, kissed her, and turned to go. He was still giving her space, and she reveled in his patience.

"Thank you." She called after him, her lips still tingling with his kiss.

He turned around and bowed to her. "I will see you tomorrow. Good night, my beautiful queen. I hope you rest."

She watched him go, his powerful backside taking deep strides up the massive hall. When he disappeared, Ashina shut the door and leaned against it. Her eyes froze over the room. He had brought in more flowers while she was gone, and the room lit up in rainbows of colors. The smell calmed her.

She wondered what Tala would say if she were alive. Ashina gripped her heart and eyed the door again, a sudden realization striking her. She was in love with Cayden. She truly loved him. He was her true mate. There was no denying the fact that her king was going to be her husband and best friend.

Chapter 27

An Endearing Hope

"I am the one who took you. I am the one who found you first."

Ashina tossed and turned in the bed until the sun was hot on her face and drenched in sweat. *"I am the one who took you. I am the one who found you first."*

She kept hearing Alaric's voice tell her that over and over as she stood cowering to him in the woods before they dove off the cliff. Alaric deliberately bit her in the forest and pursued her for power, not love. She heard his voice until her eyes flew open, and rage filled her stomach with dread.

"I hate you." She rose in the bed. "I hate that I let you bed me." Her heart filled with regret.

Ashina knew if she had stayed, she would be with his child. She rolled her eyes and huffed.

Alaric had not even tried to get to know her or woo her. He pushed himself upon her and expected her to follow his ambitions, which were evil and twisted like him. She shook her head as she thought of him. She was relieved she got out and killed the seers and that the mountain on that side collapsed.

She grabbed a biscuit and walked to the balcony to stare out. She did not wake at dawn this morning to bend into the sun. She did not sleep well last night. Every time she tried to close her eyes, Alaric loomed over her.

"I'm coming to get you." She heard him whisper. Alaric's voice was sharp like his tongue was a blade.

She dropped the biscuit. Her heart raced as Alaric called her again.

"Ashina. Ashina. Ashina."

"I am coming to burn that city to the ground, and you will come with me."

"I am coming to take you as my mate."

"You are mine, my beloved."

"Mineeeee."

Ashina gripped her heart, leaned into the railing, and blasted into the room to dress and find Cayden.

Cayden stood in his wolf form and gathered in the throne room with his council. The wolves marched back and forth talking and planning. Their roaring voices echoed past the high pillars of the magnificent splendor of the room.

"Alaric marches upon us now with the full power of that mountain." The old gray wolf sneered.

Cayden scoffed. "Let him come. He will meet the same fate as his father!"

The wolves agreed with him as the other old gray spoke up. "Alaric has proven to be as wicked as him, and the humans will suffer."

"They have been suffering all along. The only way to secure those lands and save their kind is to kill Alaric and bring down his kingdom and his wolves with him. I have only just gotten my queen from his grasp; we still have a lot of work to do." Cayden huffed.

"Yes, his wolves are treacherous." Another one spoke up.

Cayden agreed with them and let them continue.

One of the black members growled. "Yes, he has whole life-times of seer power at his call now! The only way to defeat him is to empower your mate to kill him."

Cayden sighed, thinking. "She is not ready for that yet. She is still healing from his abuse."

The old gray wolf eyed him. "You love her."

"I do love her."

"When is the wedding?" He asked.

Cayden shook his brawny wolf shoulders. "It is supposed to be decided today. As soon as possible."

Another black wolf chimed in, a female, her voice high and echoing. "You need to bond to her Cayden, so Ashina is empowered in her strength. Have you bitten her yet?"

Cayden shook his snout. "No." He roared, hoping. "I will not force her."

The doors blasted open, and Ashina barged in. Her hair was loose down her back, and she wore a loose tunic top and trousers. Her face was firm, and Cayden glared at her with wide wolf eyes because she had something on her mind. As she neared the court, she blurted out.

"I need you to break this bond Alaric has on me now. Today. As soon as possible."

The court gasped.

"What." Cayden gasped.

He stood there in his magnificent wolf form, perking his ears up higher at her even as a moan left his snout, excited.

"Alaric still calls to me. He is on his way. I need his bond on me broken today."

The wolves stood around Cayden, and Ashina froze at the expressions on their snouts. They were wide-eyed, and one of them cleared his throat. Cayden turned to them and then back to her. Ashina sighed and turned her head. As she turned back to Cayden, he lighted off the throne as if a wind pulled him to her. He turned back to his human form at her face and pressed his palm against her cheek.

He smiled into her eyes, but his face was hard. "I will kill that son of a bitch." His voice was firm.

"Please break this bond." She pleaded.

His face lit up with longing, and his cheeks were flushed. "I will break it, but you do not understand what you have just asked."

Ashina narrowed her brows. "Seers can break it..."

Cayden shook his head, still smiling, his whole face red. "No, Ashina. That is not how we break a bond."

She craned her eyes to the council, their eyes still wide and embarrassed. She met Cayden's eyes again but he was still smiling ear to ear as she took his palm from her face.

"What did I ask?" She questioned herself. "I do not understand."

Cayden pulled her with him to the doors. "You just asked me to mate you before the court." He smiled. "And you want it today. As soon as possible." He raised an eyebrow. "Happy to oblige." He laughed.

She met his face. "What." She rolled in laughter, her cheeks flushed.

Cayden nodded his head. "I must bite you to begin our bond, and then we become impassioned to mate. I know my limits, so we will be in my bed..."

"For a long while." He added, his eyes exploring her face.

"You have no self-control." She laughed, butterflies growing in her stomach.

"With you, never." He warned her. "But you must be ready. I will not live with regrets."

"No regrets." She whispered to him.

Cayden smiled. "You could at least wine and dine me first." He laughed out loud.

Ashina laughed with him, shaking her head even as he led her away from the embarrassed wolves gawking at her. She pressed her fingers to her forehead and dropped her head, but Cayden continued laughing with her. They laughed with one another.

"What do you want to do." He asked, his voice deep and excited. "Do you want to do this today because I am so damn ready…"

Ashina bent into his lips and dove into his face like a fire eating her up. He kissed her back and rolled his eyes over her. He pulled her in tight against him, and as they kissed, he moaned on her lips. "Is this a yes?"

Ashina breathed in his face, her eyes closed. "Yes."

He stopped kissing her and smiled, his whole face clenched in passion. "Let's go, beautiful. It's about damn time."

Ashina held her breath. She loved him. She laughed as he smiled into her face, the longing in his eyes cascading his passion into her loins.

As dawn crested the horizon and bled down the walls of his suite, they fell into one another. They fell into one another, and the fire they started burned so brightly it filled the space of their kingdom.

Cayden breathed in Ashina's mouth as she fingered his black beard. She touched his face and lips with her fingers, exploring his passion. He held his breath as her fingers raked down his neck. Her palms glided down to his forged chest and lingered on the hardness of his groin, and he sighed. He met her eyes, his face soft and beckoning. He kissed her like a gentle rain as his fingers grazed her face. He pressed against her on the wall, his pecs and forearms flexed. Their naked bodies rushed with anticipation, his loins hard and throbbing.

His forearms bulged in her palms as his golden eyes sparkled in her face. He kissed her with desperate passion, rolling his tongue in her mouth, and she met him there. He seethed at her beauty, gripping her waist to pull her to him. She grabbed his forearms and slid her hands down his muscular back, anxious.

Cayden rolled his fingers down her neck as his tongue rolled in her mouth and filled his palms with her breasts. He raked his hands down her stomach to her groin and then rolled them around her thighs. She straddled him as he lifted her by her bottom, gripping her tight. He dove inside her against the wall, lunging up and down, moaning in her open mouth.

She gripped his back to hold on, sinking her fingers into his tattoos. Their mouths craned open into one another. He pulled her off the wall and walked her to the bed. He pressed on top of her, his body a haven of strength against her. He thrust her hard and deep, slow, and rolling. He lived inside her until she bent her spine and arched her back, pushing her breasts against his chest.

Her whole body shook to her core, tense against him. She let him go, stretched her arms out, and grabbed the sheets to hold on. He lingered his eyes up and down her curvy sides, her navel thrusting in synch with his mighty strides.

He plunged hard inside her until he hit her soul and stretched out, moaning in her mouth with her open kisses. Ashina moaned and rolled her head back as he bent into her neck and shoulder, and kissed it with an open mouth. His breathing was hot on her skin as his fangs burst out.

He bit into her neck, rocking her back and forth. She yelled, grabbing the sheets in her palms as the bed rocked. He moaned into her blood, his eyes a fierce fire of gold at her power.

Ashina moaned in passion as he continued to grip her hips and thrust her hard with her in his mouth. She writhed in sweet surrender as he took his time with her. Her body was tense and inflamed at him. She rolled her head back further and grabbed his forearms hard in her palms, her moans filling the room.

He raised from her neck and pushed harder inside her, his breaths deep and bellowing. He belted out a roar from the pits of his guts, her blood filling his veins with her hope and power. She met his face, and they smiled at each other.

He breathed into her moaning mouth and whispered. "I love you. I love you." She continued to be eviscerated by his passion, inflaming her to her toes.

He cupped her breasts and sunk into them. He slid his palms up her sides until her whole body was in his arms, and he roared in her mouth again. Ashina met his kisses, but her mouth did not move because he shook her to her core. It rocked her soul. She raked her palms down his muscular back and gripped his buttocks in her palms. She pushed him inside her deeper.

He exploded inside her, yelling in her mouth, the vibration of his surrender filling her lungs. They breathed in one another, their loins on fire as their hearts beat together.

He closed his eyes and continued thrusting in slow motion, his seed draining from him. He pressed his lips against her neck as her heart beat hard against his. Ashina's legs shook against him, her body writhing under him. She wrapped her long arms around his back and pulled him tighter against her. He rested against her neck, exhausted and engorged with splendor.

He rolled his palms down her curvy sides and gripped her buttocks, pulling her into his groin harder. He continued spilling his seed and moaning while thrusting her slowly. He raised to her face, breathing wildly. She met his eyes and smiled at his face. Their eyes lit up with their amazement at one another.

"I love you." She whispered.

Cayden sighed, his voice exasperated. "You are the love of my life." He melted in her lips, his voice aching.

He rolled off her, pulled her against his chest, and closed his eyes. Ashina laid a long leg over his groin and sunk into him, breathing heavily. He bent his face into hers and she breathed on his lips again.

He clasped his strong arms around her body, kissed her lips, and met her face with longing. They smiled at each other's faces. Their eyes lighted upon one another as unbridled bliss forged an impenetrable bond within them. As he grew hard again, he lunged atop her and caressed her to the chasm of her soul, their aching moans filling the night with sweet surrenders.

Chapter 28
The Gathering

Serimi stood with Galin and Kylo on the street of the city of the falls. The wide cobblestone street was vast and rolled around the falls. The roaring beauty spilled into a vast ravine down high rock walls that encompassed it. They had been able to explore more of this hidden gem, and as the weeks went by, it became apparent this city's engineering was done so with meticulous design.

Serimi had split his army into patrols in all directions of the city, monitoring the wilderness. He needed to ensure the safety of the territory surrounding this kingdom. The warriors spaced out within fifty miles and began setting up outposts.

Brovia gripped her staff and sighed, even as vibrations of humans flocked in. The throne room where they had stood towered over the city, and even though the falls made it look sunken, it was a rolling plain. The mountain had collapsed in ancient days, and the wolves of old had carved their city within its towering walls. All around the mountain walls were flowing falls bursting from the deep river and a vat under the earth.

As the weeks passed, more and more humans came in, brought by wolves. They were scared and hungry, and many of them had small children. Alaric had his wolves terrorizing the humans and taking them, and the ones who escaped only did so with the help of the wolves.

Kylo growled, sighing heavily. "I will show them to the houses. They can rest." Kylo met them with his wolves and led them down the winding street.

Serimi narrowed his brows. "Well, this city has officially become the white wolf queen's new hope for wolves and humans."

"There is no going back now." Brovina smiled.

Galin crossed his arms. "Yes, and more will come. More come by the day."

"Have you received any word from Randon yet?" Serimi fretted.

Galin shook his head. "Not yet. But we know Alaric will have his wolves patrolling the southern border of his lands, so it is a matter of time before they find him or Randon runs into Hardulph."

Brovina huffed. "That is not his name."

The men glared at her.

"That is Cayden, the king. We often wondered why Conri was at the forefront for so many years. It is apparent Cayden did not want it known..." She gazed up and around this magnificent city, her eyes lighting upon the falls cascading rainbows around them. "There is something greater going on than we can see right now."

"Randon said he is one of the ancient primordials..." Galin questioned.

Brovina narrowed her gray brows. "This city has been lost and empty for centuries. I must find out why." She pondered. "Regardless, Ashina will come to a full city of her council, warriors, and wolves. Impressive."

Serimi huffed. "Well, while you do that, we are preparing to march upon Cayden to get Ashina back."

"We ride at dawn!" Galin confirmed.

"We will leave two hundred warriors here to keep order with one hundred wolves." Serimi nodded. "I have fifty men going back to Serkily for supplies and food. They will not go hungry but must garden and hunt soon."

Brovina swallowed. "We do not know the vastness of Cayden's wolves. No one has ever breached his kingdom. He just lost two hundred thousand to Alaric's power, so we must assume that was nothing compared to what he had in there. You risk much by going in, and we cannot risk losing you or Galin, Serimi." She warned.

"His wolves must be numbering in the hundreds of thousands. They outnumber us, and there are not enough seers to help with battle." She worried.

Serimi rubbed his fingers through his red beard and cleared his throat, smiling. "There is something Galin and I have been meaning to ask you to do for us."

She widened her eyes at them.

"The silver blades we use to chop up the wolves, can you make them repel harder and faster against our magnetized swords?"

Brovina thought a moment. "I can." She held her breath. "Why."

"If we find ourselves outnumbered, which we will, we will need to be able to pummel through the lines of wolves using the same blade." Serimi crossed his arms.

Brovina gasped. "Ingenious. I will do it today." She turned away from them. "Give me a few hours to craft the spell upon the silver."

Galin eyed Serimi, both fully armed and adorned in their battle armor. "I hope this plan of yours works."

Serimi huffed. "It is the only weapon we have been able to forge that takes them down. It must work. Our spiked armor only deters them for a moment. Our long swords only breach so far."

They stood there watching more humans flow into the city while the wolves led them on, their eyes craning to the solemn faces of pain.

Galin shook his head. "Either way, we have no choice now. Ashina will be delivered from the wolf kings. She is our queen."

Serimi nodded. "I hope Randon gets her back."

S erimi led his army west with Galin across the plains through the forest at dawn. He had around one hundred thousand. Thanks to Randon's efforts, the wolves began flocking in to serve the white wolf queen and rid the kingdoms of Alaric. The wolves who had bred with humans sent their wives and children far into the east to keep them away from Alaric's grasp. But many were still coming into the city.

They were a week south of Alaric's Mountain and hoped to avoid his wolves. But the mountain remained silent since he destroyed Cayden's wolves on the plain, and weeks already passed. Randon was tracking Ashina by himself. Serimi expected to receive a falcon with news any day now, but nothing had come, and he suspected Randon had been killed or taken also.

In the distance, the mountain loomed on the horizon, but it looked different. That meant a pivotal event also happened to Ashina, and Serimi worried what it had been. It was no secret that once Alaric had his mate in his hands, he would bite and mate her. He thought about what Ashina had endured there with him. But now, Cayden had her, and the deep city at the falls made it clear that the Black Mountain kingdom was evil.

Serimi left around four hundred wolves in the city at the falls. It had sat empty for years, and they cleaned it and were repairing some damage. In the weeks he prepared his army to march, humans from all over their kingdoms flocked into the wilderness, desperate.

Alaric was taking all the humans now. He was hell-bent on it because he still wanted Ashina. Nothing would stop him because if rumors were true, he also had the power of the mountain. Serimi took a risk marching upon Cayden, but had to save the white wolf. She was the only power that could bring the kingdoms together. She was the only thing that could destroy the wolf kings.

They marched in solidarity, both man and wolf. They filled the lands with their vibrations of retribution. Their silver breastplates adorned their muscular bodies, and silver spikes shot up from their pauldrons. The gauntlets were spiked, too, and much needed in case they needed to stab the wolves in battle. Serimi's army looked like silver demons with spikes, even their silver helmets had horns they used for weapons.

The march would be long and uncertain toward Cayden. But they had no choice. They were also facing encountering Alaric's hoard, and Serimi weighed his options with both wolf kings. He hoped Ashina could hone her power and that Randon could save her again. He also hoped that Alaric would not march behind them, but in case he did, his army was ready.

The wolves may outnumber the humans, but they were formidable and did not give up.

On the rolling plateau just miles outside Worgen, Rieka hunched down on his knees and eyed Serimi's army. It had been another week, and now the human faction was finally marching on the outskirts of Worgen. It looked like the human warlord had a little over one hundred thousand, and he recognized wolves among them.

"Wolf traitors." He growled, his face clenched.

He shook his head and laughed, craning his head to his wolf pack sitting on their horses behind him.

"They march to Cayden." They all laughed.

"They think Cayden is evil," Rieka added, his laugh a thunderous roar. "Fools."

He stood up and lunged on his horse. "We will let Alaric know they have begun marching. We follow at his command."

Then he turned his ear again, and his wolves pulled their bows. The falcons had been more numerous, but they had killed them all. When they tracked their fall, they saw where Randon was trying to send messages to the warlord Serimi, and some were trying to get messages to Serkily. Rieka scoffed as he watched another one fall, shaking his head.

"They march upon Cayden to start a war, and we will ride up behind them and kill them all." He huffed. "It is time the human warlords died."

He craned his eyes back to the human faction and growled. "The humans will stay down this time."

Chapter 29
The Truth of the Heart

Cayden ensured the wedding happened as soon as possible, and once Ashina approved it, they moved forward. He had already moved move to his suite to be with him weeks ago. That was the day they first made love. And every day since then, he doted upon her, loved her, and encouraged to her. But now she would be Cayden's official queen.

Ashina walked down the massive aisle to the throne as the light cascaded upon her beauty. Her hair twisted in ribbons on her head, looking like she already wore a crown. Her silver and white gown strung behind her as the train kissed the rose petals up to Cayden. The gown lingered below her shoulders, accentuating her curves. The light blasted upon her, lighting her eyes.

Cayden stood in awe of her, his eyes glowing in her beauty. He wore his intricate leathers over a long blue robe to his boots. His long black hair spilled down his back under a slender golden crown. He had trimmed his beard; his face framed seductively while his golden eyes sparkled as she neared him.

He held his hand out, and she took it. They smiled into one another as he pulled her to him at the throne. Then she joined him there, and they married one another. The council stood over them, officiating the ceremony. The old gray wolf handed Cayden a golden crown slightly more elegant than his, and she bent her head for him to place it. As he laid it on her head, he closed his eyes, thankful.

She raised back up to face him, and they smiled. Cayden grabbed her around her waist and lunged into her lips, their kiss like a roaring storm. The court and lines of wolves and humans of the kingdom erupted in roars as wolves and humans were present.

When they stopped kissing, Cayden pulled her hands into his chest and breathed in her beauty. "My beautiful wife."

Ashina smiled at him. "I love you. I will love you the rest of my life."

He bent in and kissed her again, their love filled with light and hope. And then the court raised their paws, and the crowd silenced as Cayden and Ashina stood to face them.

The old gray wolf sighed. "The kingdom of Cayden presents our king Cayden and our queen Ashina!"

Ashina gripped Cayden's arm in her palm, and he stared down at her.

The old wolf roared again. "Our kingdom is united stronger, and the wolves have become one!"

The roars and screams echoed around them. As Cayden led her out, his eyes lighted upon her as if she were a meticulous treasure he could not risk letting go of. Ashina's heart lit up in fire and joy, and she could not begin to describe the release given to her.

Randon gripped his heart aside Kira and watched this beautiful spectacle of miracles. He stared down at her, her long blonde hair kissing her frame in a tight royal blue gown. "Dine with me tonight." He asked her, smiling.

She met his face, and her eyes lingered upon him. "I would be honored."

Randon pulled her hand into his arm as they stood there and roared for this happy wedding together. He would be biting her very soon.

Cayden led Ashina out into the streets and flower petals danced on their heads. The wolves mingled with the humans of the villages, their snouts and faces bright and joyful. Ashina raised her chin to gaze upon the sky that seemed to spill in soft petals, her heart singing. Cayden watched her do it, his eyes upon her. He joined her in looking up at them, laughing.

They stood in the street, basking in the glory of the screams of joy. They basked in the hope of their union, reveling in each other's power. Cayden grabbed her around her waist again and twisted her around, laughing. She laughed with him, and they danced in the street, the petals singing at their feet.

They danced together, holding one another tight as their souls burst into surrender. They had gotten to know one another in the past few weeks. Cayden had courted her and doted upon her. She opened her soul to him, and he made her feel safe. He was patient with her but passionate. Ashina did not want this to end, ever.

She had spent a lifetime running and hiding and trained for the worst things to happen to her. But no more. She had found her wolves. She had found her love. She had found a strength forged from the kingdom.

As the day bled into an evening abyss and crimson kissed the horizon, Cayden approached his wife on the balcony. He pressed his body into her backside and leaned into her. She was still wearing her wedding gown, and he was in his regal robes. She stood gazing upon the rolling plains, her heart still in sweet surrender. The wedding was simple and beautiful.

He put his arms on either side of her from behind and engulfed her, kissing her neck. He pressed against her back and a mountain of hope filled her. She leaned into him and closed her eyes. "I love you, Cayden."

Cayden breathed against her skin. "I love you, beautiful. Come to bed." He smiled, anxious.

She leaned her neck and smiled, turning to him. "Coming, my love."

He led her to their bed by her hand, and they fell into one another again, over, and over. They dove into each other like roaring falls had burst up from a deep chasm. There was no end or beginning. It just was.

And it lived and breathed. It bled hope, and from the depths of their impassioned chasms, their souls breathed within them. It whispered of a new beginning. It filled them with gentle whispers and erupted into vast ravines of passion. From the depth of their unbridled moans, they both lived and breathed each other forever.

By dawn that next week, Cayden and Ashina walked to the keep together. She lingered off with other wolves as a horn bellowed from the wall. Kylo lunged into the city from the black plains, his survivors still numbering in the thousands, luckily. Cayden met them at the keep with the council, his eyes narrowed. Kylo blew in frustration, his eyes wide at his king.

"My king! Alaric has turned against all the humans and is taking them to that infernal mountain. Rumors are spreading that the deep city of the falls is back, and the human warlords are there. The humans are fleeing to them."

Kylo huffed. "Alaric has spent the last many weeks doing this."

Cayden raised his brows. "It is a pivotal location for the humans to go; it makes sense to bring it back."

Kylo slid from his stallion as the army pelted around the streets to the stables at the back of the city. The roaring sounds of his survivors vibrated over the plain.

"That is not all." He turned to Cayden and huffed, sliding his gauntlets off.

"The human faction is marching upon us, numbering one hundred thousand. Coming for the white wolf." He warned.

"There are wolves with them also, numbering in the tens of thousands."

Cayden pursed his lips and turned to see Randon and Kira join him in the street at the keep. Randon gasped.

"I have sent falcons every week to them..."

Cayden sighed. "I bet Alaric's wolves are shooting them down. They would be patrolling those lands since the battle at Serkily."

"So, of course, Serimi marches upon us..." Randon rolled his eyes. "Damnit."

Kylo nodded to Randon and Kira, his respect adamant. "They will be upon us in two weeks."

"Alaric will follow them and kill the humans to hurt Ashina." Cayden sneered, thinking.

Silence.

"What is your command, my king." Kylo sighed.

Cayden turned to Randon. "You will ride out to them as they near us. We will ready our wolves to help them fight Alaric."

"What about his powers? He took out your whole army." Randon wondered.

Cayden took a deep breath and gazed upon his beautiful wife. She walked the street toward him with wolves of the city, talking to them and making fast friends. Her face glowed, and her hair accentuated her frame. He swallowed, his heart heavy.

"My wife will have to use her powers to kill him." He turned to Randon and Kira. "It is up to us to protect her from him."

Randon watched Cayden march to Ashina and bent to kiss her. His heart beamed at their love for one another. Ashina truly loved her husband, and it showed. Randon crossed his arms over his chest and narrowed his brows. Kira glared up at him, her eyes wide.

"It is up to us to protect her, Randon. We cannot fail her."

Randon gazed upon his mate Kira. His eyes lingered over her body, her neck still red from him biting her. He sighed at her, his eyes shaking.

"I cannot fail you either."

She met his stare and smiled. "We will not fail each other, and our queen will live."

She turned her stare back to Ashina and Cayden, her eyes firm. Randon met Kylo's glare, their faces clenched as the dawning of war was coming again.

Chapter 30
When the Reckoning Begins

Alaric watched his army march from the mountain. His wolves filled the plain at the pass like a wave of blackness thrust over the lands. They numbered three hundred thousand, with his archers on horseback numbering in the tens of thousands.

His eyes craned to the sunken mountainside. He shook his head and sighed. Ashina set him free, but he had lost her in the process. He had not meant to lose her. He closed his eyes and pulled at his chest. He could not sense her, and a hole had engorged his heart because of her.

She had broken the bond he had put on her and given her heart to Cayden. He knew she had given herself to Cayden because she was his mate. All Cayden had to do was take her, and he sacrificed a whole army to do it. The ancient king was mighty, but Alaric was stronger.

Cayden had a reckoning coming to him one way or another. Alaric seethed inside. That wolf king had killed his father. But his father did the right thing by twisting fate to take Ashina. It was the only way to get back at Cayden.

Alaric needed Ashina back on the mountain. She was the only primordial white wolf born, and her power was mighty like his. She would bring value to his throne, and their offspring would be mighty kings. They would rule the world of man.

He sighed and rolled his eyes. "Looks like I will be using your power against you after all my love. You will join me on this mountain again."

His army marched from the mountain, following behind Serimi. They would meet them from behind at Cayden's gates. The humans would die and suffer, and Ashina would watch. It would compel her to come out and face him. Then he would take her because he was stronger than her. He would get her again.

He would kill Cayden. He would bring down the walls of that city. He would send his wolves into the abyss with his powers. Ashina would grovel back to him, and he would finally stay free.

Alaric thought these things as he sat on his horse and over-looked his massive army of wolves. He matched their intimidating armor with his obsidian armor. His breastplate, pauldrons, and gauntlets fitted his war-tuned body like a blessed wind. He had his hair in a ponytail down his back, but it slithered in braids and bent in the wind like snakes.

His greaves and tassets kissed his muscular frame down to his sabatons over his boots. He was a bleeding obsidian nightmare, and his eyes raged crimson from the power of the mountain. His fangs burst up, thinking of Ashina and what she had taken from him. He turned to lead his army through the pass, his soul lit on fire, his face clenched.

He breathed in the heavy wind through the pass as a storm lingered. He rubbed his fingers through his blonde beard against his neck, his heart on the mate he was destined to keep.

Chapter 31
Where Life Breathes

Cayden took Ashina to the black plains that next morning at dawn. Randon and Kira walked with them for miles under a looming sun and stopped when he felt it was far enough away from the city. They walked west of the city from the roaring falls. They had sparring spears and turned to face one another.

Cayden needed to do this with his wife to help solidify her power. He stood behind her, his shoulders high, his eyes glistening upon her backside. Randon and Kira stood behind him as their commanders.

"You will pivot your fears through us, Ashina. On the battlefield, we will be your sword. We will be your hope. We can sense your fears. We will follow your commands at your lead, and the wolves will move as one." He kissed her lips sweetly.

"Now close your eyes..." Cayden's voice was strong and edgy.

Ashina closed her eyes and breathed in the rising sun.

"The commanders of our army are pivotal to the success of beating Alaric. They will be your backbone in battle, and the wolves will follow their lead. It is important you control your emotions in the heat of battle..." Cayden warned her.

Ashina stretched into the sun, her eyes lit up golden as she faced the black plain. The ground vibrated at their feet, and the black rocks rolled as the earth moved.

"You have ancient seer powers in your bloodline, Ashina. It is the same as Alaric. You must control your emotions to use it wisely to defeat him."

Ashina seethed inside.

"Breathe, my love." Cayden calmed her. "Now take that anger you have for him..."

Cayden bent with her. "...and throw it into the wind."

Ashina rolled her arm by her side, twisting her spear and thrusting it out, just as Alaric had done when he took down the wall at Serkily. The horizon rolled in the distance and the echo of the hill collapsing filled the sky with dread. As it collapsed, the crack melted to their boots, and she stepped back.

A black wall catapulted up from that hill, and the horizon filled with darkness. The wall moved. It seethed in agony, alive and screaming. Ashina glared at it and bent again, her eyes flaming red. The wall burst further west as the quake from its power shook the heavens to the city walls.

Cayden stopped bending and glared at it. Randon and Kira joined him, too, and Ashina stood to see what she had done. The horizon filled with black soot to the clouds. The ripple effect from the wind pushed the earth and rock high in the air like a wall. When the wall stopped moving, it plummeted down as the ground shook beneath them.

Randon twisted his spear and gazed at Kira as she watched the catastrophic devastation.

Cayden sighed. "Alaric will use your power against you to take our city."

Ashina closed her eyes.

Cayden pressed a firm grip on her shoulder and smiled. "Again."

"You do this because I must face him again." Ashina fretted.

Cayden froze when she said that and met her face. His powerful body lingered close to her. "If something happens to me or Randon, you will face him alone."

Kira gazed at Randon. "Why Randon?"

Cayden met her stare. "Because they have bonded. He is the closest thing to me that will be able to sense her if I fail her."

Randon's heart ached. He had also bitten Kira, so now he had two wolves to fret over. Kira pressed a firm palm on Randon's forearm and smiled at him. "It will be okay. We get through this together."

He huffed. "Yeah, because I will kill him if he harms either one of you."

Cayden smiled at him. "Spoken like a true commander." He stretched his neck and stared at his wife, but Ashina was not smiling.

She craned her neck to see what she had done and held her breath as her fangs burst up. She lunged against the sun and belted out her rage toward the plain. The blast from her rage blew everyone away from her. The plain catapulted up, and the wall moved and rumbled.

She clenched her face and pushed it further out, where it writhed in agony in the distance. The rumble filled the span of the heaven as the ground vibrated. Cayden, Randon, and Kira flew back from her. They landed on their feet and braced themselves. When they realized what she had done, Cayden lunged back up, his face wide. But Ashina stretched her neck and turned to them, her face hard.

"In case I cannot change to my wolf in battle..." She watched their faces fall.

The silence hit them as if the wall had come to them. Cayden froze when she said that, his heart skipping a beat. Ashina swallowed at their faces, but a light glowed within her.

"I will be able to fight this way." She believed. "I am good with a sword."

Cayden's breathing became erratic with this dawning. His eyes fell upon her stomach. "Ashinaaaaaa." His knees grew weak.

Ashina turned back to the devastation, ignoring the unbridled passion of joy her husband was giving her. "Again." She commanded.

Randon met Kira's wide-eyed expression but said nothing. They followed their queen back into formation so she could continue honing her powers. They followed her command and held their breaths at their queen's courage.

Cayden did not follow them. He stood there gawking at his wife and this painful reckoning that filled his bones to the core. He stood there, his whole body tense at her perfection. They had to kill Alaric and wipe out his wolves. He would be damned if that wicked wolf would hurt his wife and offspring.

As Ashina bent down again, Cayden lunged into her and pulled her up by her forearms. She pressed into his chest, breathless. He gripped her head with his palm and stared at her face, his jaws clenched. He wrapped a strong arm around her waist and gasped in shock.

Ashina met his powerful grip and sighed on his lips. "You're going to be a father." She smiled.

Cayden's heart busted with joy. He met her with a moan. "I told you, you are my hope. And you are." He kissed her. "I am so excited for this little one." He breathed against her lips.

Ashina kissed him back. She closed her eyes and pressed her head on his chest, sighing. The heaviness weighed on her. She was excited, but fearful.

Randon sighed. "Now I have three to worry about." He glared at Kira and held his breath, his eyes wide.

She shook her head. "Do not look at me like that, we have only begun mating. Bearing offspring is inevitable."

Randon took a deep breath and blinked his eyes, his face hard. "That is true."

Kira laughed at him. "When I know, you will know. It'll be a little shit like its father."

Randon burst out in laughter, but then he swallowed and gazed at her again. "Do not die on me."

She smiled up at him. "Don't plan on it."

That night, Cayden lay in the bed on his side, his bulging arm twitching as he propped himself up. He loomed over Ashina's naked body. Their legs stayed intertwined, and their hearts raced from ravaging one another. He pressed his forehead against her face and sighed. He put his palm on her belly and breathed her in deep.

"No." His voice was deep and harsh. "You will not be joining the battle."

Ashina sighed in his face.

"You will stay behind these walls." He fretted.

Ashina swallowed and met his eyes. She watched his face clench up, his eyes lit in fire. Something burst up from the deepness within him, his protectiveness over her adamant.

Cayden shook his head no at her, his eyes roaming from her eyes to her belly. "No."

"You will not be able to change to wolf form while with child." He added. "You will be vulnerable."

Ashina pressed into his chest and he wrapped his arms around her naked body and sighed.

"I love you, my king." She confirmed.

Cayden closed his eyes atop her head, fingering her long hair. "I love you with all I am. I will not lose you."

They held each other in silence for endless moments before Cayden blurted out. "I will kill that son of a bitch."

Ashina closed her eyes and sighed deeply inside. In the morning, they would walk the black plain again, and she would continue honing her power until she blew Alaric and his army into pieces.

Chapter 32
The Coming

It became apparent that Alaric had his wolves shoot down the falcons Randon had sent. Week by week, there was no word back. Week by week, the silence pestered him. It was an eerie silence among the chaos Alaric was now inflicting upon the lands. Randon had a sinking intuition that the wolf king was planning something horrific, or else he would have already marched upon Cayden.

Now Ashina was with child, and she was the only thing powerful enough to take him down, and even then, Randon questioned it. Alaric had ruled for many years and waited for the hunter's moon to get Ashina. He had many more years to hone his powers and become formidable with his wolves, which he did.

Alaric had years of experience using and commanding it. While he had bonded to Ashina, he forced her to use it. Randon sighed as he remembered the things Ashina had told him. Alaric had also mated her, but Randon was relieved the child was Cayden's. If she had gotten pregnant with Alaric's child, the world would burn because he would never stop until he had her back.

Alaric would always come for her. He would chase her to the ends of the world. Kingdoms would burn. His rage would fill the lands with darkness until he had her. Alaric would never stop.

Randon sat naked in the bed, Kira lingering behind him under the blanket. He turned to her and kissed her face, and she rolled her arm around his waist. "You tossed all night." She worried, opening her eyes. "You did not sleep."

"I never sleep when war comes. I sense it. It fills my bones with dread." He mumbled.

Randon rubbed his face. "I need you to stay with her in battle until she faces Alaric. You know she will not listen and stay behind these walls. She will confront Alaric."

Kira swallowed. "I know."

"She will confront him, and he will try to take her. He will hurt her on purpose so he can take her. He must die." Randon belted out, his face clenched.

"Yes, he is as evil as his father."

He turned his face to her. "She is like a sister to me; I love her very much." Randon stared at Kira. "I worry for her."

"I will stay with her. Promise." Kira confirmed, her eyes wide.

He shook his head. "You stay with her until she faces Alaric. He will kill you."

"What, you just said to stay with her. I will not leave her alone with that wolf." She narrowed her brows.

"If she faces him, she will do it alone, and they will rage at one another with their powers. I will not lose you. Trust me. The army will take it from there. We have a plan…"

He gazed into the light. "As long as Serimi does what I know he is good at doing."

"Okay." She stretched out in the bed behind him. He smiled into her face and lunged on top of her. Kira laughed. Randon kissed her ferociously and then stared into her eyes.

"When this shit is over, you are mine."

Kira smiled in his face. "I am already yours. I knew it the day you came to protect Ashina from Cayden."

Randon kissed her and raised back up to get dressed, and she watched him, her blue eyes sparkling.

"You head to meet Serimi today." Kira swallowed.

Randon's back was to her, his eyes craned out the window as daylight streamed upon their bodies. He slid into his trousers and huffed.

"You stay back. Serimi will not listen to anyone else. I will be back by nightfall."

Kira watched him get dressed and sighed. She stared at the rising dawn and kissed Randon as he marched out. She sat up, realizing the frame had broken. As she stood up, the bed wobbled and slid to the floor.

She huffed. "Going to need a stronger frame with that wolf." She raised an eyebrow.

Randon lunged out of the city on horseback, the hooves echoing on the cobblestone. He was formidable to look upon with his six-foot-four stature. He gripped the reigns, his silver gauntlets beaming under the morning sun. His whole physique demanded presence. He dressed for war, his silver body armor accentuating his black hair.

The wolves stationed along the walls watched him leave the gates. The bellowing horn blew after him. He pressed his nose into the horse's mane, his eyes clenched toward the black plain.

Behind him, another horn blew from the wall. This one was deep and painful to hear. It signaled the arrival outside the black plain that the human faction was getting closer. Randon was meeting Serimi there to warn him. He had to tell him this was all just a trap so Alaric could come and wipe them all out because his numbers far outweighed theirs. He had to warn him Alaric had shot down the falcons.

Cayden marched along the wall to the watchtower, watching Randon lunge out of the city toward the black plains. By the time he reached them and returned, it would be dark. Below him, the streets filled with his formidable army in their wolf form, and they marched out the gate to fill the rolling plain before the city walls.

They marched out, all four hundred thousand, and spread miles wide to cover the city at the black plain line. Below the human villages, wolves marched and filled the city streets. He had another one hundred thousand of them. They were there to protect the human villages if Alaric took the city. Though his numbers were great, Alaric was more powerful.

His black wolves' shadows stretched over the plain, their twelve-foot statures powerful. They snarled, marching in formation out the gates, their roars thunderous and echoing over the plains. Cayden nodded his head at their bravery. His wolves were adorned with obsidian wolf armor, and their battle axes hung on their wide backs. They had broad swords and the back lines of tens of thousands had bows.

Cayden did not plan on Alaric winning. His army outnumbered Alaric's, even after losing the two hundred thousand. His army always outnumbered Alaric's, and it would stay that way. He clenched his fist atop the wall, his golden eyes raging fire. He clenched his face and peered out to the black plains, his heart pinged a warning of a darkness coming behind the human warlords.

He turned to face Kylo and huffed. "The wolves will be the buffer for the humans once they have dispatched their silver, understood? Ensure they get behind us."

Kylo nodded. "Yes, my king."

Cayden watched Kylo go to command the army on the plain, his black beard trimmed to his handsome jawline, his long hair braided down his back in thick knots. He too, wore his obsidian armor from head to toe, but it did not matter. He knew he would be changing to his wolf in battle anyway.

The seers of old had done a service to the old wolves. It had taken them a long time to turn when the moon came. When the seers endowed them, it gave them the power to change like a wind. They changed anytime they wanted, and when turned back, they were still clothed. They had to hold on to their weapons, but in battle, they had limited weapons because of it. It was easier to stay in wolf form when preparing for war.

In time, that magic helped the wolves take the kingdoms and conquer. It further divided the lands and pitted humans against them. Cayden sighed, thankful for the old seers. But now it was time for a reckoning, and the humans had risen.

He gripped his long sword, his black cloak blowing in the wind. He stood rigid with his wolves along the towering city walls. His arms were flexed in glory, his shoulders high. His breathing was calm until Ashina approached him from the corridor.

He held his breath at her. She had gotten dressed in her glorious silver body armor and was armed. Her hair was in sloppy braids at the base of her neck hanging down her back like a rope. Her face was hard, and her eyes were golden and on fire, like his.

"No." Cayden shook his head at her.

She calmly pressed against him while he leaned down to face her. He towered over her, his face longing, his mouth smiling at her beauty. His face lit up at her presence, his smile wide as he stared into her face.

"Absolutely not." He smiled in her face.

"You are so handsome." Ashina gazed into his eyes. "You are so brave."

Cayden laughed in her face. "The answer is still no." He shook his head. "Beautiful woman." He enjoyed the view of her.

"I will ravish you tonight." She whispered.

Cayden held his breath. "Yes, you will." He leaned back. "The answer is no, still."

Kira rushed out of the corridor and chased her, her face flushed. She froze and rolled her eyes as she noticed Ashina taunting Cayden. "I have her, my king. I promise."

Cayden huffed and met Ashina's face again. He sighed, caressing her face with his fingers under his gauntlet. He bent down and kissed her and breathed in her lips. "I love you. Stay behind these walls with Kira." He turned away from her and marched down the wall to his wolves.

Ashina watched him as Kira joined her. They stood together, formidable wolves waiting for war. Ashina swallowed. "Remember what I told you."

Kira rolled her eyes, meeting Ashina's stare as they stood the same height. "Yea. Randon is going to kill me." She gripped her long sword at her side and nodded. Her obsidian armor starkly contrasted from Ashina's glorious silver, but these two wolves stood as one.

"You will only get one chance. I trust you." Ashina smiled at her.

Kira nodded. "And you?" She gazed at her belly.

Ashina took a deep breath. "I feel like throwing up."

Kira pursed her lips. "That will be fun out there." She shook her head, her blonde hair in a sloppy braid down her back, her amber eyes upon the queen.

Randon rode until the black plains ended, and his eyes recognized the vast human armies with Serimi leading. They spilled over the rolling hills as the wolves dispersed between them and the mounted archers at the back lines. When Serimi recognized Randon, his face fell pale and his eyes wide.

Randon lunged up to him and shook his head. "You haven't been getting my messages!"

Serimi sighed as the army continued to march around them. "We feared you were dead!"

Serimi's face lit up at him. "The white wolf, is she?"

"She is well. Married and happy, and with child."

Serimi gawked. "What the hell?! You wolves do not play around, do you."

"Lots of changes in the last weeks, my friend," Randon warned him, craning his head to see Galin rush up to them from the back lines. "Cayden is a good king," Randon added.

"Then why does the city show him to be the dark mountain?" Serimi questioned.

"It is not true. This king is good." Randon stopped as Galin rushed up to them. "The stories told showed Alaric's father as altering that history."

Galin met them and huffed. "Scouts say two days behind us rides Alaric's wolves."

Randon raged. "I knew this was a trap!"

Serimi pressed his gauntlet over his lap and shook his head. "The number?"

Galin huffed. "Hundreds of thousands. He more than triples us."

Serimi stared at Randon. "Will this wolf king work with us to kill Alaric?"

Randon nodded. "The city awaits your arrival. We are ready for war."

Serimi turned to Galin. "Once we reach the city, have the archers turn to face Alaric's army. We will begin with the wolfsbane and silver blades."

Galin nodded and turned to lunge to the rear again. Randon turned to trot alongside Serimi, his eyes glaring over the army. "Did you find the city of the falls?"

"Indeed. It is beautiful and big! Families are coming in to flee Alaric. He is taking all the humans now, even the old men. It seems he is set on fulfilling his wicked father's wishes like in the old days." He rolled his eyes. "Wolves are coming more by the day also."

Randon sneered. "He does this to get Ashina's attention. Alaric must die. He will not stop until he has her again."

Serimi paused, and they turned to face the rear of the army as the ground vibrated beneath them. Randon had felt this before. He clenched his fists and turned his horse around to face it. The air shook in the heavens, and the ground cracked through the army.

"Alaric is here!" Randon warned them. "Prepare yourselves!" He yelled.

Randon lunged off his horse like a mighty wind breathed through him and changed to his twelve-foot wolf. He snarled and gripped his broad sword in his paw, clenching his paw tight over the hilt. He growled, his body writhed in scathing muscles. His eyes were a fiery gold, and he pressed his snout toward Alaric and roared.

Galin huffed. "Show off." He pressed into his horn and blew, and the army turned to face the onslaught.

As the scorched earth billowed beneath them, a dark cloud rose before them. A wind bellowed into the air, and Randon realized Alaric would kill them all. He would kill them all and take Ashina, because she was all that mattered to him, no matter the losses.

Chapter 33
The War of the White Wolf Queen

Alaric filled the span of the world behind the human warlords and wolves. He marched toward the city, leading his army on horseback in his human form aside from Rieka. For miles behind him, his army marched in their wolf form. Their axes poked up over their backs while they gripped broad swords in their paws. Their muscle-riddled wolf forms sported golden breastplates and pauldrons that kissed their broad shoulders.

They wore a slim tunic to cover their midsection, adorned with a wide belt and sheath with a short sword and dagger. Their roars echoed into the heavens as retribution filled them with rage. They were a seething walking nightmare as they neared the black plains, and the ground shook beneath them.

Alaric laughed, turning his head to Rieka, who met his stare with a smile. Rieka nodded his head to his king. "Go get your queen, my king."

Rieka pressed his face toward the path ahead. "We have the humans."

Alaric took a deep breath as his eyes filled with crimson. He commanded the black plains to rage upon the humans. His heart was upon Ashina and her betrayal to him. His head raged against Cayden for taking her. The city would pay, and the humans living in it. Alaric clenched his face as the ground split open to the human warlords.

Cayden watched a black cloud rear up miles out and lunged down the corridor into the city streets. He jumped on his stallion and raced out of the city to face Alaric as his wolves lunged toward the humans. Alaric was here, and now the humans would face his wolves alone before his army could reach them.

Ashina stood beside Kira, her heart racing as her husband left the city. Their wolves met him on the plain on horseback and galloped to the humans. They filled the plain with a dread she could not describe, but a knot filled her throat. She glared toward the darkness rising, her back tense.

"You will not take me, Alaric." She belted out. "You will not take my husband nor this city."

She turned to Kira and swallowed. "Ready?"

Kira blurted out. "Ready."

"I will use you to buffer the wolves. What I command, you will do, and the army will sense and follow."

Kira's eyes glowed amber, and she growled, ready.

Ashina yanked the long-magnetized sword Randon had given her and nodded. "Here we go."

They raced on horseback and headed west from the wolves to flank Alaric. They headed west because that is where Randon had thousands of silver blades in the ground, waiting.

Serimi met his archers at the rear and faced the darkness blowing at them. He sat on horseback aside Galin, and they pulled their swords. Galin blew the horn and the archers readied their silver arrow shanks. They filled the plain for miles in the tens of thousands, with wolves sitting aside them, ready, too. As the black cloud neared closer, Alaric's wolves snarled, marching in on them.

Galin sounded the horn, and the archers fired into the dark wall. The wolves pressed in on them, and the arrows catapulted back into the humans. The arrows plunged straight back and hit the rear line of archers, and Galin and Serimi dove off their horses.

Randon met them there and hunched down to protect them. Serimi and Galin readied their swords. "Alaric is using his power! He uses our weapons against us!" Galin belted out.

Serimi yelled. "Damnit!"

He turned to see many archers gored through, and the horses turned and fled from them. His whole archer line was now compromised and weak. The ones who did not take direct hits stood to face the wolves alongside them.

Around them now, bodies piled up as Alaric's wolves plunged into them, darting out of the dark wall he had made with his powers. The wolves lunged into the humans with their axes and tore into them on the front lines, blood and screams spraying on the plain.

Randon lunged into them as his wolves from Serimi's army joined him there. They lunged through them together around Serimi and Galin. Randon beat through them and cut their heads off or gored them with his sword, his roars filling the plain.

When he turned to kill another wolf, Rieka lunged off his horse into his wolf form and catapulted into Randon. He writhed in his black wolf form. Rieka stabbed his claws into Randon's shoulder, pushing him away from Serimi and Galin. Randon roared in pain and bent his snout to the ground, his eyes sneering at Alaric's commander.

Rieka rounded him, pressing his long blade out. "You are the reason we are in this mess, primordial. You." He growled.

Randon faced him as the plain erupted in roars. All around him, the humans banded together, but the wolves took them three to one. The wolves ripped them apart limb by limb, leaving chunks of them with their armor shimmering in the darkness.

Rieka twisted his neck and wrinkled his snout as his amber eyes pierced him. "You hunted our queen and took her from Alaric."

"And I'll do it again!" Randon growled and lunged at him. Their swords slipped off their blades as Randon plunged his claws into Rieka's bicep and slashed him open.

Rieka roared at him as his blood seeped down his arm to his paw. Randon's rage filled him with fire as he rose over Rieka in midair. He belted into his snout as he pressed his claws into his chest. He lunged through Rieka's breastplate and ripped his heart out. As Rieka gasped, Randon pulled his heart out in his palm.

Rieka's body fell, and Randon turned to Alaric's wolves. They engulfed the humans and throttled them.

Serimi was separated from Galin as three wolves pressed in on him. A haze was thrust upon them thanks to Alaric. One of his archers lay at his feet run through with an arrow, and Serimi pressed his long sword against it. It moved away from it, he belted out in rage. He gripped the hilt tight and twisted his arms toward the wolf, and the shank bolted out of the body. It sunk through the wolf's snout and out the back of his throat.

Serimi ducked as a paw came at his shoulder through the haze. The wolf catapulted over him and his snout craned to bite his head. Serimi lunged his long sword up through its snout, falling to his knees to avoid its attack. He pushed the blade through its skull, pulling it back out as the wolf fell. As a shadow loomed behind him, he flung his sword backwards, and it lodged through the throat of the third wolf.

As he killed three of them, Galin met him through the haze. They assembled toward the silver arrows and lunged into the wolves. But they had taken losses already, and Alaric was just getting started. From behind them, his army heard deep belted roars from the city.

They craned their necks to see Cayden lunging in to fight with his wolves. His wolves were bigger than Alaric's and had more weapons. They spread among the plain for miles to back up the human army and the wolves fighting with them. Cayden raised off his horse and changed to his wolf in midair, meeting Alaric's wolves over the humans.

His roar thundered through the darkness filling the plain, and Alaric heard him. He waited until Cayden reached the warring plain and laughed. As Cayden's wolves filled the breadth of it and covered for the humans, Alaric lunged his horse into the cloud and bent his arm by his side.

A wall of earth rose and moved toward his wolves. The wall picked up the silver shanks as Alaric pressed his arm out and growled. The wall plunged into Cayden and his wolves and gored them. Cayden was tossed back to the rear of the lines and run through with arrows in his shoulders and one in his stomach. The injuries changed him back to human, but he was still alive.

Alaric's roar rumbled from a pit of hatred. As he pressed in with his wolves to finish them off, Alaric lunged off his horse. His army met the rage of a wall of silver blades. The blades shimmered from the western plain and flanked his wolves. They sunk into his raging army and decapitated them. As the bodies fell around him, Alaric was hit twice in his shoulder.

The blades flew through the bodies, and they fell by the thousands. The silver dispersed onto the plain before Cayden's surviving wolves, shining and ready.

Alaric pulled the blades from his shoulder and moaned in anger. He turned his eyes toward a familiar figure emerging from the dust. As the ground cracked around him, he faced Ashina. He stood up, his face clenched. He glared at the thousands she had just killed alone with her power.

He growled at her and pulled out another blade from his forearm. Kira plunged from behind Ashina and belted a raging roar for the army to follow her. She changed into her magnificent black wolf form and picked up a silver blade. She gripped it tight in her paw and tossed it straight out, flinging it wide with her long sword. The blade shot into Alaric's wolves.

Kira galloped away from Ashina as the blade flew midair away from her sword. She lunged into the shard and killed Alaric's wolves with the same blade as it stayed suspended in midair. Cayden's wolves heard the call and pressed into Alaric's wolves, following her. The plain shimmered of bloody deaths as Cayden's wolves picked up the dead humans' swords and met the darkness in fits of rage.

When Cayden realized it was Ashina and Kira, he pulled an arrow out of his arm and moaned. "Noooo!"

Randon met Serimi and Galin, and the humans pulled together with the wolves. They plunged into Alaric's wolves even though losses were apparent.

Cayden yelled. "Ashina!" He ran toward her to get her away from Alaric. As he pulled the last arrow from him, he raged into his wolf again, his heart a desperate race.

A laric took a deep breath and pressed into Ashina with a mighty wind. She pushed away from him, even as he met her face and ripped her up into his arms. He pressed her further into the western plains, away from the city. She yanked

out her dagger and pushed it toward Alaric's chest, but he met

her wrist with a firm hand, and she could not hurt him. He

ripped the dagger from her grip.

"Ashina!" He yelled.

She growled at him, her eyes meeting his as he dropped her

onto the plain with his mighty wind. They landed opposite of

one another on their knees, facing one another.

Alaric stood up, now well away from the wolves fighting and

dying. Ashina gripped her stomach from the sudden sickness

and slowly stood to face him, her face pale. Alaric's craned his

face at her, his jaws clenched.

"You reek of Cayden!" He yelled at her.

"He is my mate! You knew that and took me anyway," She

yelled at him. "You defied fate with seer magic and it will be your

demise."

Alaric belted out a growl at her face, his jaws clenched. "Yes."

Ashina froze, gasping.

"I knew Ashina!" He growled at her. "I took you anyway and

bit you! I took you and mated you! I did! I wanted you then,

and I want you now. That will never change."

He walked back and forth and paused, suddenly gazing at her belly. He dropped to his knees as if his wind had been taken from under him, lifted his chin in the air, and gasped. "Ashina." He stared at her belly.

Ashina backed away from him, even as the ground cracked further around her. "You are not the father. My mate is the father." She warned him.

Alaric closed his eyes and took a deep breath. "Did you think I would not sense the life growing inside you? The life that was supposed to be mine. You denied me even that." He gripped his heart.

"If you had stayed with me, you would be having my child." He bellowed. "You would be with my child, and we would be together. Forever."

She bit, pulling her sword to face him. "How dare you!" She growled. "You deny rights to others, even me. You are evil!"

Alaric met her eyes with a hard face and stood up slowly, sneering at her. "You have destroyed my kingdom! You set me free, then ripped me apart!"

He lunged out his long, muscular arm and belted it toward the city. Ashina gasped as the land roared, just like he did it at Serkily. His eyes were red, and Ashina met his rage with her sword. Alaric pulled his sword and met her blade, and they pressed into one another.

"I love you!" Alaric screamed at her face, pressing her off his blade. "I love you, Ashina!" He pleaded with her.

Ashina lunged into him again, their blades ricocheting off each other. Alaric met her eyes, his face clenched. She growled, denying it. She pushed him away and took deep breaths, her eyes tearing up.

She shook her head no. They rounded each other, glaring. "What you have done to me and the world is not love! You do not love me, Alaric! You want to control me. That is not love. There is a difference."

Alaric shook his head, disagreeing with her. "I am protecting you."

Behind them, the wall raged into the western wall of the city. The ground cracked and echoed like thunder. It hit the base of the foundation. The crack slithered to the watch tower, and the turrets fell onto the plain. The stone chipped from the ground up, and the western wall buckled.

The wolves on the city walls raced back through the corridors and into the streets to prevent loss of life. But the rounded gatehouse buckled and fell onto the plain, taking the whole western wall with it. The stones collapsed into the city streets to the keep.

Ashina yelled at him. "Stop it, Alaric! You can do what is right and stop this war now. You can let me go! You can choose to live!" She pleaded with him.

Alaric laughed, his whole body flexed at her. "I will never let you go. I will do what I must to ensure my kingdom's survival."

"You can walk away and still rule your kingdom. You can still be a virtuous king." She pleaded, crying. "Please Alaric. Please do not make me..." She held her heart at him, her stomach in knots.

She stared at his eyes. "You will force my hand today, and I am in pain because of it!" She warned him.

He glared at her face, noticing her tears, and stared at her. "I will never stop hunting you. I will never stop wanting you." He growled. "I need you, Ashina. You belong to me."

He stopped rounding her and held out his hand. She stared at it and backed away. His hand was smeared with blood, and his eyes beamed at her, sparkling crimson.

"Come with me, and this will all end. Come home with me, and I will forget what you did."

"I did nothing wrong! You are the one who is wrong." Ashina pressed her arm out and roared at him in rage. She turned her head toward the devastation he sent to the city and met his wall of earth with her wind. The wind roared into his wall and pressed it flat. It was too late to undo whatever damage he had done to the city wall. Alaric watched her use her power and seethed at her, the blackness from the plain dissipating at the ground around the armies.

He gripped his hilt tight and held his breath as his fangs burst up. "Is that a no?"

Ashina's fangs burst up, but she could not turn. "No, Alaric."

He laughed at her, her defiance intriguing him. "You turn me on with your defiance, Ashina."

He smiled and pressed his sword toward her belly. "That child will call me father! You will come back with me to the mountain." His voice was as hard as his face. "You will submit to me, and we will bring our own heir into the kingdom."

"Your seed is nothing but evil and will spawn more evil." She moaned.

Alaric froze when she said that. "So. I still want you, Ashina."

Ashina raged at him. "You want power even as your wolves are dying, Alaric!"

He growled at her, his fangs showing. "So are yours! And your wretched mate will die next. This city will fall to me."

Ashina stepped away from him as he transformed into his magnificent primordial wolf. He loomed over her. "Did you think I would just let you go, white wolf? After what we shared in the bed, after you released me from the seers, and your power..."

He stretched his shoulders, his snout snarling at her face, his eyes bright and crimson. "I will never let you go. Ever." He moaned.

His ears stood upright and he took in a deep breath, and flexed his whole body at her. "You cannot change into your wolf because you are with child. It has made you weak."

He stepped closer and clenched his paws. "Together, we are powerful. We are powerful mates, Ashina."

Ashina held her breath at him, shaking her head. "You will die today because you refuse to repent and do what is right." A tear fell down her cheek. "Alaric, please." She pleaded with him, her heart aching.

Alaric laughed, his snout rolling, his eyes sparkling. He stepped closer to her, his paw cracking the ground beneath him. He sneered at her. "I am everything to this world, and you are everything my kingdom needs to keep growing."

As Alaric stepped closer, a shadow rose behind him and lunged through the haze. Ashina froze as Alaric turned to face Cayden. Cayden ripped into him midair, his roar raging at Alaric's snout. He throttled Alaric from above as the two primordials flung claws into one another. They ripped into each other's shoulders, and swiped their claws into their snouts. They ripped into their stomachs and fur danced around them. Their blood sprung in the air as they raged into one another.

"No one touches my wife!" Cayden roared at him, and drug Alaric's shoulder with a claw.

Alaric roared in pain and pressed his claws at Cayden's chest, latching his fangs on his arm. Cayden punched his snout and catapulted himself over his shoulder in midair. He punched Alaric's snout from above, and a fang broke off in his arm. Alaric jerked his arms up, grabbing Cayden's fur at his bloody chest. As Cayden roared into Alaric's head, he was jerked back over Alaric's shoulder and slammed on his back at his snout.

Cayden met Alaric's arms with firm grips and roared in his face, pushing him off with his bulky paws.

As he pushed him off, Alaric lunged into Cayden's fur at his chest. Alaric pressed his claws toward his heart just as his body went stiff. The light in his eyes dimmed as he froze and gasped. His body jerked as his paws shook in pain, and then the breath of his life left him. Cayden growled at his snout, pushed Alaric's body off, and rose to face his wife.

Ashina bent to her knees behind Alaric, with his heart in her palm. The blood of him rolled up her palm and pooled on the ground. She gazed at it for a moment in shock. Her hand shook to her soul, and as her tears fell, she cried. "I am sorry you chose not to live." Her lips trembled. She dropped his heart to the ground and cried into the air.

Cayden gasped at her and slid over Alaric's body. He pulled her into his wolf arms, engulfing her with bloodied biceps. He cradled his wife in his bloody arms against his bloody chest, pressed his snout atop her head, and moaned. She melted into him as he changed back to human, and he engulfed her pain. She cried into him, gripping his muscular forearms, her mouth open and wailing. Cayden sighed a breath of relief, wrapping

his arms tight around her, his legs straddled as she fell between th
em.

He pressed his face into hers as his arms shook around her. "My brave wife! My beautiful, white wolf!" He kissed her face and head. "Oh, my love!" His tears met hers.

Behind them on the plain, Cayden's wolves and the humans continued pressing into Alaric's survivors. They lunged into them with the silver blades and cut them down. They moved through them for miles until every wolf of Alaric was dead, and the rolling black earth bled in red.

Ashina melted into her husband's strong arms and closed her eyes into his chest. Cayden continued to kiss her face and head, overwhelmed. Cayden raised his face as Randon and Kira met them there. They were still in their wolf form, both a powerful couple to look upon.

Serimi and Galin emerged behind them, and Cayden acknowledged the humans and nodded at them. Serimi raised his blade to his head and bowed to the king. They were bloodied and injured, but their resolve was still strong.

"Wolf king, the wolves of Worgen are dead." Serimi smiled at him. "We hunt the deserters as I speak."

Galin stretched a long arm toward the city and shook his head. "But the whole of the western wall fell."

Cayden pulled Ashina tighter against his chest and sighed on her head. "Replaceable." He answered, engulfing his wife in his arms.

Ashina raised from his chest, her eyes meeting Cayden's. "I love you."

He met her face and wiped her tears. He bent to her lips and kissed her. "I love you." He held her face in his palm. "You saved us. I cannot begin to describe what I feel for you, my love."

Cayden pulled her up with him, and she leaned into his chest, still weak and drained. As she turned to face Randon and Kira, she bent over and vomited. Randon bent his snout down and watched her, sneering at her.

"We love you too." He smarted off. Kira laughed at him.

Cayden sighed, meeting Serimi and Galin's stares. "She is with child." His heart beamed.

She continued heaving as Kira patted her back with a gentle paw to console her. "Oh, you poor pregnant wolf."

Galin grimaced. His face was cut and bloodied, and his arm gashed open to his shoulder, where his pauldron was ripped off. "Congratulations."

Chapter 34
Liberation of the Mountain

Serimi and Galin had lost more than a third of their army, even with the wolves helping them fight. They had lost so many because Alaric was powerful. He had used their weapons against them until Ashina saved them all.

As the kingdom of Cayden mourned the dead, the valley spilled with floating lanterns in the tens of thousands. Their hearts ached with the kingdom survivors and their families. The sky filled with flickering lights into the night even as their hope lingered in the heavens.

Alaric was dead at the hands of Ashina. She did warn him, but he did not do what was right. He never repented. After the war, and everyone had rested and buried their dead, the surviving wolves and human warriors went to Worgen. The kingdoms had a lot of work to do to be whole again.

The wolves and humans followed Ashina through the narrow pass and stared at the collapsed side of the mountain for endless moments. Her eyes teared up as her heart burst in her chest. She trotted down the road, stopped on the plain before the city, and waited. Cayden joined her side, and waited until their wolves and human armies flooded the mountain city.

They surrounded the road and the plain. Randon sighed next to Ashina and nodded to Galin. As Serimi met them at the front line, he gave the order. "Warn them."

Galin pressed the horn to his lips and blew, and the war horn sounded a shrieking bellow upon Worgen. Alaric's army burst from the mountain in wolf form, filling the plain with blackness drenched in hate. They froze as they recognized Cayden, his golden crown sitting high on his regal head.

"Your king is dead!" He roared at them in his human form, his fangs showing.

"You can choose to live this day or die. But you will release the humans!"

Silence split the horizon until Alaric's wolves growled, their defiance echoing.

"Release the humans, or I will bleed this mountain dry." That was his final warning.

Cayden, Randon, Serimi, and Galin pressed out in front of Ashina on their horses. Cayden waited and watched, his body flexed and tense, his eyes firm. Alaric's wolves growled and hunched to the ground as their fur spiked down their backs to their tails. They seethed at him.

Ashina stared at Kira and sighed. Kira huffed. "They are choosing this day their fate, my queen."

Stretched to the pass behind her, Cayden's wolves sat on their horses as burly men in their human forms. Their bodies were scathing in muscles and writhing with power. They readied their axes and broad swords and held their breath for war. They spread out in the hundreds of thousands to take the mountain.

Mingled among Cayden's wolves were the human warriors. Their fine-tuned bodies echoed the wolves' aggressive intimidation. Their silver horns and armor shimmered against the obsidian armor. The blended as one and melted onto the plain, waiting. They gripped their long swords and spears, their muscular arms flexed and ready for blood.

Ashina held her breath as Alaric's wolves lunged toward her husband. They numbered in the tens of thousands, still. Randon and Cayden changed to their wolf form and met them on the plain. All around Ashina and Kira, the wolves of Cayden and human warriors plunged around her to join them. The mountain carried roars of vibrations from their power high into the heaven. Cayden's wolves changed to their wolf form midair on the horses and split through them to the city.

Kira pulled her broad sword and guarded Ashina, but they had to do nothing. The human faction with Cayden's wolves ripped into Alaric's wolves and slaughtered them on the open plain before the city. They roared as they died, their blood pooling on the fields to form rivers of pain.

When they finished the slaughter, Ashina melted over the bodies on her horse beside Kira, and Cayden met them in his human form again. He climbed on his horse and followed the road into the city toward the throne, where they met some women with their children there.

The women were armed but not a threat. Ashina gazed down at them, realizing she had seen these women when Alaric brought her there. A middle-aged woman clutched her toddler to her waist and sighed at Cayden and Ashina, her eyes craning to the city now overrun with human warriors and Cayden's wolves.

"My husband is a wolf. I love him! Please do not kill him. He refused to partake in this war." She pleaded. "There are a few of us who do love one another…"

Cayden raised on the horse and eyed a group of wolves in their human form lingering behind the women from stone houses. They bowed to him, their bearded faces grieved.

"We are not like them and love our wives. Please, let us live." The wolf begged, his bulging arms under his tunic shaking.

Cayden sighed. "You did not serve Alaric's army?"

The wolf shook his head. "Many of us stayed back to care for our families and to hunt, to build and care for the city. Alaric only took the biggest wolves for his army. A pack of us remain to come and go here with our families freely."

"I see." Cayden huffed. "Where are the humans he has taken?!"

The wolf swallowed and gazed at his wife.

"Where are they?" Ashina demanded.

The women pointed to the western side of the plateau, their faces wide as it became apparent their king was dead. The wolves of Cayden and the human warlord faction had come to liberate the mountain.

Cayden stared at them with their human wives and children and smiled. "You beautiful families, but you will not stay here. You will accompany us to the city of the falls. I am destroying this mountain once everyone is free."

The wolves and human women bowed to him, relieved.

Cayden followed her over a winding pass atop a plateau to a cavern. A stone pressed against the opening, its shadow stretched over the grassy plateau.

Randon, Kira, and some of his wolves pushed it open. And it was there the travesty of Alaric's Mountain became evident. As the light burst in, shadows stood to face it. Ashina met the hordes of humans, most women, and she grieved. Her fangs burst up in anger as she pointed to Serimi and Galin.

"Get them out. Give them food and water and provisions." Then she stood in the light. Her shadow stretched over them as they stood to face her. There were hundreds of them.

"I am Ashina, the white wolf queen. I have come to free you from the reign of Alaric."

A woman approached Ashina, gripping her younger sister in her arms. Their brown hair was disheveled down their backs, and their wide eyes were as pained as their faces. "Can we go home?"

Ashina swallowed and sighed. "Alaric has destroyed your homes. My kingdom, the city of the falls, will be your home until you can rebuild. It will take some time, but Alaric is dead, and his wolves cannot harm humans anymore."

The women closed their eyes and shook their heads. Ashina gripped their shoulders and smiled at them. "I am sorry. I promise you all my city will give you everything you need. Our wolves are virtuous and will protect you and help you rebuild."

Their eyes teared up as they met Ashina's face, but they were not smiling. They had all endured a harrowing experience since being taken. Ashina led them out, and the human men met them on the plateau.

As the days dragged on and the travesty of the mountain was evident, Serimi and Galin continued to direct their warriors to liberate the humans. Cayden and Ashina sat beside them on horseback, ever watchful. They had battled Alaric's wolves left there and taken it. The wolves left serving Alaric were hunted and killed if they refused Cayden's reign. The brutality of Alaric's throne had been bred into his wolves, and their human mates suffered for years.

The wolves left behind with wives and children who wanted to start over led their families out of the mountain. Ashina watched them with their human wives and children as a longing pain hit her. They were the happy ones.

Serimi shook his head as Galin masterfully guided his warriors to help the human women. Alaric had another keep of them in a cavern under his throne and more stone houses strewn about the plain full of them. It was obvious he planned on having breeders to build his army. Alaric had emptied the kingdoms for hundreds of miles of humans.

Many of the women had children, and some were pregnant. Serimi's warriors pulled them out of the mountain and set them on horses. Every human Alaric had taken were put into wagons or on horses, and liberated out of the mountain. They were free.

They were taking them to the city of the Falls to rebuild their lives. Alaric had destroyed every village in the kingdoms for hundreds of miles and ripped families apart for years. Serimi sighed as the plain filled of humans getting freed. He clenched his jaws, craning his head to Ashina and Cayden.

"Thank you." His eyes teared up.

Ashina met his stare and swallowed, gripping her growing belly. "I am sorry." Her eyes became teary.

Cayden bent over, gripped her hand, and smiled at his eyes met Serimi's. "We can rebuild, and the humans will be given rest and hope. Whatever they need to heal, they will have it."

Serimi cleared his throat. "Yes. We will."

As Galin pulled the remaining humans out with his warriors, what Alaric had done for many years hit them with pained hearts. Galin lit a torch and his warriors followed. They burned the mountain behind them and liberated the humans. They turned away from the rolling plain inside the insidious mountain, the fires raging behind them into the heavens like the world was on fire.

But it was a new beginning.

Chapter 35
The Era of the White Wolf Queen

The throne room had stayed in darkness for a long time. It was apparent as Ashina melted into her heritage of the deep city of the falls. Her eyes lighted upon the massive cavern wall and craned to the ceiling and the black mountain. Randon and Kira explored the tunnel behind the wall beside the throne and found a skylight not opened. A round pivot lay inside that wall, like a hidden gem.

As they craned it to turn open, the light filtered in. The light blasted the whole breadth of the cavern ceiling, telling the story of the ancient primordials. Cayden was the dark mountain but not evil. The kingdom of Cayden was the liberator. It stood tall and dark, shrouding over Worgen, pulling man and wolf to its gates.

Ashina smiled, her belly now evident as the months had flown by. When the light came in, she stood on her throne aside from her husband and reveled in the glory of man and wolf. Their golden crowns kissed the tops of their heads as regal robes danced on their powerful bodies. Below her stood Serimi, Galin, and Louve. King Meltivi joined Brovina, smiling up at them.

Randon and Kira stood aside Ashina on the throne as commanders and advisors. They wore regal robes in crimson and black. Their leather armor kissed their strong bodies and gave them a demanding presence in the court. Randon kept eying Kira, and she met his stare. They loved one another.

The ancient primordial wolves stood split in half on either side of Ashina and Cayden. They stood in their regal stances of the court with their power.

Ashina smiled at the warriors and wolves who filled her throne to the trickling falls. The whole cavern wall seeped in the kingdom's beauty as the river flowed on the wall behind them. She doted upon Serimi, Galin, and Louve. She awarded them with commander status in the court. Cayden joined her in approving them.

Outside in the bustling city streets, humans mingled with the wolves. They danced, ate, drank, and laughed. The fires burned with cauldrons of stew, and the racks filled with bread baking. The city smelled of feasting and full hearts.

The rolling plain had stone homes that trickled from the falls into fields, and gardens stretched from one side of the mountain to the other. The women taken from Alaric's Mountain had homes, hope, and rest.

The human warriors of Serimi's army filled the plains too, reveling in freedom, finally. They danced with their human women, filling the night with laughter and love.

Ashina smiled at the old primordial gray wolf. He pressed before her and raised his long arms, his massive paws stretched wide before the masses. "Now enters the age of the white wolf queen!" He roared. "Man and wolf are at peace!"

When he said that, Cayden took his wife's hand, kissed it in front of the world, and bowed to her. The whole court of wolves and man bowed to their queen, and the city erupted in bellowing horns and cheers. Ashina held her bulging belly at her husband, his face lit up.

Then Cayden stood up as the silence grew around them, and his eyes met her face. He flexed every muscle in the fiber of his being as he spoke to her and gripped his heart.

"You have healed our kingdoms. You have healed my heart!" His deep voice echoed.

Ashina gasped in a state of wonder with him, her heart racing in her chest, her stomach tied up in knots.

"I love you!" He shouted so the whole world heard him as his handsome face dove into hers.

Ashina's eyes filled with tears as she clutched his face in her palm. She took a big breath and moaned. "I have never been so empowered in all my life." Her knees grew weak at his commanding presence. "You are my best friend and my hope." She smiled at him.

He held her face, tears filling his eyes. Their eyes met as rivers of hope flowed through them into one another, and the whole world devoured their love. He kissed her lips as she met his embrace back, their love falling on one another.

"I love you." She met his lips.

They clung to one another, his face pressed into her face, breathing into her. He caressed the side of her face with his fingers and cupped the back of her head in his palm as he gently kissed her.

Cayden gazed at her belly and took a deep breath. His heart raced as he pressed a palm on it and sighed at her face.

"I wonder if it will be a stubborn daughter like her mother." He smiled, and everyone laughed with them.

Ashina laughed with him, hopeful. She turned her head to see Randon smiling ear to ear at her. Randon pulled Kira's hand in his own and smiled at her. They beamed at one another, gazing down the throne at the brave warriors and wolves they had survived with.

Louve cleared his throat, his eyes tearing up. "That is beautiful. Look how beautiful they are."

Galin turned to him, shaking his head. "Clearly, you were adopted."

Louve scoffed. "I was not adopted! Our mother was a whore."

Serimi burst out in laughter, turning to go with King Meltivi and Brovina to join the celebrations.

Brovina narrowed her brows. "I didn't know you two were brothers!"

They laughed out loud at her.

Serimi smiled. "You could not see the resemblance in their attitude? Their hair and beards are the same, just different colors."

Brovina laughed at them all and walked out with them. "I see it now." She eyed them.

King Meltivi patted Serimi on the back as they left. "I heard they have honey wine here. I am famished. And hungry."

Serimi laughed as Brovina joined them. "Yes, come! It is time to rest and dine!"

Louve and Galin turned to follow them out as the masses trickled out behind them to join the feasting. The two brothers rolled their eyes at one another while giving each other battering pats on their backs at the same time.

"I love you, brother." Galin smiled, pressing his long arm over Louve's shoulder.

Louve met his stare as they were the same height and sneered in his face. "Love you too, smart ass."

T he next few months were busy for the deep city of the falls. It was busy because they prepared for fall harvesting and Winter coming soon. They continued to build houses and cut firewood. The city bustled with purpose and hope.

By then, it was too late for Ashina to travel back to Cayden, her home. The wolves were rebuilding the whole western wall, and the humans were busy repairing Serkily. The kingdoms were rebuilding and free as the world breathed again. It breathed again, and life was born.

Tala would have been proud to see the ancient city come back to life with humans and wolves living together. They worked together to rebuild their lives. She would have been a wonderful grandmother, too, Ashina thought.

So, when the time came for the little one to be born, Cayden was torn up in knots. He reveled in the glory of the wife who held his whole heart as she birthed them black-headed white wolf queen.

The End.